Victim in the Violets

Lovely Lethal Gardens 22

VICTIM IN THE VIOLETS: LOVELY LETHAL GARDENS, BOOK 22
Beverly Dale Mayer
Valley Publishing Ltd.

ISBN-13: 978-1-773367-65-1
Print Edition

Books in This Series

About This Book

A new cozy mystery series from *USA Today* best-selling author Dale Mayer. Follow gardener and amateur sleuth Doreen Montgomery—and her amusing and mostly lovable cat, dog, and parrot—as they catch murderers and solve crimes in lovely Kelowna, British Columbia.

Riches to rags. ... Old cases never die. ... Love spans decades, ... even if unrequited!

With her estranged husband still pestering her, Doreen is looking for a new case to keep her interest and to help her dodge Mack and his brother's scoldings. So she decides to delve deeper into the Bob Small case, especially since it pertains to Nan's now-deceased friend.

Only to have the case suddenly connect to a current friend and Rosemoor resident. When this woman's sister ends up murdered, and there's a connection to Bob Small, Doreen and her animals are off on the trail, ... much to Corporal Mack Moreau's disgust.

Anything to do with Bob Small is big. He was linked to dozens of unsolved murder cases, and no way will Doreen do anything private on this case. However, even she isn't prepared for the ending that suddenly shows up—with gun in hand and a story for the ages ...

Sign up to be notified of all Dale's releases here!
https://geni.us/DaleNews

Chapter 1

Midway Into the Fourth Week of September

DOREEN LAY BY the river, a cup of tea and a mystery book in her hand, dozing, resting, dozing, until Mugs barked. She looked up to see Mack coming toward her, a big box of pizza in his hand. She beamed as she recognized the crest of the eatery, one of her favorites.

He chuckled. "I didn't call to say I was bringing dinner, in case maybe you were still resting."

"I am, been here most of the day ..." She motioned at the creek that trickled gently beside her.

"It is a beautiful place," he noted, as he sat down and opened the box, offering her a piece.

She frowned. "Do you eat anything other than pizza when you're busy?"

He nodded. "I do, but this is fast, easy, and it holds me."

"Right. Well, I won't argue because you brought it."

"Good thing," he said, then gave her a grin. "Everybody was so curious about this find that all our officers—even those off duty—worked in shifts, straight through yesterday, all night, and throughout today. So everything's already been itemized and set up in a locker," he noted. "They'll do a big press release, and the captain wants you to attend."

She rolled her eyes at that. "I can attend, just keep me out of the news."

He burst out laughing at that. "I think that's a little hard to do at this point. Of course the press was there soon after its discovery, so they already know that you're involved."

She smiled. "That's why I'm at the back of the house, because yesterday the Japanese tour buses started coming by with extra runs." She sighed. "Richard's barely even talking to me."

"That may be a blessing in disguise," Mack noted, with a chuckle.

"Yeah, I don't know. I may need a secret way in and out of my house now."

Mack frowned and asked, "Is it that bad?"

She shrugged. "It is, but whatever. It's all good."

"What about Stuart?"

She nodded. "I talked to him several times."

"Good. What about?"

"Well, now that he has some money coming to him, he's thinking about maybe going back to school."

"Oh, wow, that's not what I expected."

"No, but I think he's starting to understand how much that job and criminal lifestyle crippled his father."

"And that's a good thing," Mack agreed. "At least if he understands that, Stuart can do something better for himself."

"I think he will. At least I think he is trying hard to find a way forward. Losing his dad suddenly like that was hard."

"Of course it was, but he's done pretty well."

"He has, indeed," she murmured.

"Grab a piece of pizza."

She snatched a slice of pizza, sat up, and washed it down with water from her bottle. "And has work calmed down for you now?" When he glared at her, she apologized. "I know. It's my fault again."

"No, now, in this case," Mack explained, "we needed to find that second hoard before everybody looted the grave-yard. The fact that you found it is really no surprise."

"I think you would have found it too, if you'd gotten that far," she said, "but it was fun to see it uncovered. Buried treasures are everybody's childhood dream."

He chuckled. "It is, indeed, and it's still the talk of the cop shop."

"And will be for a while," she noted, with a smile, and he nodded. She added, "As long as no other cases come to light, you should be doing okay now."

"We were doing fine *before* this case," he stated, giving her a hard look. "It's just *somebody* keeps giving us more cases."

"True, and I'm sure that's a pain, but just think—between all the guns and now the loot—how many cases you guys could solve."

"Oh, don't worry. The captain's gloating all over that." Mack let out a big belly laugh. "He did say something about making sure that I treat you right, so that you never leave town."

She looked at him and then started to chuckle. "That's nice for a change. I figured he would offer you a bribe to get me out of town, so that you guys wouldn't work so hard."

He laughed even harder at that. "No, it's all good. And the fact that you've taken off a day or two and rested," he noted, "that's seriously good news."

"Of course I haven't done much of anything. That

Mathew returned home without contacting me is even better. I could actually relax."

"And you only took these couple days off because Ella Hickman is away on a trip, isn't that right?"

She nodded. "I'll talk to her when she gets back."

"The police want to talk to her too. She's coming back today."

"Right, well, that would be good," Doreen noted. "More things to tie up."

"But you're hoping for more information on Bob Small, aren't you?"

"Yeah, sure am." Doreen smiled. "I won't rest until that one's dealt with."

He winced and nodded slowly. "It won't be an easy thing to deal with though, right?"

"I know," she murmured. "I was hoping it would be easier, but I don't think it will be."

"No, probably not, but still I trust that you'll take whatever precautions you can take and do a decent job."

She leaned over, kissed him gently on his cheek, and said, "Thanks for the vote of confidence."

He grinned, kissed her on the lips, and murmured, "You're welcome."

"And you're sure there are no other cases now?" she asked. "I could use something easy."

"*Easy?*" he repeated. "If that were the case, we would have solved them already."

"Good point," she muttered.

"But, no, I don't think there will be anything for a while," Mack guessed. "You rattled up this town pretty well."

She glared at him.

But he just grinned, then his phone went off. He sighed as he looked down at it and then answered. "Yeah, Cap. What's up? ... Yeah, I'm sitting here, having some pizza with her. ... Okay, I'll tell her. ... Yeah, I'm coming." He got up, frowned.

"*Uh-oh*, what's the matter?" she asked.

He sighed. "Let's just say, things will get more difficult now."

"Why is that?" she asked, standing up with him.

"Because they found a body at the airport."

"A body?"

He nodded.

"At the airport?" she asked, her voice rising.

He nodded again.

She shook her head. "Please, not Ella."

He nodded again. "It's Ella. She was found in a patch of violets in the front of the airport, in one of the big garden beds, waiting for her ride."

She stared at him in shock. "Oh no," she whispered, somewhat sad and a whole lot of angry because all her dreams of getting answers on her Bob Small file were flying out the window. "Poor Nelly." The thought brought tears to Doreen's eyes.

"Stay here," he said, his tone grim. "I'll let you know what I can, when I can." And, with that, he strolled toward the kitchen.

She sank back down onto the ground, and then it hit her. "Violets." That was *V*. She snickered. She called out to Mack, "Are you still there?"

But there was no answer.

She picked up her phone and called him. "You did say *violets*, right?"

"Yeah, I did. Why?" he asked.

She heard his engine start, as he got into his vehicle. "How about *Vanquish?*" she asked. "How does *Vanquished in the Violets* sound?"

He snorted. "I think you're grasping at straws."

"Nope, I don't think so," she stated. "However, *victim* is better. *Victim* is perfect."

"No," Mack declared, "not at all because this is my case, not a cold case."

"Ah," she argued, "but it'll be connected to one of the biggest cold cases you ever saw."

He groaned. "Fine, *Victim in the Violets* it is." And then he chuckled and added, "That's a good one." He ended the call, still laughing.

She put down her phone and laughed out loud. She reached over, gave Mugs a big hug, snatched Goliath and danced around with him in her arms, and then scooped up Thaddeus and plunked him on her shoulder. "We have another case," she exclaimed, noting the pizza Mack had left behind.

"Pizza *and* a case," she proudly proclaimed. "All we need now is coffee." And she raced into the kitchen to put it on.

Life is good. Life is very good.

Chapter 2

After Lunch …

ONCE MACK LEFT, the real implications of Ella's death hit Doreen. Not only would Ella's sister now be left alone but all those answers that Ella had, that she might have shared, had died with her. As much as Doreen didn't want to believe that all was lost, it was hard at the moment to find a positive note about it all. To think how much Ella could have told Doreen and Mack—not only potentially about the guns and the treasure hoard but everything to do with that gang mess—was all gone, along with any connections to the Bob Small serial killer case too.

Surely Ella had kept some records, had kept some notes about something. The woman had been a politician. She knew how important and how damaging records were. Doreen didn't want to believe that a woman, such as Ella, who had built up a rapport, who had that savvy reputation, and who had known many powerful people, would let it all go to naught. Surely Ella would have kept journals at least. She also hadn't had a chance to come home to prep, hide, or destroy anything. She'd been taken out first, and, of course, that always made Doreen suspicious.

"Who could have done that? A lot of people *have* done that." She wandered her house, frowning and fussing over little things, until she realized that she was trying to take her mind off the information circling and rolling around in her head.

Doreen wandered to the bowl that her grandmother had given her, still filled with bits and pieces of baubles Doreen had found hidden in all Nan's clothing, including change, even a few rolls of small denomination dollar bills. Doreen had kept it all here in the bowl as a sign of affluence, a sign that she was doing okay, a sign of the changing times. But she had more than a little curiosity about the marbles, which she kept picking up and rolling around in her hand, loving the feel of them. Lots of other things were in the bowl as well, from buttons and paper clips to all kinds of miscellaneous items that made no sense.

And then she delved her hand into the bowl and pulled up something that she had meant to talk to Nan about further but hadn't yet—the keys. Nan had safe deposit boxes in her name. Doreen pondered that, wondering if she should ask her grandmother more about that. The last time she'd asked her, Nan had gotten fairly upset at her. Mostly because of Nan's confusion, and yet that confusion was there a little more often some days than others.

That condition was frustrating because, for somebody like Doreen, apparently answers were what made her tick, and she often needed her grandmother's help. With Ella dead and Nan getting forgetful, Doreen could see how getting more information would be challenging now and into the future. Yet she had to remind herself that no answers were to be had with lots of these cases. And that just drove her batty.

Finally she looked down at the animals. "Right, let's go for a walk."

Mugs immediately jumped to his feet, barking, his tail wagging as if a helicopter rotor. She smiled and gave him a couple good scratches. "It's all good, buddy. It's all good."

But, of course, it wasn't, but hopefully it would be. However, it wasn't Mugs's fault that things had gone into the sewer. Doreen still needed answers, and they would not find so many now. She could only hope that Ella had maybe left a journal or something somewhere.

As she pondered that, her phone rang. She glanced at her Caller ID. *Nan.* Doreen winced. Apparently the news was out already. She answered, "Hello, Nan."

"Is it true?" she asked in a loud voice. "Is it true?"

"I'm not sure what you're asking about," Doreen replied cautiously.

"About Ella," she cried out, almost a note of hysteria in her tone.

"Easy, Nan, easy," Doreen noted. "Calm down." But there was no calming down her grandmother.

"You have no idea how upset her sister is," Nan cried out.

"I'm sure she is. She's her only sister. Ella was her only family, wasn't she?"

"Yes, exactly," Nan agreed slowly, her tone easing back from the panic.

"Why are you so upset?" Doreen asked.

Silence came first. Then Nan reluctantly admitted, "Nelly took something of Ella's. It's one of the reasons why they were fighting all the time. Nelly wouldn't give it back."

"Why would she do that?" Doreen asked.

"Because Ella had threatened to take her away from here.

And, while we all think that Nelly is really sweet and quiet, she's got hidden depths."

"If she stole something from her sister, that sounds like sibling rivalry, which can happen at any time."

"Oh, absolutely," Nan stated. "Still, it doesn't change the fact that Nelly feels terribly guilty because now she can't give it back to her sister, and she can't ask her sister for forgiveness."

"Ah, how true," Doreen noted. "I'm sorry to say that Ella was apparently found at the airport, dead, while waiting for her ride to show up."

"Oh my," Nan muttered, her voice still shaky.

Something was going on here that made Doreen more than a little suspicious. "Nan, what do you know about this?"

Her grandmother took a slow breath. "I know that Nelly went for a joy ride of sorts this morning. She was supposed to go along for the Rosemoor shopping trip. Everybody went into the store, and the driver went to get a coffee, and Nelly hopped into the Rosemoor van, drove off, and disappeared."

"What?" Doreen exclaimed.

"Yes, yes, however, I'm sure she didn't kill Ella though," Nan added immediately.

Doreen pinched the bridge of her nose. "I'm not so sure."

"No, no. You don't understand. Nelly's not like that."

"Has she ever done anything like this before?"

"No, that's the thing. She's never left an outing like this before, especially not driving off in the van and stranding everyone. She's the most perfect person you ever saw."

"*Nan.*"

"I know you won't believe me. As far as you're concerned, this is all in my imagination."

"No, not at all," Doreen stated firmly. "Yet obviously we need to sort it out."

"You'll come down then, right?"

And such a note of eagerness filled her grandmother's tone that again Doreen had to wonder. "Come down?"

"Yes. I told you. Nelly's here, absolutely crying her heart out."

"Oh, ouch. Yes, her sister has passed on. Of course she'll be distraught."

"No, it's not that," Nan corrected in a dry tone. "Nelly won't talk to anybody but you."

"Double ouch," Doreen muttered to herself. "Okay, but, if it's connected to this case, I must call Mack in."

Silence came from the other end. "I suppose you must, don't you?" Nan replied reluctantly.

"Yes, but, of course, we don't know if Nelly's desire to speak with me is connected to Ella's death, or do we?" Doreen asked her grandmother.

"I don't know that it's connected, but I'm assuming it is," Nan stated, with unusual honesty.

"Right, in that case …"

"No, you come here first, sort it out, and then, if you feel you must, you can call Mack."

"*Great.* He may not look at it quite the same way."

At that, her spirits slowly returning, Nan declared, "Too bad. One of us is hurting, and we must help them." And, with that, she disconnected.

Doreen sighed loudly but knew what she had to do. "Guys, how about we walk down to Nan's?"

Mugs wasn't offering any argument to that at all. By the time she got everybody out of the house, and they saw where they were going, they raced ahead of her toward Rosemoor—almost as if they understood that, right now, some craziness was going on.

And, of course, craziness was one thing, but this craziness? That was a whole other problem. As Doreen walked, her mind wondered, *Exactly what is going on here?* If this was in any way connected to Ella's death, Doreen must phone her favorite detective.

She smiled at the beautiful creek, as it trickled alongside her, happily bubbling away. She hadn't realized how much the water mattered to her, but, boy, oh boy, this was hard to live without. She couldn't imagine living anywhere else now. It was such a joy to be here.

Nan had done so incredibly well, not only for herself but now for Doreen, having bought her house so long ago. And back then it must have gone for a tidy sum, even calculated in sums adjusted for that year. Doreen had no idea what its value was now because the value to her was priceless. She couldn't even imagine selling.

As Doreen came around the corner and headed toward the Rosemoor parking lot, Nan impatiently shifted from foot to foot outside her patio on the grass. That was disturbing in itself because Nan was always this calm, at-peace person. Sure she got excited about events, but she rarely got this distraught.

As Doreen drew nearer, Nan saw her, smiled, and came running. "Hey."

"This has really got you rattled, hasn't it?" Doreen asked, giving her grandmother a hug.

She nodded, and then she lowered her voice. "I don't want to think that Nelly killed her."

At that, Doreen stopped in her tracks. "Oh Good Lord,

do you really think that's what happened?"

"No. ... I don't know," Nan muttered, "but, of course, I'm worried about it."

"Of course you are." Doreen gave Nan another hug. Almost immediately Mugs jumped up to get into the middle. Nan chuckled and bent over, giving him a big hug and then one for Goliath, while Thaddeus jumped onto her back, surprising her. Still chuckling, she slowly straightened, as Thaddeus worked his way up to her shoulder and snuggled in against her neck.

"Thaddeus loves Nan. Thaddeus loves Nan."

"And you, my dear, are such a sweetheart," she replied warmly. She spent another moment just cuddling the animals, looking over at Doreen. "Every time somebody here loses family, it reminds me how grateful I am that you're with me, dear."

Doreen winced. "I was thinking something along that line too," she said softly. "We've had an awful lot of cases where people have lost family and friends, and it's been pretty rough."

"Absolutely," Nan agreed. "And, when you think you know all about what's going on, and then something like this happens, you realize you really don't have a clue."

Doreen had definitely considered that too, time and time again. Nothing she could do but agree with Nan. "Let's hope that this one's fairly simple," she suggested in a reassuring manner.

"I hope so, but I don't know," Nan murmured. "Nelly's pretty upset."

Instead of going to her patio for tea, Nan took Doreen inside, through her small apartment, and down the hallway to a completely different section of Rosemoor. Doreen followed along, not at all sure where she was going. When Nan finally came to a closed door and knocked, they heard a soft voice inside. Nan stepped inside and motioned for Doreen to follow.

Doreen came in behind Nan to find Nelly sitting there on her couch, a great big wad of tissues in her hand, several boxes of them beside her, with multiple balls of them all around her on the floor. Nelly's face was puffy and red, looking as if she had lost her best friend. Or, in this case, her sister.

Doreen walked over and sat down and gave Nelly a gentle hug. "I'm so sorry for your loss," she whispered. At that, Nelly started to bawl even louder. "I am sorry," Doreen repeated and gave Nelly several moments to compose herself, looking at Nan.

Nan said, "I'll put on some tea." She disappeared out into the hallway again, presumably to get tea from Rosemoor's kitchen. Doreen wondered at that, but, hey, sometimes you couldn't make sense of anything around this place.

Doreen waited, but, when Nelly showed no signs of calming down, Doreen mentioned, "Nan brought me here because you wanted to speak with me?"

At that, Nelly nodded, took several deep breaths, trying to bring her emotions under control, and then whispered in a low tone, "I killed her."

Chapter 3

SHOCKED, DOREEN WASN'T sure what she was supposed to say to that announcement. She stared at the tiny woman beside her and asked, "What do you mean, you killed her?"

She stared at Doreen. "I killed her," she repeated more stoutly. "I got so angry."

"How did you kill her?" Doreen asked.

"I hit her. I knocked her down. Boy, was she surprised," Nelly admitted, and then she started to cry again.

"Okay, and then what did you do?"

She frowned. "What do you mean, what did I do?"

"Afterward."

"I ran," Nelly shared. "I was scared. I didn't mean to hurt her. Well, I did mean to hurt her, but I didn't mean to *hurt her*, hurt her."

It was a little garbled, but, through the tears and the tissues, Doreen finally managed to get the rest of the story.

Earlier this morning Nelly had gone to the airport—stealing the Rosemoor van for this—to pick up Ella, knowing her sister was arriving. When Ella saw Nelly, the two sisters got in a big argument, and Nelly had hit Ella and then had run away. She'd come back in the Rosemoor van to the shopping mall to meet up with the other Rosemoor residents and had been in a terrible mood ever since.

The fact of the matter was, Nelly wasn't allowed to drive the Rosemoor van, and she wasn't allowed to go to the airport on her own. So all kinds of things were wrong with that scenario, but all kinds of things were right too.

"Were you supposed to pick up Ella?" Doreen asked.

"No. She had texted me from Vancouver, and we'd been having a doozie of a fight ever since. … When she landed, she still had to clear customs and had to get her luggage, but she was texting me the whole time, telling me what a rotten sister I was, how she would pull me out of Rosemoor, make me go to another home, one I don't want to go to," she added, her gaze flashing, as her temper kicked in.

"Did she have the power to make that happen?" Doreen asked curiously.

At that, Nelly frowned at her. "I don't know, but she told me that she did."

"Which makes it as good a threat as any," Doreen noted.

The other woman nodded slowly. "It sure felt real."

"Yes, of course it did," Doreen agreed. "Okay, so what else?"

"Isn't that enough?" Nelly stared at her.

"No. You hit her, knocked her down, hopped into the van, and came home, right?"

"Yes. Exactly."

"Okay, so having told me that, why would you think that killed her?"

"She was found at the airport," she stated in astonishment, "and I hit her."

"So you think you hit her hard enough to kill her?"

"Yes, yes, that's exactly what I think," she admitted. Then she stopped and asked, "Don't you?"

"I'm not so sure," Doreen replied. "That's not how I thought it happened."

Nelly sat back and frowned. "Really?"

Doreen nodded. "Did you hit her with your hand?"

She winced. "I hit her with a book."

"Okay, what book?" At that question, Nelly picked up the nearby book. As the self-help title flashed by, Doreen eyed Nelly and barely held back her smile. "That looks like a good book."

"It is. I'm trying to be a better person," Nelly stated.

Doreen wanted to note how maybe Nelly was failing at that but didn't think that was terribly fair to say right now. "The book is about controlling your emotions. I gather you have a problem with your emotions flying out of control?"

Nelly nodded, shamefaced. "Yes, and Ella's been on my case since forever to fix it. I thought I was."

"I'm sure you were trying," Doreen said. "This isn't easy."

"No, it isn't," Nelly wailed. "It's terrible. And it always seems as if I'm the one in the wrong."

Doreen didn't say much to that, but she'd certainly known of quite a few relationships where one person was made to feel as if they were always in the wrong. "Okay, so what was Ella doing when you left?"

Nelly shook her head, then shrugged. "I don't know. After hitting her, I hopped in the Rosemoor van, and I left."

"Okay, well, at least that's something. Was she lying down?"

Nelly nodded. "Yes, she stumbled and fell backward."

"Okay, I must tell Mack about this," Doreen stated,

"but I don't think this is as bad as you think it is."

Nelly stared at her, but a glimmer of hope filled Nelly's gaze. "You don't think so? How is that possible?"

"I'm not sure yet. So I won't say too much at the moment, not until I get this figured out. However, we *will* get it figured out," she explained calmly.

Nelly looked at her hopefully. "Seriously, will you help?"

"Oh, absolutely I will help," Doreen confirmed. "What was the reason behind the argument?"

The poor woman flushed. "I took something of hers."

"What did you take?"

At that, Nelly pinched her lips together. "I don't know that I should tell."

"Your sister can't get it back, so it's too late to ask for forgiveness. However, the police are looking at who killed her, and they need to know all the details," Doreen shared in a reasonable tone. "So, regardless, you'll need to hand it over, and I would like to know what it is first."

"Why?" Nelly asked bluntly.

"Because Ella's connected to several cold cases," Doreen replied. "And we were all really hoping to get answers from her as soon as she landed."

Nelly nodded at that. "She was pretty upset that you talked to her when she was here." At that, Nelly stared at Doreen.

"Yet she didn't appear upset at all—not at the time," said Doreen.

"She was," Nelly stated bluntly. "She was upset that you brought up Bob Small."

"Okay, what can you tell me about Bob Small?"

"They were lovers, for quite a while."

"And did Ella know about his ... activities?"

"I don't know. I don't know what activities you're talking about."

And, of course, that would always be the next thing. Did Nelly know? For that matter, how much did Ella know? "Okay, what broke them up?"

"He disappeared. We don't know how, why, or when, but they had a big fight, and he just disappeared."

"Okay, and how long ago was that?"

"A long time ago," Nelly noted, "at least ten years, if not twice that."

"He went to jail, didn't he?" Doreen asked.

Nelly frowned at that. "I don't know whether he did or not. He should have. He was a bad man." She had said it in such a simplistic way that it was obvious *she* believed it. Yet, from her tone of voice, Nelly didn't really expect anybody else would believe it.

"I certainly believe that too," Doreen admitted.

Nelly eyed her in surprise. "My sister always told me that he was misunderstood."

"I don't think he was so much misunderstood as much as he was a bad man," Doreen replied bluntly.

At that, Nelly immediately nodded with enthusiasm. "I kept telling her to leave him alone, to stay away, but she wouldn't listen."

"Sisters are like that," Doreen noted, with a smile. "Particularly older sisters. You're not supposed to know more than them."

Nelly chuckled. "I often had a problem with that. … We used to fight a lot growing up, but somewhere along the line," she added, her tone turning sad, "I lost the fight and then the will to fight."

"And maybe that's because you weren't necessarily the

type of person who wants to fight all the time, whereas—I'm not sure but—your sister enjoyed the fighting and wanted more of it in her life."

Nelly shrugged. "I don't know why anybody would."

"No, but sometimes we must do what is right for us, regardless whether other people like it or not."

Nelly looked at her oddly. "That's very true. I kept telling Ella that I had to live my life. But she kept yelling at me, saying that, if it was my life, I should be paying for it."

"And you weren't?"

"I was and I wasn't. According to my sister I wasn't capable of looking after my affairs. I would help all the wrong people, and the money would be gone in no time."

"Depending on what you did with your money, I can understand your sister saying that. If you want to stay in Rosemoor, it costs, and it costs a lot."

Nelly swallowed hard. "I really want to stay here," she cried out. "I don't want to be sent away."

"I don't know anything about sending you away," Doreen murmured. "Let's see if we can get to the bottom of one problem first. And the next problem would be sorting out your finances to see if you can stay."

Nelly stared at her. "But, if my sister's gone, then I should get the money, and I could stay, right?"

Doreen studied Nelly's face for a long moment, not liking the thoughts crossing her mind, but how could she not consider it? "I guess that depends on if you had anything to do with your sister's death. If that's the case, then, no, you don't get to stay because you don't get the money, and, of course, you would be in jail," Doreen explained, looking at Nelly cautiously, trying her best to not upset the poor woman. "However, if you didn't have anything to do with

your sister's death, and your sister left everything to you—
and I don't know that," Doreen pointed out, "then possibly
money is not a problem, depending on how much money
she had. Now do you have money of your own?"

Nelly looked confused. "Some, but I don't know how
much."

"Right, so that's something else we'll look at then."

"But you'll help me?" she asked almost desperately.

Something held Doreen back. Then, thinking about it,
she nodded. "I'll help you sort it out. I don't know what
that'll look like at the end of the day."

Nelly's shoulders sagged. "Of course. My sister was right.
I'm a bad person."

"You're not a bad person," Doreen corrected instantly,
"and, even if you did something wrong, that doesn't make
you a bad person forever. You can certainly fix things."

"Not my sister," Nelly pointed out, shaking her head,
the tears starting again. "I can't fix my sister." And, with
that, she burst into tears again, and the conversation was
done.

Chapter 4

DOREEN SAID GOODBYE to Nan soon afterward and slowly walked toward the creek. As soon as she got around the corner and away from Rosemoor, her fingers were already busy phoning Mack. When he came on the line, he appeared distracted.

"Doreen, I'm really busy."

"I know," she acknowledged. "I'm not sure how important this is."

He hesitated. "What's the matter?"

"How was Ella killed?"

"She was shot."

"Oh, good," she muttered.

"Good?" he asked, with a note of amusement. "How is that good?"

"Because her sister was hysterical, thinking that she killed Ella."

"Back up. How is that?"

"She was there at the airport this morning, before Ella was shot. Nelly argued with her sister over the phone the whole time Ella was in Vancouver, even while Ella traveled home again. That all happened over texts, and then Nelly was so mad that she drove the Rosemoor van from the mall to the airport to see her sister, and they had a big fight, and then Nelly hit Ella up the side of her head with a book. Her sister fell down. Nelly hopped into the van, thinking she killed her, and drove back to the mall, where the Rosemoor residents were. Now terrified of what she'd done, she's crying her eyes out at Rosemoor."

"What?" Mack cried out.

"Yeah, so Nelly feels terribly guilty, thinks that she killed her sister but, at the same time, is obviously hoping that she didn't."

"I needed to know that anyway because the autopsy would indicate a blow to Ella's face that wouldn't have made any sense."

"And that's why I'm telling you," Doreen noted calmly. "I can also tell you that Nelly's beside herself with worry that she'll get kicked out of Rosemoor because she may not have enough money. I don't know what the sisters' fight was about because Nelly won't tell me, but I understand that she has something of her sister's but wouldn't return it to Ella, and it's been a bone of contention for years. Nelly also told me that Bob Small is a bad man."

Silence came from the other end. "Good Lord." Then his tone changed. "She has something of her sister's?"

"Yes, apparently she stole something from her sister and has been using it against her these past few years. So she could stay at Rosemoor."

"Interesting family dynamic."

"Their relationship is complex. That's the problem. You and I both know what we've seen in the past with these cold cases, how ugly that family dynamic can end up looking."

"Oh, yeah, that is very true," he muttered. "Seems I need

to go have a talk with her."

"I told her that she would need to tell you guys exactly what happened, but she is a mess."

"Of course she is," he muttered. "I still must talk to her though."

"No, I get it. I understand," Doreen muttered. "I thought you should know. She did mention Bob Small but not much. Honestly she got kind of cagey then."

"Did she now?"

"Yes, and I told her that I'll come back later and talk to her a little bit more when she was calmer. She's in shock over her sister, so that wasn't the time." They talked for several more minutes, as Mack tried to sort out what was going on.

"And do you really think she had anything to do with her death?" he asked.

"No, not at all," Doreen stated. "However, I do think that Nelly had a big argument with Ella, probably hit her in the face with a book, panicked, and left."

"That helps, and I appreciate it. I need to talk to her about Bob Small, but first my focus is on Ella's murder."

"And I presume you'll talk to Nelly soon?"

"I have to," he said. "As much as I don't like to put her through that, obviously a hit to Ella's face will show up in autopsy." And he quickly ended the call.

Doreen pondered the information, as she walked along the creek back toward her house. She stopped, kicking a rock into the water a couple times to send up a splash, making Mugs run in delight. She picked up a stick, tossed it down the path, and he raced after it. She smiled, as she watched his antics. "I'm glad you're in a good mood. Heaven knows this will be a hard-enough day for lots of people."

As she continued home, she pondered why no mention

of Ella had been in any of the notes Doreen had on Bob Small. *Of course not, because everything I had read came from Hinja so far.* With that irking thought in mind, Doreen headed home, thinking she needed to go to the library and to search anything and everything else she could find on Ella, Hinja, and Bob Small.

After she locked up the animals in the house, she drove off, headed to the library. The librarian raised an eyebrow, but she was busy checking people through. As Doreen raced to the back of the building where the microfiche section was, she couldn't help but feel that, for some reason, time was now of the essence. At the self-help desk, she sat down and started researching these people.

Shortly thereafter she was deep into her research when her phone buzzed again. She looked down to see it was Nan. Being in the library, Doreen had to keep her voice low. She hesitated and then decided not to answer it, turning off her phone instead, finishing up what she was doing. She would call her grandmother as soon as she left. She directed her attention back to the screen in front of her, saving as many articles that she could, sending them to her email to read later. By the time she was done, Nan had called two more times.

Feeling bad, Doreen raced out of the library, without even saying anything to the librarian, knowing that would cause more eyebrows to go up. But it wasn't the time or the place to explain. As soon as she got outside, she took out her phone and called Nan. "What's the matter?" she asked.

Nan groaned when she heard her voice. "There you are," she cried out. "Why didn't you answer me?"

"I was in the library, and we're not allowed to talk in there."

Nan went silent for a moment. "Oh." Then her tone turned brisk. "Nelly is calling for you."

Doreen wasn't sure what to say to that, knowing that Mack should be there already, talking with Nelly.

"She wants to talk to you again."

Doreen winced, knowing that this was delicate ground. "Has Mack talked to her yet?"

"I don't think so. Nelly was just talking to you."

"Fine, I'll head back down again." And this time, leaving the library in her car, she drove straight to Nan's, parked, walked into the little patio area, where Nan sat, waiting for her. Doreen studied her grandmother. "Are you okay?"

Nan nodded, but her features worked with various emotions. "I'm fine," she murmured. "It's been a tough morning."

"It has," Doreen agreed in an undertone, "but we'll get to the bottom of this."

Nan smiled up at her. "You're a good child. I know you will."

She laughed. "Hardly a child anymore," Doreen corrected affectionately.

"Do you really think Nelly killed Ella?"

"No, I don't," Doreen stated.

Nan looked at her in surprise. "But she's telling everybody she killed her."

"I think, in her mind, she did, but she hit her on the side of her head with a book." Doreen lowered her voice and added, "You can't tell anybody because it's not public information yet, but Ella was shot."

Nan looked at her in horror and then in relief. "That's an entirely different case then," she cried out, her hand going to her chest.

27

"Exactly, but it doesn't change the fact that the police must talk to Nelly because that hit to Ella's face or anywhere else will show up in autopsy."

"Yes, of course. Oh my. Why the devil would Nelly hit Ella with a book of all things?" Nan asked, staring at her granddaughter. "It's hardly effective." Nan gave Doreen a hug and muttered, "I'm glad one of us has some common sense. Come along. You need to talk to her, so we can put an end to this."

Doreen wasn't quite so sure it was that easy, but, hey, if it were so simple, she was all for it. As she headed to Nelly's room, Nan looked at her.

"She's worried about not being able to stay."

Doreen nodded. "Nelly needs to sort out her finances. I don't know if she has any money of her own or if Ella handled it all."

"*Ella* did? Why?" Nan stared at Doreen, then gave a dipped nod.

"Right, that's a very good question," Doreen noted. "If it wasn't Nelly's money, then it'll depend on Ella's will, won't it?"

"It'll depend on her will and whether there are any stipulations on previous wills," Nan reminded her. "It's possible that Nelly's care was some kind of a legacy from their parents."

"I wondered about that too." Doreen tapped her cheek thoughtfully.

"Let's solve one problem right now," Nan stated, "and then we can work on solving the others."

"Not so easy to do," Doreen reminded her grandmother. "Lots of pieces come into play, and, having said that, Nelly thinks she killed her sister, so absolutely no way she could inherit."

Nan winced at that. "Well, as you mentioned, she did hit her with a book of all things." Nan frowned at that. "Good God, I can't imagine."

"I don't think we always are rational in these emotional states," Doreen suggested. "Nelly probably just reacted to something her sister said."

"Maybe, but I will tell you one thing," Nan stated, clearly thinking over how to proceed with the upcoming conversation with Nelly. "Ella was not a nice person. We saw her here irregularly, and we certainly saw the negative effect she had on Nelly with every visit, as Ella came and went."

"Maybe, but you also don't know the family dynamic," Doreen mentioned. "So let's withhold judgment on that." When Nan frowned at her, Doreen smiled in response.

Finally Nan gave a hard sigh. "Fine, but you're starting to sound more and more like Mack."

Doreen stared at her in shock at those words. "Seriously?" she cried out. "That's what you say to me?"

"Well, you are," Nan muttered. "The old Doreen wouldn't have been anywhere near quite so logical or reasonable," Nan declared. "I'm not saying it's a bad thing. It's just something we all must get used to."

"As I learn a little more from each of these cases," Doreen began cautiously, "yeah, we do pick up a bit more of the rhyme and reason of how things happen. If Ella was murdered, we want to ensure that whoever did it pays, don't we?"

At that, Nan turned to her. "Absolutely. I still don't understand what you mean."

"We must follow protocol to get the case tried and won. We must follow rules so we don't get the case thrown out,"

Doreen explained. "That's what I've learned from Mack," she stated simply. Wherever this conversation was headed, she needed to steer it toward a productive side. "As much as I don't like it, as much as there are bits and pieces that I would just as soon throw out the window—and I get into trouble for that myself all the time—we still must follow a certain legal system so that criminals can get prosecuted. We don't want any of these people to get away with their crimes. Look at some of these old cases. See how many killers would have gotten away with murder? Plus now, with my interference in a couple of the early ones, well, they could still get away with murder."

Her grandmother looked at her in horror.

Doreen shrugged. "It's something to keep in mind. I know that, if I keep interfering, Mack's right when he says I need to be aware that sometimes my assistance isn't as much assistance as I thought."

Nan chuckled. "I do like to hear that. You have all that passion and yet a hint of common sense"—she smiled—"which makes for a great combination."

She laughed at her grandmother. "I don't know about that, and I'm not sure Mack would agree with you."

Nan waved a hand dismissively at that comment. "What are you doing for his birthday?"

Doreen groaned. "I don't know, probably have him over for dinner."

"Will you cook?"

"I guess I can't really ask him to come over and cook his own birthday meal, can I?" she grumbled.

Nan chuckled. "You could, and he'll probably be happy to."

"Maybe," she muttered. "Maybe I should ask his brother

if he'll be up for a co-hosted party."

"Oh, that's a good idea." Then Nan shook her head. "You won't cook for both of them, will you?"

She glared at her grandmother. "Wow, now that's a vote of confidence."

"I don't want to scare Mack off, but how are your cooking skills, dear?"

Doreen winced. "Not that great. I've been working on it, and I can do a lot of simple things, ... so I don't want to try something too fancy."

"Don't try anything fancy," Nan noted. "Much better to do something simple yet very well than to go fancy and do it terribly." On that depressing note Nan led the way to Nelly's room again.

Chapter 5

NELLY STILL SAT frozen on her couch, her used balled-up tissues forming a perimeter around her.

Doreen sat down beside her. "I'm back," she announced. "You wanted to tell me something?" But Nelly remained nonresponsive, now staring at Doreen's grandmother.

Nan raised both her hands in frustration. "Fine. I'll leave, but, Doreen, you tell Nelly that I won't keep calling you back here unless Nelly speaks to you each time." And, with that, Nan left.

It was an odd thing for her to say. Doreen looked over at Nelly. "Sounds as if my grandmother is a little bit upset over all this."

Nelly nodded. "And with good reason." Nelly gave a heavy sigh. "I've been fairly emotional."

"You've lost your sister, and you're afraid that you've had something to do with her death," Doreen recounted, "so you're entitled to be emotional."

Nelly smiled. "You really are a nice person, aren't you?"

Doreen winced. "Not sure that'll get me any accolades in this world," she noted. "Nice people don't seem to do very well."

"And that's too bad," Nelly declared, her tone firm, "because it really does take nice people to get anywhere."

"Maybe," Doreen hedged. "Now what did you want to talk to me about?"

She sighed. "It probably seems wrong, and I should talk to the police." She glanced sideways at Doreen.

Doreen nodded. "Yes, I agree. ... Your sister, by the way," she shared in a hushed tone, "and I'm telling you in confidence, and you can't spread it around, ... but she was shot to death."

Nelly stared at her, her mouth forming a rosebud circle, and then she sagged in place. "So I didn't kill her," she whispered at that.

Doreen shook her head. "No, you didn't, but you still must talk to the cops because the blow to her head from the book will likely show up during the autopsy, and they won't understand what that was all about. This will help give them some answers too."

She nodded. "I can talk to them." She looked at Doreen. "I really am sorry."

"I know that," Doreen acknowledged. "Sometimes our emotions get the better of us."

"She was always there and yet always such a pain in my butt," she murmured.

"And that's family," Doreen noted, with a smile.

Nelly looked at her mistily. "That is very true. I just hadn't realized."

"Of course not, and stop blaming yourself. Now, what did you want to talk to me about?"

Nelly sighed again. "I wanted to give you the stuff that I stole from her."

"Okay." Doreen studied her. "What is it you stole?"

"Her journals."

"Okay, why did you steal them?" she asked curiously, watching as Nelly tapped a small notebook beside her.

"Because it pissed her off," Nelly admitted. "She had three of them back when I first took them, but I returned them all not too long ago. However, Ella was mean to me, so I took one journal back again."

"Why didn't you give this one back?"

She winced. "Because it was a way to ensure I stayed at Rosemoor."

"Meaning that you were blackmailing your sister?" Doreen asked cautiously.

She shrugged. "The way family does," she quipped. "Although it wasn't really blackmailing her, but I had something she wanted, and she had something I wanted."

"What was it you really, really wanted?"

"The funds to stay here."

"So you don't have any money of your own?"

"I don't know," she wailed. "I was supposed to have my care taken care of until I died," she shared. "That was part of my grandfather's will. However, Ella kept telling me that it didn't include care here, although I was pretty sure it did. She wouldn't let me see anything. She wouldn't give me any proof that what she was doing was per the will either."

"Right." Doreen stared off in the distance. "How we do like to mess up our family."

At that, Nelly smiled gently. "As you said, it's family. I still loved her though."

"Of course you did." Doreen smiled at her. "What's in this journal that she didn't want you to see?"

"I'll give it to you. I suggest you read it before you give it to the police." Nelly kept her gaze steadily on Doreen. "Lots and lots of details are in there. Some about Bob Small."

"Did she know what Bob Small was like?"

Nelly shook her head. "She should have. I mean, she should have known he was a bad man. I kept telling her that, but she didn't want to believe it."

"Right. Did she love him?"

"She said she did, but how can you love somebody who's bad like that?" Nelly asked, looking at her. "I don't think that's possible."

"I think people tell themselves lies in order to avoid dealing with the truth," Doreen offered. "And you can't really blame them, when they're trying to stay hidden away in their own happy bubble."

"I blamed her," Nelly declared bluntly. "I blamed her a lot for it."

"Why?" Doreen asked curiously.

"Because I think she did things to keep herself safe but not others."

"Maybe," Doreen agreed cautiously, not sure where this conversation was going. "But I guess it depends on what she was keeping herself safe from."

"Prosecution," Nelly stated in a hard tone. "She helped Bob, and, when he took off on her like that, she was devastated, but she still wouldn't turn him in."

"Ah, that's an even harder thing."

"Maybe, but she had no right to let him get away with what he did."

"And yet you think she knew?"

Nelly pondered that. "I want to say she knew, but I don't know how the sister I knew and loved could have helped this man *if* she knew."

"And, to be clear, what is it that you think Bob Small

did?"

Nelly stared at Doreen in surprise. "You know he's a serial killer, right?"

At that, Doreen nodded. "I just wanted to make sure we were talking about the same Bob Small."

"Oh, yeah," she muttered, still with a smile. "We're definitely talking about the same man."

"Did you ever meet him?" Doreen asked, looking over at Nelly.

"Sure, decades ago. Not since then. My sister didn't want me to meet him. She said I was already prejudiced against him."

"Were you?"

"Oh, absolutely," she admitted, "and I did try to talk to the police about him back then, but I didn't have anything outside of my so-called crazy suspicions."

"Right, and suspicions are not anything that the police can work with. Circumstantial cases are a nightmare for prosecutors."

"So they kept telling me, but they also didn't make it easy to find out more information."

Doreen pondered that. "Maybe they couldn't have. Maybe they needed more from you."

"Maybe," she muttered. "I don't know. Just so much was wrong with so much back then that it's really hard to say."

"Just out of curiosity, did Ella mention a man by the name of Pullin?"

Nelly grinned. "Oh, yeah. He fell for her bad. She went out with him for quite a while, during the same time as she was seeing Bob, but then Bob was around for decades. Pullin wanted to marry her, and it took Ella a long time to decide, but it was a no in the end. She couldn't leave Bob on a permanent basis."

Doreen tucked that away in the back of her mind. It confirmed what she already knew. "And what does this journal say?"

"I only read the first part, and then I didn't want to read anymore."

"Why is that?" Doreen asked.

"Because my sister knew," Nelly stated. "She *knew*, but she didn't ever really admit it out loud."

"Does it share anything that would help us find this Bob Small?"

She frowned at Doreen. "Do you think he's still alive?"

Doreen thought about it and shrugged. "I don't know for sure, … but I guess a part of me wants to confirm one way or another. If he isn't, that's fine. We can still close a lot of cases. However, if he is alive, I really don't want him around, causing trouble."

"No, I wouldn't want that either." A look of horror overtook her features. "That wouldn't make me very happy." She pondered that and added, "He was older than Ella."

"And that's another thing. Your sister wasn't very old," Doreen noted, "so, if this Bob Small guy had taken care of himself, no reason not to suspect that he's still alive."

"Right," Nelly agreed, pondering that. "In which case we really need to ensure he stopped."

"Do you think he's still killing?" Doreen asked her. "We haven't heard of any other cases."

"He traveled a lot," Nelly shared. "He was a trucker and moved through the States and all across Canada. I wouldn't be at all surprised if he hasn't been active the entire time. You know that he's good at what he does."

"That's not a reassuring thought, is it?" Doreen held out her hand.

Nelly gave her the journal. "This is it. I feel as if I'm still betraying my sister, but she's now dead and gone. I don't know, but maybe this man didn't kill her."

Doreen stared at her in shock. "Are you saying Bob Small *could* have killed her?"

"I'm saying that I saw a man not very long ago, and I wondered if it was him. I even asked Ella about it, and she laughed and told me there was no way. But she looked disconcerted, so maybe there was a chance that Bob is alive and kicking."

Doreen's hand closed around the journal, as she slowly pulled it toward her. "Now I feel as if I should go home and scan this in, so that, if it disappears, we still have a record."

Nelly stared at her, then nodded in gratification. "Could you please do that?" she asked. "I've hung on to this for a long time, even though my sister used to come in and search my room for it."

Doreen winced at that. "Wow, obviously some hard feelings were there."

"A lot of hard feelings," Nelly declared, "but none quite so much as the fact that I knew my sister was harboring all this herself."

"Right, ... and you feel very strongly that you saw Bob Small recently?"

"I do," she confirmed, "and, if that's the case, he could easily have been the one who shot my sister. I didn't do right by her at the end. So, if you can scan this in, keep it safe, and use it to capture her killer, please, please do so."

"I understand."

"I am sure you do, but the guilt will always be with me,"

she murmured. "It's something I need to do for my sister."

"Do you really believe she's had no contact with him all these years?"

"She was devastated when he disappeared. They'd been fighting, and I guess she was really sorry at that point in time because a life without him was not what she wanted either. I can't imagine how anybody with the brainpower of my sister, with that intelligence, knowing what Bob was like, that she could still stay with him."

"But that is your assessment," Doreen pointed out. "You must keep in mind that it may not have been what Ella understood to have been his actions."

Nelly looked over at Doreen. "You give her too much credit, too many good qualities. She's dead, and I shouldn't say anything, but there was an awful lot to *not* like about my sister." And, with that, Nelly shut up and wouldn't say anymore.

Doreen wasn't sure what to do with that information, but she tucked the book into her pocket. "I'll go scan this in right away."

She nodded. "And then you'll need to give a copy to the police." She winced. "I'm not looking forward to the conversation coming up, but it is needed."

Doreen looked at her questioningly.

"I *knew.* I knew about Bob Small, and I held that book over my sister. Even when I had the book, I didn't take it to them. So maybe"—Nelly shrugged—"maybe I'm just as guilty as Ella was." She lay her head back on the couch and closed her eyes.

Doreen got up and slowly wandered back to Nan's place. She found Nan talking with somebody else.

Nan caught sight of her and waved. *I'll talk to you later,*

Nan mouthed.

And, with that, Doreen headed out to the parking lot, hopped into her vehicle, and drove home. As soon as she got home, she reset the security, walked into the kitchen, and propped open the back door for her animals. Then she headed to her little scanner. There, she very carefully, page by page, scanned each in, making sure she had a clear image of every individual one. And then she phoned Mack. "I'm sending you something," she said, her voice quiet.

He asked, "Are you okay? You sound off."

"Yeah, I'm off," she confirmed. "I was called back to Nelly's place. She thinks Bob Small may have killed her sister, and she gave me the item she's held over Ella's head all this time."

"What do you mean?"

"She said that Ella knew about Bob Small, and I've got Ella's journal that Nelly kept and used as blackmail to keep herself in Rosemoor, when her sister kept threatening to take her out."

"Oh, good God," Mack replied, his voice rising. "You have that journal?"

"I do. I've scanned it. I haven't read anything yet," she shared, "but I've scanned every page, and I'm sending you the digital copies right now."

"Any particular reason?"

"Yeah, because Nelly is pretty sure she saw Bob Small not very long ago here in town. I don't know whether it's connected to Ella's case or something else."

"But bottom line, Nelly saw Bob Small, and Ella Hickman is dead." Mack's words had a hard tone to it, and Doreen knew they were both thinking the same thing.

Bob Small killed Ella Hickman.

Chapter 6

Midafternoon ...

D OREEN MADE HERSELF a cup of tea, and, with Ella's
journal in hand, she sat down in the living room and
started to read. She couldn't explain the need to be inside,
where she and the journal were locked up and safe. The
journal told a tale of emotions, love, betrayal, acceptance,
and then almost seeing the pathway to Ella trying to sort
through how to make this okay in her world and to keep
Bob Small in her life. Apparently they'd known each other
for years and years, and she'd had a secret crush on him for a
long time.

Bob was older, and yet it never changed anything for
Ella over all these decades; Ella even knew about Hinja. And
that had been a sour point between the two of them, when
Ella had found out. Bob promised that he would take care of
it and that he would break up with her, and sure enough he
had. Doreen had to go back through her notes to see
whether it had been during the same time frame that he'd
declared he would do so or he had chosen to tell Ella that
and then hadn't followed through. She suspected that the
Hinja relationship was not a case of on again, off again but a

case of whenever he was in town.

Doreen thought about Ella—the woman she had met at Rosemoor—and it didn't seem to fit that a successful professional woman would sit around and wait for her man to show up. But that also didn't mean that Ella had waited nor that she didn't play around on her own. After all, Ella had Pullin and his love for her. There was talk back then about her marrying, but she hadn't. She'd waited for Bob Small to return to town and had realized very quickly that only one man was meant for her, and that was it.

Again, something that Doreen found very difficult to imagine. This was a smart, intelligent woman, who had held a powerful position in town, and yet she had continued to hold the candle for a man who she refused to admit was a serial killer.

Doreen sat back, studying that whole theory, and couldn't make any sense of it. She suspected, when all this came out, it would be one for the case books for a long time. Something that would be held up as an example of unexplained behaviors and misplaced affections and God-only-knows what other words would be attributed to Ella's attraction to Bob Small. But what was it that prompted Nelly's behavior?

If Nelly knew her sister was dating a serial killer, why didn't Nelly do something more about it herself? And, of course, Ella's actions paled in comparison to everybody else's. In Ella's case, she got to keep this man in her life. Somebody she obviously cared very deeply for. Whether that affection was misplaced or not, surely there was some way to understand a woman who had obviously been immersed in an emotional life with this man to the point that she willingly overlooked everything.

Yet both sisters had made interesting decisions. Doreen was trying hard not to judge the sisters herself. An awful lot of family history existed, likely starting with their own father, that would help to explain this.

Doreen pondered that for a long time, making notes for herself, questions to ask Nelly down the road but preferably not too far down the road, so they could get this solved and the case permanently put away. Although, with so many cases attributed to Bob Small, it would be a massive manhunt, and Doreen wasn't sure what it would entail.

That thought brought her back to the fact that Nelly thought she had seen Bob locally, recently too. With so much information to go by and such stunning bits and pieces, Doreen was quite vexed with herself for not having asked Nelly more about her Bob Small sighting—where, when, and what did he look like?

She picked up the phone and managed to connect to Nelly. When she identified herself, Nelly said, "I suppose now you'll be bothering me all the time."

"Until we can get to the bottom of this, quite likely," she admitted calmly. "I am sorry about that in advance."

"I'm already regretting having given it to you. Call it momentary guilt."

"It doesn't matter what we call it. This needed to happen."

"Maybe, and now everybody will look at my sister and hate her."

"I don't know about that either," Doreen replied. "This journal is sad in a way."

"Is it?" Nelly asked in disgust. "And I think that's partly one of the reasons I hung on to them. They say so much that I just couldn't understand about my sister. She obviously loved him, loved him deeply. Have you read it all?"

"I'm more than halfway through. I haven't finished it though."

"You should finish it," she stated bluntly, "and then call me back." And, with that, Nelly hung up.

Worried about what she would still find, Doreen kept reading. When she got to the end, there were several blank pages, and she thought it was such a weird place to end it because Ella had basically written that he was gone from her life and that she didn't know what she would do. Yet obviously Ella had gone on for many years, had picked up the pieces, and had found some purpose in her life.

But, as Doreen flipped through to the end, she came to another few pages with no date, where the woman was practically screaming with joy, writing, *He's back. He's back. Oh, my God, he's back. My life is so full. My heart is so full. He's back.* And then there was nothing.

Doreen stared at that in shock. "Oh, good God," she whispered. "If he was back ..." That was incredibly bad news, for everybody, for every woman in this world, particularly ones with curly hair. Doreen remembered that little detail. It jumped at her. She phoned Mack back.

"What now?" he asked.

"Did you get the attachment?"

"Yeah, I got it, but I haven't had a chance to look."

"One of the last entries she made, Ella's saying, *He's back.*"

"That's nice. Who?" he asked, again distracted.

She waited until she had his attention. "Bob Small. She's adamant that he's back, and she is filled with joy."

"Good God, please don't tell me that Bob Small is in town."

"There's no specific date. Just a month—June."

"And you don't know what year?"

"I don't. I need to find out when Nelly stole this, the second time, … but I'm wondering if Nelly isn't correct when she told me that she saw Bob recently."

"So now what?" he asked.

"I'm thinking that Bob Small might be your number one suspect in Ella's murder." She couldn't see his face, being on the phone.

"I'll take it into consideration." And, with that, he said, "I've got to go."

She heard people calling him in the background, then heard the *click* of the phone call ending. She winced because she kept butting into his life, and he was busy. He had other things to do.

Yet, as she stared down at the journal in her hand, she realized she was busy too. She now had something she needed to work on in a big way. This would come down, and it would come down big.

She phoned Nelly back, and, when she answered the phone, Nelly said, "You have the most terrible timing."

"I'm sorry. Were you napping?"

"No, I was starting a game of snookers," she replied.

Doreen stared down at the phone. "Oh, I didn't realize you play."

"Yes, I do. I play lots of games here, but my sister didn't understand. She told me it was a waste of time and a waste of her money."

"If you are happier for it, then it's not a waste," Doreen stated.

"I *was* happy. Now, of course, I don't even know what to think. I was trying to take my mind off all this."

"I can appreciate the need to do so," she murmured. "However …"

"Right, however, there are things to be settled. I get it. Now what do you want to know? And did you read the end?"

"I did read the end, and, yes, I understand that your sister thought that he was back."

"More than thought, I'm pretty sure she set up several meetings to see him."

"Did she ever say anything to you? And how long have you had that journal?"

"About three months ago, this time, maybe. I knew that she'd gone to meet him. She didn't tell me any of the details, but I told her exactly what I thought of her for it. She glared at me, and one of the threats that she made to me, one that she did tell me, was that, if I didn't return her journal, she would tell Bob that I had it."

Doreen sat back, as yet another bombshell slammed into her world. "I really hope she didn't do that," she replied cautiously.

"I hope not too, and I did wonder. I did ask her about it. Ella laughed and said, *Why not? If I was holding this information against her, no reason for her to not tell him.*"

"And yet she knew what he was like."

"Yes, she did. And when I told her that she would put my life in danger, she laughed and said, *So? Since it was obvious I hadn't cared about her at this point in time, why should she care about me?*"

"Ouch."

"Yeah, as you can tell, some hard feelings remain over this whole thing."

"I would say so," she murmured. "That's not helpful

though."

"Maybe not, but it is what it is."

"And you saw him not very long ago, right?"

"Yes. I told Ella that. She laughed and said that I was lucky. Maybe not," Nelly murmured, "but Ella implied that I should be grateful for having seen him."

"Or was it a case of being grateful for having seen him before he saw you?"

A gasp came on the other end of the phone. "I don't know. Believe me. I've thought about it many times. It's not an easy thing to get answers on."

"No, I'm sure it isn't, but, at the same time, now that we have this information, we must get to the bottom of it. I need a description of Bob."

"Good luck with that," Nelly said.

"Wouldn't Ella have pictures?"

"He wouldn't let her take any pictures, so no pictures were ever allowed."

"Did she sneak any?"

Nelly sighed. "I don't know. She was the kind of person who would, but I don't know."

"Do you have access to her house?"

She stopped and thought about that. "I guess. I have keys."

"And, if I showed you any pictures, could you identify him?"

"I don't know," Nelly admitted. "It's been a long time."

"And yet you saw him recently."

"I did, but it was the look in his eyes, that square chin."

"Tall, short?"

"Tall, six foot at least, if not taller. My sister was tall, she was five ten, and, in heels, he still towered above her."

"In that case, he must be at least six-two."

She repeated, "I don't know."

The fatigue in Nelly's voice worried Doreen. "Do you think your sister told him about the journals?"

"I don't know. Another reason I don't sleep well anymore."

"Of course not."

Nelly laughed and added, "I know his victims were all young. I certainly don't fit that category anymore. So that's a comfort."

"You might not fit," Doreen noted, "but who's to say that he might not make an exception."

"Thanks for that thought," Nelly grumbled.

"I just want you to be careful," Doreen explained. "Your sister's gone. At the moment, we have no way of knowing who killed her."

"She had enemies. You saw several times that she wasn't the nicest person at Rosemoor. But, boy, she was the worst of them all. She wasn't nice at all, but lots of people loved her. Lots of people admired her abrasiveness."

"Good enough," Doreen noted. "I still need some description of this Bob Small guy. What was he wearing? How did he move?"

"He wore jeans and a T-shirt. He was fit. I can tell you that. Even though he's got to be seventy*ish* now, maybe a little older. I can't be sure. Ella was only sixty-six. Even at seventy or so, he was still fit, with muscles and all."

"Okay, so probably works out at the gym. How about his face and all?"

"Bald, like seriously bald, yet not going bald, but he always rocked that look anyway."

"Okay," Doreen murmured, as she took down notes.

"Do you know what he was driving?"

"A truck—a blue truck."

At that, Doreen winced. "That's the most common vehicle. Almost everybody around here is driving a truck."

"I know. Ella used to laugh and say that he spent his life behind the wheel of the eighteen-wheeler, yet no way when he retired would he have anything but a truck."

"And did she ever say what company he worked for?"

"No, he was a contractor, and, as far as I know, he changed his name constantly."

"I don't know about that part, but you would think that, if his name were Bob Small in this world, he might have changed that."

Nelly laughed. "Maybe. Look. I need to go."

"No, that's fine. Be careful, will you?"

"Oh, don't worry," Nelly agreed. Then she hesitated before ending the call. "Look. If you want the keys to my sister's place, come and get them. I'll leave them with Nan."

"You don't mind if I go take a look for myself?" Doreen asked.

"No, don't mind at all, but, if you find out something about my finances, please keep me in the loop."

"There should be a lawyer, and he should contact you," Doreen noted gently.

"Find the lawyer's name for me, and I'll contact him myself," she said tiredly, and, with that, she was gone.

Knowing she would get in trouble because Mack was obviously crazy busy, she phoned him again.

"*Doreen*," he said, with a note of warning.

"Can I go to Ella's apartment?"

"No," he replied immediately.

"Have your guys not been through it yet?"

"I don't know if anybody has or not," he stated, "but we certainly need to. And why would you be going?"

"Her sister has asked me to go find Ella's lawyer's name. I also asked Nelly for a picture of Bob Small, but she said that Bob Small wouldn't ever allow her sister to take photos. However, knowing Ella Hickman, she was the kind to have snuck one anyway."

Mack sucked in his breath. "I'll meet you there. That's the best I can do."

She smiled at the phone. "When?"

"I'm off at four today—if I get this all done."

"Right. I do have an address, but I must look it up."

"It's not an apartment. It's a house in a nice gated community area. I have the address myself." He stopped and added, "Look. You stay put. I'll pick you up now."

"That's probably for the best."

"See you in about ten minutes."

Chapter 7

DOREEN WAITED ANXIOUSLY inside her home. She wanted to take the animals with her to Ella's house, just to see if they picked up on anything.

However, when Mack stepped up to the front door, he called out, "No animals." She glared at him; he shrugged. "Still connected to our crime scene, so the last thing we need to deal with is all the hair, fibers, and everything else coming off them."

She nodded. "Fine." She grabbed her purse and headed out. She hopped into the front of his truck.

He noted, "You've had a heck of a day, and it isn't near over yet."

"Sounds like you have too, right?"

"Yeah, you could say so," he murmured.

She watched the traffic go by, as they drove up to a posh area. "Did you get most of your work done?"

He gave a long-suffering sigh. "Let's just say I still have some things to deal with that I need to work on before the day ends."

"I'm sorry about interrupting you so much today," she muttered.

He flashed a grin her way and said, "Hey, it's all good. At least it's helpful, and you weren't tearing to go on your own."

"I thought about it. I do have the keys to Ella's house, and I have her sister's permission."

"Sure, but you also know how we would have felt, if we'd found out afterward."

She nodded. "So this way, it's even better," she replied, with a bright smile. "Besides, if Bob Small's in there, terrorizing the place, you'll be there to help out."

He shot her a look. "Bob Small?"

"Yeah, you have been listening, right?" He nodded. "Ella had a relationship with him starting a long time ago. And that part about him being back?"

"Which you told me that you didn't have a specific date for."

She pondered that and then nodded reluctantly. "This is all speculation up until now. However, I do know Nelly said she thought Ella met with him a few weeks ago."

He frowned at that. "How did Nelly find out about that?"

"I don't know. The sisters were having a huge fight over these last few months, and, for all I know, it was all about Rosemoor and money."

"Most families fight about money," Mack noted, "and it's the next most popular reason for fights in relationships."

She sighed. "Both of those make sense in this case."

Finally they pulled up in front of a really nice brick house. She stared at it and said, "Wow, Ella Hickman was doing very well, obviously."

"She was, but I'm not so sure about Nelly," he added. "We did track down Ella's lawyer, and he's yet to get back to us on her will. He hadn't even heard about Ella's death yet."

"No, of course not. It's not exactly news." As they hopped out, Doreen walked up, pulled out the keys that she had been given, and unlocked the front door. She looked over at him. "Have the cops been here?"

"No, not yet, but it's in the process."

"Good," she muttered. "Let's go take a look." As they moved into the front hallway, she gasped and stopped. He immediately grabbed her arm, pulled her toward him, and muttered, "Stop. No going in."

She understood the warning because the living room had been completely upturned—books and loose papers were all over the floor; the couch had been flipped, its cushions scattered all over the place. She slid closer to Mack and whispered, "Do you think the intruder is still here?"

"I'm not sure." Yet he already had his phone out and was talking to somebody at the station. She stepped out of his arms and peered around him to look at the kitchen. Same thing there.

Drawers had been yanked out, cupboards opened. She knew in her heart of hearts it would be somebody after those journals, but it was also possible that it could have just been a simple robbery. Maybe somebody had found out that Ella was dead and took advantage of the situation. There were enough lowlifes who would have decided it was a perfect opportunity to take anything of value.

But then they would have put themselves in danger of being charged with murder or linked to the murder, so maybe that didn't make sense after all. She wandered through the kitchen, following Mack, who then headed back to the center of the living room, a grim look on his face.

He looked over at her and whispered, "I'll go upstairs."

She nodded. "Do you think it's empty?"

"I'll go give it a look," he said, but he was staring at her.

She got it. "Right. I'm in the way. Stay down here."

"Let's say I would much rather you weren't here at the moment."

She shrugged. "Yet the safest place for me is with you. Therefore, if this guy isn't hiding somewhere close by," she muttered, "he may be inside. So let me come up with you."

He stared at her and then nodded. "Fine, but you'll listen to me if I tell you to get out of the way?"

"I got it. I really do."

He looked at her for reassurance and then sighed. "No, you don't, but come on. Let's go."

She followed behind him, careful, listening as they went. She murmured, "It sounds empty."

"I think it is, but I can't be sure." As they got to the second floor, he quickly searched through the upper level of the house, while he made her stay at the top of the stairs. Once that was done, he stepped out and nodded at her. "It's empty."

"Good," she said, and they moved into the main bedroom together. She stopped and stared. "Wow, it's hard to believe that this kind of luxury is even around."

He turned toward her. "This isn't very luxurious, and it wouldn't be even close to what you had with your husband."

She laughed. "But, after all these months basically destitute, I've already forgotten about that. This is really nice." And it wasn't even so much that; it was as luxurious as Ella could afford. Mack was right. Doreen had seen better at Mathew's house, but there was something very lived-in and cozy here. "I really like this room," she announced.

"Good," Mack replied. "So you stay there, looking at the

decor, and I'll search the contents."

She winced at that. "No, I'll help." She dove for the closet, and he went for the night table. As she opened up the closet, she gasped. "My God, there's a fortune in clothes here."

"She was in business, and I'm sure she still had lots of power clothing," he replied.

"I guess, but still, if Nelly sold all this, she'll get thousands and thousands of dollars out of it."

He burst out laughing. "Trust you to be thinking about how to make money from it."

"Hey, I've been broke just long enough. Almost everywhere is an opportunity to make money," she claimed, with a smile. She spied a small step stool in the back of the closet; she pulled it forward and immediately opened it up and stepped onto it, looking at the top shelf of the closet.

He turned and watched her. "What are you doing?"

"The only reason you keep a step stool in your closet is because you use it to reach something," she explained. "So let's see what's up here."

He stepped beside her and noted, "Remember. Ella's tall. So, even if you might reach the top shelf, you still may not know what's up there." Mack pulled out two pairs of gloves, handing her one before putting his on. He flipped on the light switch.

"Oh, that helps too. I like having lit closets." She studied the top shelf. "Interesting. All kinds of boxes are up here." She pulled them down, handing them to him.

"You think this is interesting?" he muttered, as he stared at her.

"Yeah. Did you know there are lots of journals?"

"Ah, but then again you have the one that's important,

right?"

"I have one of them, but we don't know what else might be in all of them that could unlock the case."

He laughed. "You're starting to sound like a real detective."

"Not that you'll like that"—she chuckled—"but, hey, it's something."

By the time they had everything down from the top shelf, he heard movement at the front of the house. "Company is here. ... And you won't like this," he muttered, "but you'll no longer be active in this case."

She turned to protest and saw the look in his gaze. She raised both hands and glared at him.

He smiled. "I'm sorry. I know that you're really getting into this."

"Of course I am," she cried out. "How can you do this to me?"

"I'm doing this *to you* because this is a case that we need to lock up for the courts, and, whether you like it or not, you are still a civilian."

"Who has full rights to be here," she reminded him.

He nodded at that. "You can stay, as long as you represent the sister." When she looked at him with a question in her gaze, he added, "Nelly told you to come and to find her sister's will, and she wanted the name of Ella's lawyer and if there was any information about her finances, right?"

"Yes."

"That means there is a loophole for you to exploit. It gives you a probable cause to be here. Nelly really doesn't know about her finances?"

At that, Doreen shook her head. "No."

"So definitely something is involved here that we need to

get to the bottom of," Mack stated.

Doreen added, "But the lawyer should help with that, right?"

"Yes, I just need him to call me back."

"It's a lawyer, so …" She gave a wave of her hand. "Chances are, he won't get back to you very quickly."

Mack chuckled. "Remember? We're working on your attitude toward lawyers."

She winced. "Right. Speaking of which …"

"No, I haven't heard from Nick." Mack sighed. "Some days I wonder if you'll ever get a divorce."

"You and me both," she said, with feeling. "It's hardly fair, but sometimes I really worry about it too."

Then the front door opened, and Arnold called out, "Mack?"

He yelled back, "We're upstairs in the closet." He looked at Doreen. "Now step back." She frowned but followed his orders, stepping back as Arnold came in.

He took one look and chuckled. "You again, *huh*?"

"Sorry, but Ella's sister asked me to come look for paperwork that would let her know about her finances."

"Her finances?"

Doreen nodded. "Ella managed Nelly's finances at Rosemoor. They had quite a few arguments lately about Nelly not being able to stay at Rosemoor."

"So the poor lady is beside herself thinking that she'll have to leave, *huh*? Well, she might," Arnold guessed, "particularly if she had anything to do with this."

At that, Doreen smiled. "I've already explained it to Mack, so he'll fill you in, but, as much as Nelly might have thought she had something to do with it, what she did is minor enough that she won't be involved in your case."

Arnold looked at her in confusion. She shrugged.

Mack chuckled. "Don't worry about it, Arnold. I still need to talk with the sister," Mack explained, "but considering Doreen was on her way over …"

"Right, got it," Arnold noted, "and then you got here, and there was already an intruder."

"Yeah." Doreen smiled. "Hence why you're here."

"*Great.* Forensics is on its way too." Arnold looked over at Mack. "You're thinking this has something to do with Ella's death?"

"I'm thinking that we don't have any other way to look at this but to take it at face value."

"No, I get it." Arnold rubbed his jaw and scratched at the unshaven stubble he was sporting. "What was the intruder looking for?"

Mack faced her. She shrugged. "Probably journals."

Arnold stared at her. "I guess that was real popular back then, wasn't it?"

She laughed. "It was real popular back then and still is today."

"Journals are helpful if they have anything useful. However, what they often are," Arnold shared, "is romantic nonsense or musings of a depressed mind."

"I know," she agreed, "and that just complicates our world."

"Sure does," Arnold declared. Hearing another vehicle, he turned. "I've got to go."

As soon as he left, Doreen asked Mack, "Anything in the boxes?"

"Lots of paperwork, old legal cases, contact files, business cards, and maybe a backup of her stuff."

"Surely she would have gone digital," Doreen suggested.

"It's hard to say, but I would think so too." He frowned at that thought.

"So then why are all these documents still here?"

"They may not have gotten to the scanning part," he told her. "Remember? Not everybody gets to where they want to be as fast as they want to. She may also have been scared to get rid of the physical copies. Not everyone trusts the cloud."

Doreen shook her head at that. "Or she didn't want to keep a digital record of it."

"There are a lot of materials that *we*," he said, with quiet emphasis, "must go through, and that won't be a fast process."

"No, but if it's all connected …"

He winced. "If it's all connected, I'll sit here and read through a ton of journals. Not exactly what I want to do with the rest of my day."

"Won't be just your *day*." Doreen chuckled. "Would be your evening too."

He glared at her. "I'll run you home."

She nodded. "Fine, you do that." As she glanced around again, she asked, "Can I go into her office first?"

"No," Mack said. "We'll contact Nelly and give her Ella's lawyer's name."

"But what about her finances?"

"We'll talk to the lawyer and see how that's been set up."

She groaned. "That's not *me* helping her. That's *you* helping her. And actually I don't know how much help there is in that because a lawyer is involved." He glared at her. She raised her palms and sighed. "Fine. I'll call her when I get home. What's the lawyer's name?"

He gave it to her, and she nodded. "At least he's not anyone I know."

"They're not all bad. Remember that."

"Nope, they're not all bad. Your brother may be the exception to the rule."

He smiled and dropped her off, with a final warning. "Stay out of it now, please."

She nodded, crossing her arms, as she turned around on her top step, watching him drive away from her.

He wasn't giving her a whole lot of choice, but she also knew where the line had been drawn. Trouble was, she was already involved in the current case because of somebody else. With that, she headed inside and phoned Nelly. When she answered, she seemed tired, worried. "Have you talked to the cops yet?" Doreen asked her. "I have the lawyer's contact information for you." She quickly rattled it off for Nelly to write down.

"Thanks. And no, I keep expecting the cops to show up, but so far they haven't." Then Nelly cried out, "Why haven't they?"

"I've already talked to them myself, so Mack knows what's happened between you two, and he will be there soon, but I went to your sister's house with him," she added.

"You find anything?"

"Somebody had already gotten to it."

"What do you mean?" she cried out in horror.

Doreen quickly explained. "Now there's an investigation going on into your sister's place."

"Oh, good Lord, this nightmare is getting bigger and bigger."

"The problem is, when there are secrets like this, and somebody dies, other people want to bury the secrets, while still others really want those secrets to come out."

"I wouldn't want to ruin my sister's reputation."

Doreen stared down at the phone. "I think it's well past that point now. Your sister's been murdered, and her life will get completely turned upside down, as the cops find her killer."

"But what if they don't sort it out? What if they get it wrong?"

"It doesn't matter," she murmured. "It's the play we've got. Once there is a death—and in this case, a violent murder—all bets are off. It's in the cops' hands now."

"You make sure that they sort out her death properly," she instructed.

"I don't really have any pull in that department," she muttered, wondering how people assumed she could do any of that.

"You should," Nelly declared. "You work with the cops."

"Sure I do, but I don't have an official position," she shared, "and you know that, when it comes to an active case of this magnitude, they do try to keep everybody out."

"*Sure*," Nelly replied. "That's what'll happen to my sister, and then they'll forget all about it, and she won't get any justice, while they focus on Bob Small."

"I don't think that's true," Doreen disagreed, hoping it wasn't. "I think there will be an awful lot of justice, but it might not come down the way you think it will."

"Meaning?"

"I don't know yet," she hedged, trying not to get pigeonholed into anything. "I think it's a case of we must wait and see."

"I don't want to wait and see," Nelly wailed. "Can't you do something?"

At that, Doreen winced. "No. Right now, there's nothing I can do but go back over the journal, take notes, check out timelines, see where this Bob Small guy is and whether he's been in Kelowna recently or not. We need a picture, and once I got to Ella's house, everything had been tossed. So there was no easy way to find anything. I'll go back, as soon as the police have cleared the crime scene, and they can let me back in again."

"When will that be?" Nelly asked in a nervous tone.

"Probably tomorrow," she murmured. Of course she could also quite possibly be way wrong here.

"Hopefully that would be fast enough," she muttered.

"Fast enough for what?"

"I think I saw him again," she told her nervously.

"When?"

"Today."

"Today?" Doreen repeated, straightening up. "What do you mean, *today*? Did you go anywhere else today, other than the mall and then the airport?"

"No, I didn't," Nelly snapped. "I'm not supposed to go anywhere. That's why everybody was so angry when I drove the van, but I needed it for that quick trip. I thought I saw him outside Rosemoor."

"And you have a driver's license, right?"

"I did. I certainly drove a lot. I don't know whether it was still valid or not. I didn't really care either, at that moment."

Doreen winced at that. "Which would also explain why everybody got upset."

"Sure, but believe me. I won't be allowed to do it again."

"Good," Doreen declared. "If nothing else, you could have put other people in danger."

She snorted at that. "I don't care about anybody else.

And, if I didn't kill my sister, somebody did. And now I want to know who."

"And why do you want to know who?" she asked cautiously.

There was silence on the other end. "What do you mean? I want whoever did this to pay for it."

"Interesting," she muttered. "We still need to get an awful lot of answers yet. So hold on tight, and I'll get back to you with any answers, as soon as I get some." And, with that, she ended the call.

Chapter 8

NOT EVEN AN hour later Doreen found out that she really wasn't good at waiting. Particularly waiting for answers or waiting for Mack to get back to her. She wasn't too keen on waiting for things to happen in life to give her a direction to go in. She felt beyond stuck, and, when it came time to go outside and relax and do nothing for a bit, she took the animals down to the river and sat there pondering life and what this latest mess could mean. So many people were affected by this Bob Small.

She'd texted Mack about the possibility this guy had been outside of Rosemoor, but without proof, he'd told her to keep it to herself but be careful.

If he was alive, he would do everything he could to avoid capture. Particularly after all these years, no way he would roll over and let somebody take him down. And was that what had happened with Ella? Had she decided that she'd had enough and would turn him in?

Had Ella warned Bob about Nelly? Had Ella gotten pissed off enough at Nelly that she'd set Bob Small on Nelly? However, instead of taking her out, Bob had taken out Ella first? In a way that would make more sense. Now who was there to protect or to give a hoot if Nelly was taken out?

And considering she's the one who had the journal, that would be a logical next step. If Bob had taken out Nelly first, then Ella would know who had done it and may have had a spell of remorse over it all. Yet she might not have, considering how that sisterly dynamic had been working out lately. However, if so, then Ella may very well have turned Bob over to the authorities, and he couldn't have that happening.

As Doreen pondered that and the vague description she'd gotten, she wondered if there were any security cameras at Ella's house. She quickly texted Mack. When she got back **No**, she frowned at that and sent another text. **That's very strange for a woman living alone, a former politician and a savvy business person too.**

Mack gave her a thumbs-up in agreement. Not that that was a help, but it also meant that he at least was on the same page as Doreen was. It was so strange for this successful and well-off woman to have not safeguarded her life and her expensive home with a security system. Maybe she had a security system, but it wasn't on, or maybe she was changing companies or something else. Or maybe Bob Small had removed it. The man appeared to be quite capable, and anybody who was that capable was seriously dangerous.

Not that anybody would ever listen to anything Doreen had to say. As she'd come to realize, so many people didn't want to hear the truth, no matter what. And what if Bob Small went to ground now? What if he decided that he'd covered his tracks enough, so he could just run? Who would stop him then? That was one of the things that really bothered her.

This guy had shown himself to be resilient in way-too-many scenarios. He could cheerfully take out a lot more people. The thought that he'd changed or had become a nice guy didn't even occur to Doreen. She didn't think that level of change could happen with a cold-blooded serial killer.

With those thoughts nagging at her, Doreen went inside and grabbed the journal and her notepad from the living room. Sitting at her kitchen table, she opened up the journal and read it through again, hoping for some more insights. When her phone rang, she ignored it. She didn't recognize the number, and, right about now, the last thing she wanted was to talk to a stranger. Somehow the media always seemed to end up finding her, before she had a chance to figure out how to block them yet again.

When it rang again, she stared at it and on instinct answered it. Sure enough, it was Gary Wildorf, calling from prison. She winced at that.

"Not only did you contact Ella but now I hear she's dead. Does everybody die around you?" he asked, with a dry snarky tone.

She stared down at the phone.

"Or is it just being around you?" he suggested, his sneering evident over the phone.

Doreen now realized that *this* was an entirely new avenue she hadn't even considered. What was wrong with her? She should have had that locked down. "So anyone you know talking about it?"

He snorted. "Nobody is killing anyone around here. Remember? We're all locked up."

"True enough, but maybe they'll come back after you, realizing that Ella's name came from you."

Gary went silent for a moment. "Oh, I don't think so," he said finally. "That was way too long ago."

"Or so you hope," she murmured.

In a disgusted tone he added, "If that's the case, you should be trying to protect me. I have more information."

"So you say," Doreen stated, with an almost disinterested tone.

"Hey, how come you don't care now?" he snapped.

"Now we have another murder," she explained, "so it causes us a few more problems here."

He laughed at that. "Not my fault," he declared. "You guys are the ones digging into stuff you shouldn't be. Some of this should stay buried."

She answered him, with that same odd tone. "Seems like the same stuff you were quite willing to jump into yourself."

"If I can make my life easier, why wouldn't I?" he declared. "I've had enough of this place, and that Bob Small guy is out free and clear, so I don't give a hoot."

"Glad to hear it," she murmured. "Are you ready to give me anything useful?"

"You already got something useful." He laughed again. "You think I don't know how useful that last tip was?"

Doreen sighed. "Not my fault she's dead either. Still we obviously can't get any information from Ella, seeing as how she's been murdered."

"I didn't kill her," Gary replied, "and it has nothing to do with me that you couldn't get your ducks in a row before somebody whacked her one."

"Any idea who whacked her?"

"What? You think I run a daily news call-in for Murderers United or something?" he asked in disgust. "Remember that part about I'm in jail here? You can check the visitor's log. I haven't had any visitors."

She pondered that because having visitors was one thing but somehow knowing what was going on elsewhere? Doreen was pretty sure law enforcement was continually flabbergasted at the way prisoners managed to keep in touch with the goings-on outside in the world, maybe way better than actual law enforcement officials did. "And that may be true," she noted calmly, "and it could also be that you knew ahead of time that somebody would do this."

At that came a moment of silence from Gary. "Oh, wow, you're really giving me lots of credit. A part of me wants to accept that credit. After all, kudos to me, right?" He gave a snort. "I didn't really think you were that stupid. Guess I was wrong."

"I'm not stupid at all, but, if people are killing each other over this, I'm not sure I want to get too involved, not until all the dust settles."

At that, he burst out laughing. "Sounds so much like law enforcement. Go, go, go, until the going gets tough. Then everybody backs off and lets the chips fall where they may."

"Is that really your experience?" she asked in a quiet tone.

"Absolutely. Nobody cares about the *right* answers, as long as they get an answer. When you want to talk again, you know where I am." With that, he disconnected.

She dialed Mack.

He answered right away. "I am busy."

"And I wouldn't bother you unless …"

"Unless what?" he asked, his voice sharp. "What's the matter now?"

She stared at the phone. "We really must work on our relationship if you think the only time I phone you is when I'm in trouble."

"Or when you want something," he pointed out, a note of humor entering his tone, "or when you're hungry."

"I'm not that bad," she protested.

"Nope, you're not, but you're evading my question."

She groaned. "The inmate, Gary Wildorf, called me." After a bit of silence, Mack swore. She frowned into the phone.

"What did he want?" Mack asked.

"I'm not sure if he did want something. Sounded as if he was checking to see whether I had followed up on the information he'd given me or whether he was fishing for more information or just generally letting me know he was still there. But he already knew about Ella's death. He mentioned something like kudos for him for being correct on the information he gave me."

Mack quietly digested that information. "An interesting take on it," he muttered. "I don't know how much good that information was, since she is dead, so we'll never know."

"I told him that. Since we couldn't get any information from her, it wasn't a good source."

"Oh, I'm sure he absolutely loved that, *huh?*"

"No, not at all," she confirmed, with a small smile, even though she knew Mack couldn't see it. "I think Gary was more pissed about that whole process than anything."

"Of course. He gave us what he considered a good source, and the good source gets whacked in the meantime, and so the information isn't something that we can then work with."

"And yet there was almost that sense of curiosity to see what we were up to."

"Think about his position. Gary gave us information. Ella gets whacked. Gary thinks that we're being too slow, and now he's on the outside, watching how we run around, the whole *mice in a trap* scenario."

"Yeah, that's not very much fun," she muttered.

"Nope, it isn't, but a lot of these guys play that way."

She pondered that and then added, "I thought you should know."

"I'm glad you told me," he said, with honesty. "If he calls you again, let me know, and now I've got to go back to work."

"I guess there's no news, is there?"

"There isn't, … and probably won't be for a while."

"Okay, I'll let you get back to work then." And she quickly ended the call.

As she sat here, she wondered. Something in the inmate's tone made her question whether he'd known more about this than he was letting on. Obviously he didn't want to tell people if he was involved, Yet, at the same time, it would be nice to know if Gary knew something else that they could run on.

She phoned him back and was thankful when he could answer her call. It hadn't been very long, so maybe he was still close to a phone or in the visitor's area.

He laughed when he heard who it was. "That didn't take you long," he said in a jovial tone.

"Oh, it's not so much about taking long," she replied. "We're working on this as much as we can right now, but, without knowing who killed her, it's hard."

"Yeah, I'm sure it is, but, if you're expecting me to help you out anymore, don't bother."

"Yeah, why's that?" she asked. "Somebody warned you off?"

"Nobody warns me off anything," he declared in a dark tone. "Stop being insulting."

"Ah, well, I didn't know how much of a bad guy you are

to these guys."

He snapped, "There you go insulting me again."

"Not trying to," she noted cheerfully. "However, I really don't have any ins or outs on how you function in there, so I don't know how they look at you."

"With respect," he snapped once more. "Everybody here looks at me with respect."

The way he pronounced it made her think that it was the opposite. "Good, everybody needs to have respect in life."

"Right," he muttered. "Now if only you'll give me a little bit."

"Hey, I phoned you for information," she pointed out. "That means that I trust you have something useful."

"I gave it to you."

"Not really," she corrected. "You gave me the name of somebody who would get whacked. Yet you didn't tell me that she would get whacked, so I could go save her. Therefore, we couldn't get any information off her. So I'm not sure you gave me anything other than a decoy."

After a bit of silence on the other end, he replied in a conversational tone, "That was a bit convoluted. Yet I finally got down to the end of that, in which case, you think I gave you wrong information."

"I don't know that it's right or wrong," she clarified, "but I would prefer a lead I could verify before somebody dies."

He snorted at that. "Maybe you should talk to her sister then."

"Oh, I've talked to her all right," Doreen stated.

"Nelly is a fruitcake, isn't she?" he asked quite cheerfully.

"I won't go that far." Doreen didn't like the way he described Nelly, but maybe it was to get a rise out of Doreen. Just considering that, she was more determined to not let him have that either.

"Yeah, well, from what I heard, the sister's a long way away from being innocent in all this. Just ask Bob Small."

Doreen stared down at the phone. Then she heard the distinctive *click*.

Chapter 9

"WHAT DOES THAT mean?" Doreen murmured and wondered how much involvement Nelly did have with any of this, seemingly going back to the beginning so many years earlier.

It's not something Doreen wanted to contemplate, but was there any chance that Nelly had had a relationship with the same Bob Small? If so, why were all these women falling all over him? The fact that there was even the slightest implication that Nelly might have been involved with the serial killer guy sent chills down Doreen's back. Surely that wasn't possible?

She pondered that and then phoned Nelly. "Did you ever have a relationship with this guy?"

After a brief delay, Nelly asked casually, "What do you mean by *relationship*?"

"You never married, right?" Doreen asked.

"No, I never did. What difference does that make?" Nelly's voice gained in strength. "Just because I wasn't married, does that make me less than someone?"

"Of course not," Doreen replied. "In many ways maybe it makes you more."

The woman stopped to consider her words. "What?"

"Never mind," Doreen said. "That's just my tainted view of marriage." Nelly remained quiet, so Doreen continued. "So my question remains. Did you have a relationship with this Bob Small guy?"

"I knew him first," she shared, "but, once he met my sister, he was all over her."

"Oh, wow. ... I didn't realize that."

"Nobody does," Nelly declared in disgust, "and it happens way too often."

"You mean, you would bring home some boyfriend, and your sister would take them?"

"I don't even know that she was *trying* to take them. I would bring them home, and they would immediately gravitate toward her. She was much more dynamic than I was," Nelly admitted, with difficulty. "I was the quiet mouse, and she was the lioness out to take a mate," she shared in a dry tone, "and too often that's exactly how it worked out."

Not following, Doreen asked, "Meaning that Ella had lots of hard and fast relationships?"

"Something like that, yes," Nelly confirmed in disgust, "and she never married either."

"Any particular reason?"

"Yes, Bob Small wouldn't marry her." Nelly laughed. "That was a good thing. I'm still surprised that she would even contemplate it, if she knew what he did. Well, there's knowing what he did and then there's *knowing* what he did. She kept telling herself that no way he could have done this and that it was all a conspiracy."

"But your sister was an intelligent woman, and she knew exactly how this worked. She likely did know but couldn't accept it."

"And she was *in love*. After all the men she'd had in her life, she was in love. Besides, you've got to understand. Ella and Bob had this weird off-and-on relationship for decades. He wasn't always faithful to her. Yet, in some twisted way, they were always together. The other people they dated weren't part of their relationship."

"They were allowed to have other relationships, but, if one should call, the other would come?" Doreen sat back, stunned. "So, in that way, he was allowed to travel from place to place and not bother her, is that it?"

"Exactly, and then, when he was in town, she was there for him."

"Regardless of any other relationship?"

"Exactly," Nelly stated in a dry tone. "As I said, they had a very strange relationship, Doreen, and the more you delve into it, the stranger it gets."

"I don't know," Doreen hedged. "I've seen a couple of others where it was weird too."

"And, in Ella's case, she kept saying that she could walk away and leave Bob at any time. However, when crunch time actually came, she never could."

"Do you think that was by choice or was that by his?"

"I honestly don't know. I asked her about it a few times, and she would laugh and say that she was completely in control of the situation."

"And yet you don't think she was?"

"No, she wasn't. She could never walk away from him, and I'm not sure he would ever let her. I fail to see how any of this is important though."

"Because it helps me to understand the dynamics between the two of them."

"It was twisted," Nelly noted calmly.

Something almost *more adult* about Nelly's tone was something that Doreen hadn't heard until now. "And your relationship with Bob, after he hooked up with your sister?"

"There wasn't one," she declared. "I was pretty upset at the time, and it's probably one of the reasons why I hung on to the journal and held it over her head all this time. Just one more thing that Ella did better than me."

Doreen winced at that because how could she even begin to argue or to understand when she had no siblings of her own? "I'm sorry. I am an only child, so didn't contend with those dynamics. I don't know what that is like."

"Lucky you," Nelly replied immediately. "There's no joy to be had where siblings are always playing *one up*. Now she's gone, and I realize how pathetic the whole scenario was. And yet it's too far gone for me to do anything about it now."

"I can see that," Doreen agreed. "So let's do what we can to put it to rest and let's hope your sister finds some peace."

"She was murdered. How does anybody who's been murdered find peace?"

"I like to think that there is peace for them, and I like to think that we can find justice. I know that we don't always, and I know that they don't always go together."

"No, they don't," Nelly confirmed bitterly. "Particularly with guys like Bob Small, who had been running this place ragged forever."

"Because nobody has done anything to stop him," Doreen pointed out.

Nelly gasped. "I know I'm just as much to blame as my sister. You don't need to keep bringing that up."

"I didn't intend to," Doreen replied, trying hard to keep Nelly calm. "So I guess I must ask you, is there anything else you want to tell me about this, before the police start delving into it?"

At that, Nelly gave a broken laugh. "No. I'm not happy with any of my involvement in this up until now. The only thing I can do is try to make it right. My sister didn't deserve to be murdered. We had a lot of problems between us, but she didn't deserve that."

"No, I'm sure she didn't," Doreen murmured. "Nobody does."

"No, but that Bob Small does," Nelly snapped.

"And yet I need a better description for him," she added. "I have an approximate age, seventy-something. I need something more. Are you sure you don't have any photos?"

She hesitated and then admitted reluctantly, "Maybe. … I didn't give it to you before because I'm not sure it's him."

"Maybe you should give it to me now," Doreen suggested in a dry tone, "and let us worry about it. At least, if we have a picture, we can find out who this person is, so we can talk to him. So far he's just a ghost."

"That was what he was all the time, just a ghost. Ella never knew when he was coming into town, where he was in the meantime, and they didn't talk about it. She accepted his presence when he was here and ignored it when he wasn't. It was one of those relationships that she just couldn't give up."

"Was she ever asked to?"

"She had serious boyfriends over the years, so, yes," Nelly said. "I already told you about Pullin, a man who really loved her, wanted her to be with him, and wanted to marry her, but she wasn't having anything to do with it."

"She was never tempted in all that time, especially those couple decades where they had broken up and when she never saw him?" Doreen asked in amazement.

"As far as I understand, no," Nelly stated. "And believe

me. You're not the only one who's surprised about it. I've tried to talk her into marrying somebody else the whole time. Only once she admitted she was scared that, if she did marry, what would Bob do?"

Doreen sat back, stunned. "And was there anybody Ella was close to, who may have experienced something unpleasant from this guy?"

Nelly gave a startled exclamation. "I don't know. She was quite serious about another man, and she talked to him about marriage at one point in time, before deciding to break it off. But I don't know whatever happened to him after that."

"You want to give me a name?" Doreen asked. "Maybe I can track him down and see what that was all about."

"His name was Lucas, Lucas Donovan," Nelly murmured. "He was a real estate agent in town."

"Maybe he won't be too hard to track," she noted.

"I don't know. I lost track of him years ago. He upped and moved to another province."

"Is that what Ella told you?"

"She said that he got upset and wanted to go find himself or something like that," Nelly explained. "The end result, as far as I know, was he changed provinces."

Doreen didn't know what to think about that, even after she had disconnected. She checked out Lucas Donovan locally, but found no sign of anybody with that name. She frowned, contemplating what it would take for somebody successful and well-set to pack up like that and start all over again. She knew it happened. People certainly did it, but was it the most logical thing for them to do? Not likely.

Would they do it because they were fed up and upset? Possibly. And would they do it because they've been threatened to an inch of their lives? Absolutely. But it still didn't mean that this Bob Small guy had anything to do with Lucas's move. She had to talk to this Lucas Donovan first. She checked the time, surprised to see it was just three o'clock. This day seemed to go on forever. Regardless, if she were to make calls to real estate companies, she had to do that before they closed for the day.

She found a couple old articles on the internet with his name and the company that he used to work for. Giving it a shot, she picked up the phone and contacted the company, asking if they had any company update for Lucas Donovan.

"He moved to Alberta," the woman replied. "Quite a few years ago now though."

"Any idea what company he worked for there?"

"*Hmm*, I'm not sure, but it was one of the big ones," she noted, giving her the name of one. "You can try there."

"Thank you very much," Doreen replied.

"What's this about?" she asked curiously.

"Oh, nothing much. I'm trying to get some background information."

"Ah, I wondered because his former girlfriend was just murdered." There was almost a gossipy tone to her voice.

"I did hear that," Doreen murmured, "and I don't know if Lucas has heard the news or not."

"I'm sure he will hear soon enough, but I hope he's gotten over her. I know he was pretty upset at the time because they'd been going out for a long while. Then, all of a sudden, he asked her to marry him, but she said no. What do you do after that? It was basically a case of heartbreak. He wanted to leave town to get away from the memories."

"I'm sorry. That's got to be tough. Most guys don't extend that offer unless they're absolutely positive it'll be accepted as a yes."

"Right," the other woman agreed. "We all felt terrible for him. And he had every expectation that it would go the way he thought it would, but I guess it wasn't meant to be. And now to find out that she's been murdered," she added in a sympathetic tone, "that can't be easy. If you get in touch with him, say hi for me. He's a really nice guy."

"Have you talked to him since?"

"Nope, not at all. He came in one day and stated that he was planning on leaving and handed in his notice. There was a lot of talk about it at the time, but people pretty-well understood why he was leaving. Everybody knew he was planning on asking her, and then he upped and left. He never came back in again, and it was all arranged through bank accounts, and he was gone."

"Interesting," Doreen noted. "That's awfully fast."

"When your heart's breaking, I think *awfully fast* is the way you go. He only had to hand off a few deals in progress, and then he was on his way."

"Understood," Doreen said calmly. "Let's hope I can find him."

"I'm sure the Alberta police might have some idea of Lucas's whereabouts."

"Why's that?"

"His father lived in Alberta, and Lucas was always close to him."

"Interesting, so maybe I'll check up on the family first then."

"You could. Oh, come to think of it, I think they called here, after he left, looking for him, but we never heard again after that."

"Okay, let me dig a little bit. Hopefully nothing's happened to him."

"I don't know why there would be." Then she gasped. "You don't think he committed suicide?"

"I don't know that he's missing at all," Doreen commented in a dry tone, "so that would be a definite no."

The other woman gave a nervous laugh. "Right, that would be the first thing, wouldn't it? We did get some inquiries about him, but nobody really followed up. ... Plus I didn't talk to anybody myself. I just know that we were asked if we'd seen him or talked to him since."

"You mean, as if he'd gone missing?"

She pondered that. "It was a long time ago, so I'm not really sure how to answer that question, but I don't think so."

"I'll see what comes up." Doreen rang off, quickly searched, and found the family. Getting the phone number was a different story. Finally she managed to get one of the family members on a call.

"He went missing," she stated bluntly.

"When?"

"He was supposed to come home to Alberta, and we were all looking forward to it. I know that he was pretty upset. Some girl he'd asked to marry him had refused. Rather than sticking around, trying to work it out, he left the problems behind."

"And how did he sound at the end?"

"Nervous and upset," she noted. "Upset more than anything else."

"Right. He wasn't being threatened or anything, was he?"

"I don't think so at all, but he did sound off at the end, but then, considering what he'd been through, it's what we expected."

"Right," Doreen said, knowing that people tended to see what they expected to see. "And he hasn't been seen since?"

"No, not since," she confirmed. "If you find him, he has a big family who's looking for him."

"And presumably you put in a missing person report for him?"

"We did at the time, but, given the circumstances, the police believed that he booked it, didn't want to come home to all the sympathetic mumbles and jumbles that happen in a family, and wanted time by himself. So he's an adult, and, if he wants to take off, he gets to take off." Yet a note of bitterness filled her voice.

"I'm sorry. That must have been hard to deal with."

"It was terrible," she cried out. "Just because he's an adult, nobody seemed to care. He was en route, but he didn't tell us when he would be here, just that he'd get here when he could get here."

"But he never got there?"

"No, he never got here, and, yes, we reported it, and he never showed up since. So it was a missing person's case, and there were an awful lot of speculations that he'd done something to himself because he was so distraught."

"And was he the type to do that?"

"I wouldn't have thought so, no," she stated. "Yet there has been no sign of him since. I suspected he drove into a river, whether accidentally or on purpose, and never made it."

"What were the weather conditions around that time?"

"It was winter," she said, "and the roads were icy. The following spring, we drove up and down a lot of the roads leading here, trying to find him. However, he could have gone any number of routes, and he could have done any number of things en route. So not the easiest to sort out."

"No, and, of course, very devastating to the family as a whole because now you're left with that unsettled question of what happened."

"Exactly," she murmured. "We haven't forgotten about him. He's on our minds all the time." And, with that, she ended the call.

Doreen sat here for a long moment. If Lucas had driven into a lake, surely his car would have surfaced over all these years. She grimaced. Bob Small could have yet another victim in his tally. Then Doreen phoned Nelly back.

"Wow," Nelly answered. "Will you ever leave me alone?"

"I'm sorry," Doreen replied, with a wince. "I thought you might want to know that Lucas never showed up in Alberta. He's disappeared. A missing person case was opened, but—because he had been distraught over your sister not accepting his proposal, plus the fact that he had already closed up his accounts and had walked away from his job and was supposedly heading home—they thought that maybe he'd done something to himself."

Nelly gasped. "Oh my God, seriously?"

"Yes, seriously."

Nelly asked, "Do you think it was him? Bob Small?"

"I don't know," Doreen admitted. "I don't understand the relationship between him and your sister to begin with, and I don't know what level of jealousy there might have been or what warning level was involved."

"I don't know either," Nelly added, "but he was a killer without a conscience."

"And yet …"

"I know. I didn't do anything to stop him myself," she

said bitterly. "And, if he killed poor Lucas, I don't even know what to say."

"Would it fit with the Bob Small you knew?"

"Absolutely. I know, every once in a while, Ella was scared of Bob. Yet she called him her secret muse."

"Meaning that she was secretly enticed by everything that he did?"

"I wouldn't say that," Nelly disagreed cautiously, "because that makes my sister sound as if she's a serial killer."

"Would she have participated in any of his acts?"

"No, I don't …" Nelly hesitated. "I don't want to think so," she clarified. "But do I know that? No, I don't know anything of the sort."

"Right," Doreen noted. "And now it'll be a complete dissection of Ella's life to try and figure out how much involvement she may or may not have had."

"Oh, there was lots of involvement," Nelly confirmed. "It's not easy stuff to sort out. I'm her sister, and I don't even know her."

"And what if Bob Small killed her?" Doreen suggested. "Won't you want to do everything you can to ensure he is stopped?"

"Sure," she muttered, "but how will you protect me?"

"You think he's after you next?"

"I hope he's long gone, but after maybe seeing him outside Rosemoor earlier… I suspect he'll be one of those nightmares that I can never get out of my mind."

"Understood," Doreen said. "I'll let the police know, so it's something to be brought up."

"Do you think they would protect me?"

Doreen winced at that. "I don't know. I don't know whether they will see this guy as a threat or not."

"They probably won't," she murmured, "not until you find proof of who killed my sister. Until then, I must fend for myself."

"And what does that mean for you?" she asked.

"I don't know," she cried out, "except maybe stay inside and don't go anywhere."

"Do you go anywhere normally?"

She gave a bitter laugh. "I used to see my sister, but now I won't do that anymore either."

Chapter 10

DOREEN GOT OFF the phone and headed to the kitchen. The animals were walking sedately at her side. She looked down at them, saw Mugs's droopy tail and Goliath's twitching tail, and both appeared to be bored. She smiled.

"I guess you guys would want to do something now, *huh*? We can go for a walk? We could head down to the beach? We could stay at home and work in the garden, while we still have some hours of sunlight?" She pondered the possibilities in her head. "Or we should go back over our notes and do a little bit of work on the case?" When her animals made no sign of paying attention, she added, "What do you think?"

When the phone rang again, she was making coffee, contemplating her options. She glanced down to see that it was Mathew. She refused to answer and waited until it went to voice mail. When he left a message, she didn't even want to listen to what he said. Instead she made coffee and then grabbed the journal and her notepad and headed quite cheerfully back into the living room to try and sort out what she would do next.

DALE MAYER

Frustrated, she decided to bring out a series of index cards and started mapping out what she knew about Bob Small and the victims that she knew for sure. Of course none of it was for sure. She knew Mack would have a very different set of victims, and that was fine. They would need all of them at this point in time.

As she worked away, she wondered yet again how somebody could get away with so many murders without being caught. Back then, decades ago, sure there was no DNA, no internet, and very little interagency communication. You got a killer. And we got ours. That's nice. You keep your killers over there.

But now there were databases, all kinds of electronic stuff that would help people keep track of the killings. Yet still not great sharing though between provinces. And between countries? Even less.

She pondered that for a moment, and then added Ella's name to an index card. Now she had three—Hinja's niece, Lucas, who had supposedly gone back to Alberta, and now Ella. And of course Hinja herself had died, but she'd not been murdered. Still, Doreen made a separate index card for her.

Now would Bob Small have killed Ella and not Hinja? That was another question. It didn't make a whole lot of sense to Doreen that he would pick and choose his victims like that. But personally Doreen believed the victims were more likely determined based on the threats they posed to him. With Hinja back then, maybe he didn't see her as a threat. Maybe he enjoyed just tormenting her, being a shadow to worry about. Had Bob Small been at Hinja's funeral? Someone had mentioned they'd seen someone there. Had he been at Pullin's but, if so, why now?

92

Because if he had been at the funeral, that would fit in with his being sighted in town. But how would he have known? She pondered that set of possibilities. Was it a case of his not having wanted to kill Ella over the years, and then it had to be done, so he came back and took care of it?

When the doorbell rang a few minutes later, she walked to the front door, took a look outside the living room window, and saw a delivery person. She opened the door and accepted a small parcel. "Thank you."

The guy gave her a perfunctory smile and quickly left for his next delivery.

She brought the box inside and put it on the kitchen table, the animals now slightly more curious and alive than before. She noted the return address and saw it was from Hinja's estate—the last of Hinja's stuff that would have been tossed had Doreen not requested it. Doreen pondered that, wondering why she had even felt that it was a necessity to look over these things. She took a photo of it and then quickly grabbed a pair of scissors and cut the string tied around it. The rectangular box seemed to be reused, as if it had been something the sender had received as an order and had then repackaged.

The box itself was about ten inches by twelve and four to five inches high. As she opened it up, she was surprised to find a hairbrush, a couple books, some scratchpads, business cards—an odds-and-ends assortment. She spread them out on the table as well, taking photos of each item.

She frowned, grabbed one of her own notepads, and quickly itemized everything. There was absolutely no reason to think that this was of any importance, but she hadn't been able to leave this notion alone. Therefore, if something was here, she wanted to find it. But find what?

That was the problem. This Bob Small guy appeared to be a ghost. Almost as soon as she started itemizing things, she found a notepad similar to the one that she had for taking notes—the kind that you rip off the top page and work on the next page. But halfway through the pad of paper was a page with some writing on it.

Almost as if Hinja had grabbed it, flipped it up in haste, and started writing. But there was a date and a time, and the date was about four months ago. Doreen frowned at that.

Bob called.

And then Hinja had underlined it several times with heavy pencil marks. Doreen stared at that, quickly took a photo of it, and then found a few more notes.

Coming into town, wants to see me, oh my God.

And that was it. It wasn't a case of *Oh my God, should I see him? Oh my God, should I run?* Nothing like that. There was also a dedicated address book—the old handwritten kind from Hinja's earlier days, where contact info was manually kept, instead of on a smartphone, where you hit the Contact button. The address book also had a Notes section for some diary notations, plus a twelve-month calendar for reminder entries.

Doreen herself hadn't used an old-fashioned address book for a long time, but she knew Nan still swore by them. And, of course, being closer in age to Hinja, that made sense too. Doreen pondered what could possibly be in this address book of old, as she quickly flipped through it, looking for anything that made sense. She found phone numbers and names, but nothing really stuck out. Then she came to one name that surprised her—*Ella.* Doreen sat back and stared at it.

"Did the women know each other?" And then she

thought about it and answered her own question, "But of course they knew each other. At one time, they both lived in the same town." The bigger question was, did they know about each other having Bob as a common link? How long ago since they had been together with the same guy? And was it the same guy at the same time, or the same guy rotating between the two women, given what Doreen knew about Ella's relationship with him whenever he felt like it. He'd come and gone in Hinja's life too, but she'd always remained faithful, thinking that they were an item.

It was an interesting insight into Hinja from years ago. Outside of Ella's name, nothing in this address book made any sense, until she got to the *R*s, and there was the name *Robert*. She sat back. Wasn't Bob the short form for Robert? Would it be the same guy?

She frowned, as she looked at it. It was a number all right, but how old a number and when was the last time that number was ever in service? She pulled her phone forward and quickly dialed it. When it rang and rang, she was really surprised when a recorded voice on the other end said, "*You have reached Robert. Please leave a name and number, and I'll get back to you.*" She stared down at it in shock.

She quickly hung up, wondering what she'd done. Of course she had acted without even thinking. Still it was a scary thought to think that she may have had the number for this serial killer guy. And had called it. Should she tell Mack? Oh, boy.

She wondered if anybody else had the number, a number that she could confirm. She texted Mack and asked if Ella had a number for Bob in her cell phone. Instead of answering via text, he phoned her. "Hey, what's up?" she asked.

"You tell me," he said, his voice low. "Why are you asking?"

"You know why I'm asking," she replied.

"I can tell you the answer to that question is no."

She stared at her phone. "Seriously? She had a relationship with this guy off and on for decades, and there was no Contact for his name?"

"No name for Bob in her phone," Mack clarified, "but that doesn't mean that it's not here."

"Try Robert," she suggested.

"Robert?"

"Yes, Bob's a common nickname for Robert, and I found a Robert in Hinja's address book."

"What do you mean, Hinja's address book?" he asked, slightly distracted, as if he were looking through Ella's phone.

"Remember how I asked for whatever of her leftover stuff that they were getting rid of? I got a box today with a few items in it."

"Anything useful?"

"Not really, and yet maybe."

Ha gave a bark of laughter at that. "That sounds normal."

"It sounds completely normal, given all these crazy cases," she muttered.

"But you are getting somewhere."

"I'm not sure about that," she muttered. "*Somewhere* for you is not the same as *somewhere* for me."

His smile came through the phone when he muttered, "Give it time."

"Time's something I don't really think we have," she noted. "This Bob Small guy will go underground again."

"What do you think he's waiting for?"

She hesitated and then offered, "Honestly I think he's waiting for Ella's funeral."

There was dead silence on the other end. "Why would you say that?"

"Because I'm pretty sure he showed up at Hinja's funeral, and I'm pretty sure he may have had something to do with her death too."

"It was ruled an accidental death, I believe, or natural causes. I can't remember," he replied, confused. "I'll take a look and see what was written on the death certificate."

"I hear you," she stated. "I just don't think it'll be that simple."

"And why would Bob kill Hinja so many years later?" he asked. "There was no reason. They haven't been together for many, many years."

"For all I know, she was starting to make a stink again. And maybe it was because of Ella. Maybe Ella started to say something about it. Nelly told me that Bob had contacted her sister again. Remember the June notation with no year given?"

"Yeah. And what of it?"

"I have a note here from Hinja, with a date." She flipped back the page on the notepad, until she found it, and read it off to him.

"Interesting," Mack stated. "So Hinja may have seen him as well."

"Exactly, and maybe that's when he called Ella too."

"But we don't know that," he argued.

"No, we don't know it, but what if it's true?"

"And yet why?"

"I'm not sure why," Doreen admitted. "Maybe he's tying

up threads. Maybe he wanted to see the two women who mattered to him."

"If *anybody* mattered to Bob," Mack reminded her. "If this man is the same serial killer we've been talking about all this time, he may not care about anybody but himself."

She had to admit that Mack had a point there. "I get that," she agreed, "but what if it *is* him, and what if he did contact them, and what if he is responsible for their deaths?"

"That's an awful lot of *ifs*," he noted cautiously.

"I don't have any proof yet," she shared, the fatigue in her tone from the frustration hitting her.

"Hey," he reminded her, "don't let this get you down."

"I'm trying not to. … I wanted to help."

"Help who?" he asked curiously. "Because an awful lot of people are involved here, and I'm not sure that any of them are to be pitied at this point."

"You mean Nelly?"

"She knew about serial killer Bob Small," Mack declared. "She didn't do anything. Worse than that, she blackmailed her sister over it."

"And I think she didn't do anything because I think she didn't want her sister to get in trouble. Plus I think Ella was afraid of Bob."

"With good reason," Mack stated. "If what she knew was correct, just imagine what Bob would have done if he'd found out."

"And that's the thing," Doreen pointed out. "Nelly told Ella he was a serial killer, and Ella supposedly told Bob."

"And yet we've got the wrong dead sister," he reminded her.

"I did tell Nelly to be careful, and she gave a nervous laugh and said she didn't have any choice in the matter. She was stuck in that place. I asked her if she ever left Rosemoor because, of course, she had met her sister at the airport, after stealing the Rosemoor van. Nelly told me that she only got out for the odd times to see her sister and how that was never happening again because of her sister's death. She did say she thought she'd seen Bob today, after lunchtime, outside of Rosemoor, but also she admitted that he featured permanently in her nightmares."

"And now you're feeling sympathetic for her too?"

"No, no, I don't think so," she responded cautiously, trying to figure out the emotions fighting for a place in her head. "I'm not very happy that she didn't do something about all this a long time ago. Although she did contact the cops years back, yet she never handed over the journal, which would have given them something concrete to go on."

"Exactly, and, if she didn't give us all she knew, how are we supposed to have done anything about it?" he asked in disgust.

She smiled. "I hadn't realized how hard you guys' job was until I started doing this," she admitted.

"It's not much fun. People lie, cheat, steal, and then they turn around and look at you and give you grief because you didn't solve something, even before they did anything more to help the matter."

"So then technically they aren't to blame, you are." She burst out laughing at that.

Mack added, "I heard that used as an argument in the courts, so it may sound funny, but it's really sad."

"Wow, somebody used that as a defense?"

"Yes," he muttered, "and not the only one to do that."

"That's pretty amazing," she noted, "for defendants to turn around and blame the cops because you didn't work fast enough at catching the accused, so the bad guy's not responsible. ... The other thing is, Nelly has a picture. She has to look for it though."

"A picture of whom?"

"A picture of Bob Small."

"She's got a picture of this guy?" Mack exploded.

"I'll head down there after we hang up, giving her a chance to look for it, and then see if I can get it from her."

"She hasn't been all that cooperative yet, has she?" he asked curiously.

"No, she hasn't," Doreen admitted, "and that's another big problem too."

"It sounds as if she's a little more involved than she wants to be."

"According to her ..." Then Doreen filled him in on the lovely state of affairs between the two sisters and their own relationships with Bob Small.

"Good God. All the men out there in the world, and they're fighting over the same serial killer?"

"According to Nelly, Ella didn't believe he was a killer."

"She didn't *want* to believe it, you mean," he corrected.

"Yes, that's probably a better version," she stated in agreement. "Nelly herself was hurt and upset that this guy had gone for her sister instead of her, and so it became a bone of contention all these years."

"Then why wouldn't Nelly have turned Bob in?" Mack asked in exasperation. "Do you have any idea how many people probably died because she didn't?"

"I don't have any idea," Doreen muttered, "and I really don't want to." Then she filled him in on Lucas.

He groaned. "Nelly needs to be watching her back because, so far, *if* you're correct," he stated, with heavy emphasis on the *if*, "then there's a good chance Nelly's on Bob's murder list."

"Murder list," Doreen repeated in wonder. "Do serial killers have those? Seems to be a bad idea to write down incriminating info."

"Of course they do," Mack snapped. "Everybody keeps a list of what they'll do, and, for somebody like Bob Small, he keeps a list of all the people he still has to take out. Ones who will keep him safe."

"Or is there any other reason for why he's hitting these people now?" she asked.

"I don't know. You tell me," he said. "So far, nothing is making a whole lot of sense but that line of explanation."

"And he's how old now?"

"I don't know. Ella was fifty-eight*ish*," he guessed.

"Are you sure?"

"No, I'm not. I think that's what I heard on one of the newsfeeds."

"Nelly told me that Ella was sixty-six," Doreen claimed. "Ella was a dynamo and didn't look her age, and I think she did an awful lot to keep herself looking young. Still she was showing some age. And her sister, Nelly, is younger, about sixty-three or so, I think. And I think Bob Small will be somewhat older than Ella."

"So then why does he still murder people?"

"That's the question. I do have one thought circling in the back of my head, and, of course, it's stupid."

"Tell me," he said immediately.

"I was wondering how maybe he's ready to die, or maybe he's dying. Maybe he's got some disease or something, and he's cleaning up."

"But why clean up, if you're dying? You don't care at

that point about saving yourself from jail."

"Maybe he does care. Maybe he cared about these women. Maybe he wants to take them with him. Maybe he's making sure that nobody finds out what he did even after his death. I don't know." She raised her free hand, palm up.

"That's the part of this job where we could guess all we want, but, until we get somebody in our hands to talk to, it's pretty hard to understand." There was a definite smile in his tone when he added gently, "I'm glad to hear you're coming around to my way of thinking."

She sighed. "You're back to that rule about no assumptions. We need stuff to prove it."

"Works for me," Mack stated.

"Sure, works for you, as long as we get information, but what about when we don't get information?"

He chuckled. "And just think, in your case, how you get to sit there and play around with this one case," he pointed out. "Whereas I've got more cases, more crimes, and we only get so many days before something new pops up. Then it's on to the next new hot problem that we must deal with. So the fact that you get to sit there and do what you're doing is great and awesome and all that, but it's not something that we here at the station have time for."

"Which is also why I'm trying to help," she shared. "So we can put away some of these cases, and you guys can work on the other cases you already have."

"Yeah, you're starting to make us feel as if we need a whole team to work with you."

"I wish we could have that," she admitted, laughing.

"And it wouldn't be legal."

She sighed. "It's still not a bad idea. I could head up a cold case division."

"You're not a cop, and you don't have any credentials," Mack stated, "so park that idea."

"Of course." She groaned. "Everything's got to be done by the law."

"Particularly when it comes to court cases," he noted. "Otherwise they all get thrown out, and these criminals go free."

"The inmate told me to ask Nelly about her relationship with Bob Small, so obviously he knew a little bit more about it than she would want anybody else to know. Yet she didn't ask me how I found out."

"So she must have really known this Bob Small guy. However, it could have been a case of joking, as if he went out with the one girl first, fell in love with the sister, and that was it."

"Do you think serial killers fall in love though?" she asked.

"No, I don't. I think they have relationships, but I'm not sure how much good and decent emotions you can give them or can attribute to them."

"Right," she muttered. "It's been a long day. I was thinking I might get out before the sun goes down, do something to take my mind off this. Plus the animals need to get out."

"Why don't you call it a day?" Mack asked. "You've been going nonstop since I came by with pizza and we learned about Ella."

"I can't get my mind to stop churning on this, so I'm trying to distract myself, hoping the answers will come then. Is the cemetery open now? Can I go there?"

"Yes, you can, actually." Then he stopped and asked, "But why?"

She hesitated. "I thought I would take a look at Hinja's

grave."

He sighed. "Please don't tell me that you think Bob's hidden something there. Not like Pullin did for the other guy's grave?"

She stared down at the phone. "Good Lord, why would you even suggest that? And, no, I really don't."

"Good," he replied, a note of relief in his tone. "That's the last thing we need."

"I don't think so, but it wouldn't hurt in the least to see whether Bob Small's hanging around there or not."

"*Now* I really don't like the idea of you going at all."

"It'll be fine," she said. "I'll take the animals."

He groaned. "I get that you think they'll constantly look after you, but there'll be a scenario that you can't get out of one of these days, … and I don't want that to happen."

She beamed. "Glad to hear that, but I'll go visit Nelly first, see if I can get that picture, and then maybe I'll head over to the cemetery for a walk around. The animals are feeling housebound, same as I am."

"How can they be housebound?" Mack asked. "All you do is get out and into trouble."

"Maybe. Anyway I'll talk to you in a bit."

"Wait. I was thinking about coming over for dinner."

"Perfect. Are you bringing groceries?"

He groaned. "Do I need to?"

"Probably. I've got sandwich stuff and not a whole lot else."

Yet she said that in such a cheerful tone that he had to laugh. "What would you have eaten if I didn't come over?"

She stared at the phone. "Pretty sure I just told you how I had sandwich stuff, so what do you think I would eat?"

"You can't live on sandwiches alone."

"Why not?" she asked. "I've lived on sandwiches a lot lately."

"You need more than that for food."

"So, if you can think of something, pick it up," she countered. "Or you just tell me what to pick up, and I'll pick it up. I'll be out driving anyway."

"Okay, how about burgers?"

"Oh, a burger would be nice," she noted. "What do I need to get then?"

"Pick up some ground beef, at least two pounds, and hamburger buns and anything you want to have on them that you don't have."

"I can do that," she said cheerfully. "What time?"

"Six-*ish*," he noted, "if I can get out of here by then."

"Can't get through all the work due today?"

"Yeah," he confirmed in a dry tone. "Lots of work and I know exactly who to blame for that."

She burst out laughing. "I'll see you at six."

Chapter 11

WITH THE ANIMALS in tow, Doreen quickly drove to Rosemoor and parked. She and her animals bypassed Nan's suite and headed to Nelly's room. As she walked in, Nelly looked up and frowned. Doreen nodded, "Hi, I came to get that picture."

"I'm not sure I should give it to you though," Nelly said in a crotchety voice.

"And why's that?" Doreen asked.

"You might give it to the police."

Doreen stared at her and shrugged. "You want to hold it out for me?"

Reluctantly Nelly held up the photo, and Doreen took one good look at it. "Pretty nondescript."

"Exactly," Nelly agreed, but she still clutched it tightly.

Doreen took out her phone and took a picture of the photo.

"What good would that do?" Nelly exclaimed, staring at Doreen.

"Now *you* can give it to the cops," she stated, with a shrug. "I already told Mack that you've got it. So I'm sure he'll come by soon enough to take a look at it."

"I still can't be sure it's Bob though. I haven't seen him in a very long time."

"No, maybe not, but I can't get back into your sister's place until the police okay it. Then I'll dig deeper over there. Did you talk to Ella's lawyer?"

Nelly looked at her in pleased surprise and then nodded. "Yes, and I do inherit some of the money left," she said, with a sigh of relief. "I can stay here."

"Perfect." Doreen looked at her in delight. "That should solve the financial problem and give you some peace of mind."

"It does, but it still doesn't solve my sister's murder," she noted sadly.

"No, but at least your sister's doing right by you at the end of the day."

"Meaning that she's leaving me what she had?"

"Of course, she could have left it to this Bob Small guy."

Nelly stared at her. "You don't think she would have done that, would she?"

"I don't know what to think," Doreen admitted, trying to be brutally honest because great expectations do bring great sorrows, "because obviously she had a very strong relationship with him."

"Yeah, but it wasn't healthy."

"Maybe not," she murmured, "but that doesn't change the fact that the relationship was there, and she operated within the boundaries of it, and now we may have a dead boyfriend of Ella's from a time when this Bob Small guy was a constant in her life. It puts things in a different perspective."

"I'm wondering if that's why she never really had another serious relationship after that. Except Pullin. He was there and loved her but wouldn't play her games. It was him alone or not him. She had a lot of flings and short affairs. She always made it sound as if they were the best, but then suddenly they were no longer in her life, as if they were temporary."

"But they probably were because, if she'd already lost somebody she cared about, maybe she was afraid that Bob Small was always around."

"And yet why even start some relationship, knowing you'll end it if Bob calls?" Nelly asked. "It doesn't make any sense."

Doreen shook her head, as she studied the most recent photo on her phone. "I don't know who this person is," she noted, "but that doesn't mean that other people won't recognize him." She continued to stare at the photo.

"I think a lot of people would recognize him."

"What do you mean?"

"At one point, he had a public relations job. He must have dealt with lots of people in and around Kelowna."

"I thought he was a trucker."

"Sure, he was a trucker, but he belonged to unions, had representation, made deliveries all over the place," Nelly added.

"I see, but that would have been a long time ago though, I presume."

Nelly shrugged. "I don't know. He was heavily involved in life, whereas I was mostly an observer of life."

Interesting way to put it, Doreen thought. "Yet being involved heavily in life isn't a bad thing, but it also makes it a little bit harder to become anonymous."

"Maybe," she muttered, "I don't know."

"Did he have any health issues?"

Surprised, Nelly asked, "Did he? I don't know."

"That's what I'm asking you." Doreen studied Nelly's features. "It's quite possible that maybe he's dying himself, and he's trying to clean up his life."

"Why? By killing off everybody else?" she asked bitterly.

"It's possible, but ..." Then Doreen shook her head and added, "I can't say anything either way because I don't know."

"He has a very compelling, magnetic personality. Yes, I fell for him, but, when I realized he wouldn't even give me a second glance after meeting my sister, I got more upset because my sister had once again one-upped me. Yet I never at any point in time thought that this guy would come around and kill her."

"And we don't know that he did," Doreen stated. "We must keep holding out hope that we get answers and that we get them fast."

"Good luck with that." Nelly yawned, waved her hand in dismissal. "I'll go have a nap or maybe just go to bed early. You can leave now."

Doreen laughed. "I'll do that." She walked back with her animals in tow and headed to Nan's suite.

Nan was stepping out as Doreen arrived. "Oh my." Nan looked down at the animals in confusion. "Where were you?"

"Talking to Nelly," Doreen replied, with a bright smile. "And now I came to say hi to you."

"I'm going out for tea in the backyard," Nan said. "Do you want to join me?"

Doreen shook her head. "No, I'll head up to the cemetery to walk around and give the animals a place to run."

"Okay, dear. Are you feeling okay?"

"I am." Doreen leaned forward and gave her grandmother a gentle hug. "Just a little tired. It's been a long hectic day."

Immediately her grandmother nodded. "That's to be expected. You've done an awful lot for a very long time."

Doreen shrugged. "Doesn't feel as if I'm doing anything right now though."

"Oh dear, are you getting frustrated again? You need some more hobbies. Something you can do to help you relax."

"I'm fine." Doreen gave her grandmother a finger wave, then she turned her animals toward the front door, and she escaped before anybody else saw her. Outside she walked to her vehicle, loaded up the animals, and headed to the cemetery. After parking, she got out and stretched and took several steps, trying to figure out which direction to go. Then she asked Mugs, "Where do you want to go, buddy?"

He barked and took off in one direction, with her at the end of the leash, Goliath running alongside them, Thaddeus holding onto her shoulder. They headed up to the graves they had already visited, the ones with the weapons stashed inside, then on to where they'd found the hidden treasures.

As she came upon the last area, people stood there, talking and taking pictures, as if it were some new tourist trap. She melted away into the shadows, not wanting to bring attention to herself, and shifted in another direction.

As she walked to the old section of the cemetery, she looked up to see Dezy standing there, watching her. She smiled at him and waved.

He gave her a bright smile back. "I wasn't expecting to see you back here so soon."

Doreen nodded. "Sometimes these cases never stop."

"The same case?" he asked, his eyebrows shooting up.

She winced and shook her head. "No, not the same case. If it were the same case, I'd have something to go on."

He crossed his arms and frowned. "So another case?"

"Kind of, but also continuing on the last one," she replied, trying not to give away too much. "It's frustrating."

"What's this case?" he asked.

She needed information, and Dezy was one of the oldest guys still puttering around the cemetery, so it was worth a shot to glean anything out of him. She lowered her voice and asked, "Do you know anything about Bob Small?"

He nodded. "The serial killer? He ended up part of the riddle where the treasure was found."

"Yes, and Ella, who was recently murdered, was the other half of the riddle. In this case there's a suspicion that he might have been here in town a couple months ago. So now, of course, people are wondering if he's in town now." She held off listing him as a suspect in Ella's murder, but Dezy wasn't stupid. He could put two plus two together.

"I've never even seen him, so I wouldn't know what he looks like."

"No, and that's part of problem. He's a bit of a ghost. Nobody seems to have much of an idea of who he is. He was a trucker and kept on going through towns and of course keeping himself mobile, so that meant he could stay off the radar of the police."

"Makes sense when you think about it," Dezy muttered, "but God help anybody who crosses him."

"Exactly," she agreed, with a nod. "Not the person you want to meet in a dark alley at nighttime."

"So why are you here?"

"I came to see Hinja's grave. She is in the Rampony

plot."

"Oh, I know that family," Dezy stated. "It's over here." He led her away into another older section of the cemetery. He stopped in front of a new small stone, flat in the grass. "This is her here." And then he backed away and said, "I'll leave you to visit." With that, he turned and walked away. She wanted to ask him something, anything, but nothing came to mind that he could help her with.

Then she stared down at the grave, nice and neat, quiet, peaceful even. She hoped that Hinja had found the same level of peace in her world to make it easier on her now that everybody was once again realerted to the Bob Small case.

Chapter 12

Before Dinner …

A LONE EXCEPT FOR her animals, Doreen wandered the cemetery, enjoying being outside for a bit. There was a peacefulness to the day, and it helped to rest the thoughts steamrolling through her brain. Mugs barked a couple times, and the rough of his shoulders came up once. She stopped and looked around, but she couldn't see anybody. She bent down and gently pet him. "Easy, buddy. It's okay." He wasn't easily appeased though, so she headed in a different direction, until he calmed down.

Now Goliath wove his way through the tombstones and brushes, seemingly unaffected by anything. Thaddeus waited to speak until they came up to a group of older ladies sitting on a bench. "Thaddeus is here. Thaddeus is here."

One of the ladies looked up, her hand going to her chest. "Oh my, is that a bird?"

Doreen laughed. "Yes, this is Thaddeus, and he's very social, so he always announces his presence."

The ladies chuckled and surrounded him, preening as he preened. "Oh, he's lovely," they said.

Doreen smiled, made an attempt to move a few more

steps away, but Thaddeus wasn't done being a showman.

"Thaddeus loves Doreen," he stated, rubbing his head against her.

She sighed and responded, "And Doreen loves Thaddeus."

"Oh my," one of the women exclaimed, "You're Doreen."

She winced. "Yes, I'm Doreen."

"And the animals?" one woman asked, confused.

Her friend explained, "Remember? She's the one who does all the detecting stuff, that amateur detective who keeps solving all these cases."

The women looked absolutely delighted. One of them pulled out a little notepad and gave her a pen. Doreen looked down at it, not sure what she was supposed to do.

"I'd like your autograph, dearie," she declared, with a beaming smile.

Doreen stared at her in horror and looked down at the pen. Thaddeus immediately snatched it, and she had to grab it from his mouth. When he gave her a gimlet eye, she shook her head. "It's not your pen, Thaddeus. You don't get to keep it." She quickly scribbled down something about *Have a lovely day* and signed it, handing it back to the woman. And then she made a graceful exit.

Thaddeus, having lost his treat, immediately said, "Thaddeus loves Nan. Thaddeus loves Nan."

"Right, you love Nan every time you get in trouble, but *me* you only love when you want some attention."

"*He-he, he-he*" was the only response she got.

She sighed, but she was thankful to be away from the group of older ladies, still sitting there, now talking in a very animated way, when a new couple stared at Doreen with worry.

She whispered, "You need to behave yourself." All she got back for her efforts was another "*He-he, he-he.*" She groaned. "You can't be obnoxious all the time to me."

And of course he wasn't; he was beautiful, and she loved having him, but sometimes he wanted attention and did whatever he could to bring it their way; whereas she would much prefer her privacy, even some solitude. Especially when a killer was on the loose. Still, Thaddeus was a showman, and he wanted an audience.

It took several moments of looking around to realize she'd gotten lost again. "How is it possible to even get this confused in here," she cried out in frustration. Thankfully she was alone, so no one heard her. But that also meant there was no one around to ask for help. As she turned to look for some landmarks to help her out, Mugs started growling again.

She turned to look in the same direction he was looking and thought she saw somebody standing in the trees. She put her hand on his collar. "It's okay, buddy. People will be all over this place." And, true enough, there would be people everywhere; that was the whole point of a public cemetery. So people could come and pay their respects to their friends and family.

She headed in the direction where the man had been standing, if for no other reason than to ask for help as to how to get back to the parking lot. Yet when she got up there, she couldn't see any sign of anybody but found a signpost with a map of the cemetery, showing where she was. With relief, she studied it and realized she was not that far away and headed in the right direction. By the time she got to the car, Mugs was growling again. She stopped and looked at him.

"What's the matter with you today?"

But his back was up, and he was bristling in an ugly way. Nervously she turned and looked around but couldn't see anything. The fact that she couldn't see something didn't help. Mugs could see and sense danger at a higher level than she could. Normally he was good with people of all walks of life, but, if he was getting this upset, she would trust his judgment.

"Let's get into the car," she said immediately, keeping her voice low. As she opened the door, she let Mugs inside and then put Goliath in too. As she shut the passenger door and went to open the driver's door, a man spoke behind her.

"Excuse me."

She turned to see him staring at her quizzically.

Mugs exploded from inside the vehicle. Mugs was not happy and was not happy that this guy was outside and that Mugs was inside her car. She wanted to open the driver's side door and get in to get farther away from the stranger, yet this man looked pretty innocuous. She smiled at him. "Yes, what can I do for you?"

"I was wondering how this system here works. I wanted to maybe register a grave for one of my family members."

She shrugged. "Honestly I have no idea. I've never had to deal with that yet."

He looked disappointed and nodded.

"However," she added, "a caretaker is around here. His name's Dezy." Of course he wasn't the official caretaker, as they didn't have one, but she figured Dezy would be a place to start. "You can talk to him. I saw him last over …" And she pointed off to the side.

He looked surprised. "Oh, good. Thank you. Maybe he'll have some information."

"If not, you could phone the number for the cemetery, and I am sure they will help you out." And, with that, she quickly slipped into the vehicle and turned on the engine. He stood watching her, as she pulled out of the parking lot. She glanced at Mugs, who now seemed to be calm that they were leaving.

"What was that all about?" she scolded. "At least if you have a problem with somebody, you need to let me know." There wasn't anything familiar about the man at the cemetery, and she compared his face to the face in the photo that Nelly had shown Doreen, but she didn't get a mental hit. With that, she drove home, stopping at the grocery store.

Chapter 13

DOREEN CAME STRAIGHT home after getting the groceries and started a salad and prepping the stuff to go on the burgers.

Mack arrived a few minutes later. He put on coffee, then asked, "How was your walk in the cemetery?"

She smiled. "It was good. And yet one part was really horrific."

He stopped and looked at her. "How bad?" he asked, frowning.

"Bad," she cried out, raising her hands. "A woman wanted my autograph."

He looked at her for a long moment; then he burst out laughing. Laughter rocked his whole body with joy, as he contemplated the look on her face.

Disgruntled, she said, "It's not that funny."

"Oh, yes, it is," he disagreed, still chuckling, "and it serves you right."

She glared at him.

"With all that fame and fortune comes notoriety," he declared, still chuckling.

Her glare lightened, as she realized what he meant. "It

was terrible, … and I didn't even know what to write down."

"But did you sign it?"

She frowned at him. "How could I not? She was standing there, this notepad in her hand, waiting for me," Doreen muttered. "It was pretty embarrassing, I must admit."

He smiled. "Sounds as if you rose to the occasion, being the champ you are."

She muttered, as she studied his face, "That sounded suspiciously wrong."

"Nope, not at all," he disagreed. "I think it's great."

"You would," she muttered. "What if it happens when we're out together?"

He looked at her and snorted. "It better not."

"Right? So how is it a good thing for me when I'm alone?"

"You got yourself into this," he said cheerfully, "so it's appropriate that you'll deal with it from now on."

"That's just wrong." She shuddered. "Why would anybody want a signature from somebody else? It doesn't make any sense."

"And yet you realize that a lot of the world does that, right?"

"Sure," she admitted, "but that's for famous people."

He cocked an eyebrow at her. "See? Now you're famous too." And, still chuckling, he headed outside to put the burgers on the grill.

She sighed and went back to doing the prep work. When he returned, she added, "It really was distressing."

He gave her a hug. "Hopefully not *too* distressing because you should expect it to happen again."

"I hope not. I really do. That's so not my style."

"Yet it's likely to not be a one-off," he declared. "Accept

it and move on."

"If that's what I must do," she grumbled.

"I thought you had all kinds of training from your ex on how to handle that stuff."

"No," she replied, "not really. I knew how to keep my mouth shut and how to behave in social situations, and, when things got ugly, how to distance myself. Also … how to ask questions and get people to talk, but he was the limelight. I was the shadow." She studied Mack. "What do you do when people gush all over you?"

"I don't know," he stated, with a big grin. "It's never happened to me." She looked at him suspiciously again, and he laughed. "Honest. It's never happened."

"Whatever," she muttered. "Oh, and somebody was at the cemetery who Mugs really didn't like."

At that, Mack faced her and frowned. "What do you mean?"

"We saw a guy up in the trees, and I was a little bit lost," she explained. "It's a big place, and I got turned around. Anyway we headed to the trees thinking that, if this guy was there, maybe he could help me find my way back to the parking lot. But instead of finding him there, I found the posted map of the cemetery, and I got back fine on my own."

"Good. So what didn't Mugs like about him?"

"Mugs was growling at this guy. I think it was this guy anyway. Still, the guy in the trees upset Mugs. When we got closer, he was gone, and Mugs calmed down."

"So Mugs warned you that he doesn't like somebody, and so you went closer to him?" Mack asked in astonishment.

"I wasn't really thinking of it that way."

"No, I can see that." Mack stared at her hard. "How exactly did you think you should take it?"

"I don't know. Anyway, I got there, and he was gone," she stated for emphasis, looking over at Mack. "But then, when we went to the parking lot, I got Mugs and Goliath into the vehicle, and a man came up behind me and said *Hello*, and that time Mugs really lost it."

Mack slowly walked over to her. "How badly did Mugs lose it?"

"Kind of bad," she replied. "I haven't really heard him like that before and not mean it."

Mack asked, "What did you do?"

"This guy asked me about the cemetery and how to arrange a plot. So I told him to go find Dezy, and he could probably help him out."

"Did you recognize him?"

"No, I didn't. I had seen a picture of Bob Small, so I knew it wasn't him because it didn't look like him in the least."

"And how old is this picture of Bob Small?"

"I don't know." Then she winced. "Meaning that, over time, he would have changed?"

"Of course he would have changed," Mack declared, frowning at her. "And how bad did Mugs react to this guy when you were speaking with him?"

"Pretty badly," she said. "Mugs was not happy I was talking to him at all, and he was even less happy that I was outside the car and that he was inside the car."

"Yeah, that makes me very unhappy too," Mack stated, still staring at her. "Because, if something was wrong with this guy, so much so that Mugs would have gone after him, but being locked up in the car, he couldn't save you. You do realize that, don't you, Doreen?"

"Right." She grimaced. "I get the message. I should not have put Mugs away or not talked to this guy or something. ... I'm not exactly sure what I was supposed to do in a situation like that."

"Any or all of the above would have been a good place to start," he told her.

"It was an odd timing."

"And yet, a guy who's used to killing people would have that kind of timing down to the second."

The more she thought about it, the more she realized Mack was right. She sat down outside on the patio. "Do you really think it was him?" she asked.

"I don't know," he admitted, equally quiet. "I can't say I'm terribly impressed that somebody approached you like that, when Mugs was so obviously against it."

"No, but he seemed so ... innocuous. I didn't really think anything of it."

"Which is another thing that also blows me away. You already know that, in your mind, Bob Small took out Ella and potentially is looking to hurt or to take out Nelly. Plus you're the one who just told me about the missing ex-boyfriend, Lucas."

She nodded slowly. "Meaning that, picking the isolated opportunity like that is what Bob Small does well."

"Exactly," Mack snapped. "Guys like that, they've stayed hidden for a reason. They're good at what they do. They don't raise any alarms—in humans, that is—and they don't look the way you'd expect them to look."

"He certainly didn't look in any way alarming or how I would have thought some serial killer would look," she admitted.

"How did he look?" Mack asked curiously.

She thought about it. "I didn't think much about that either," she muttered. "But he had on a baseball cap, pulled down low, a plaid shirt, and jeans. Plus a beard and sunglasses."

"So nondescript, right? His face would have seemed completely normal." Mack sighed.

"Is that bad?" she asked, looking over at him.

"The beard and sunglasses you can pick up at a dollar store," Mack explained. "As disguises go, it's pretty common."

She didn't know what to say to that. She stared at him in shock. "Do you really think it was Bob Small?"

"I don't know, but the fact of the matter is, you're investigating a case that he won't want anybody investigating," Mack spelled out. "And, for all we know, your last little poke of the silent bear has woken him up."

"Not my fault," she stated immediately. "I think somebody else poked him way before."

"Maybe, but the chances are that you're on his radar, and that's not good. I don't want you on anybody's radar, but a serial killer? Definitely not," he stated forcibly. "That's a one-way ticket to your own plot in that graveyard."

"So what do I do?"

"What do you think you can do about it?" he asked curiously. "If this guy saw you, and he's already figured out who you are, what's your next step?"

She stared at him, realizing that he was trying to get her to think about her own safety. "I guess one of the biggest things … will be to keep the alarm on and to stay home, and, if I'm going out, then be extra careful?"

He sighed. "Yeah, that's a good place to start," he muttered, looking at her keenly, "but I don't think it'll be anywhere near enough."

"It has to be," she said, "because there's no security, not 100 percent anyway. No way you can look after me the whole time."

"No, I can't," he agreed, "but I sure would prefer that you weren't getting into dangerous situations where it was totally unnecessary."

"I was at the cemetery, having a walk. I stood at Hinja's plot, met three old ladies who asked for an autograph," she shared, "and that's it. It's not as if I was doing anything else there."

"No, but obviously it was enough for this guy to want to talk to you."

"I was the only one in the parking lot," she noted. "But, other than that, I can't imagine that he cared who he was talking to."

"Unless you were the person he was looking for."

"But how would he know that?" she asked, with a shrug. "It's not as if anybody else knew I was there."

"Who else did you see?"

"I saw Dezy," she replied, and then she frowned. "Unless Dezy told this guy who I was and that I was there."

"Pretty easy to find out, isn't it? Just ask Dezy."

"I hope Dezy says he didn't talk to him. Then my encounter with the stranger was completely innocent."

"And if Dezy did talk to him?"

She shrugged. "Then maybe not quite so innocent."

"I think we'll go for the *not so innocent*." Mack already had his phone out and tapped to dial a number.

"How is it you have everybody's number on tap?" she complained. "It's so hard for me to find phone numbers sometimes."

He smiled at her and said, "I've had to talk to Dezy a couple times over our last case," he muttered. "Having him in my Contacts makes sense." He carried the cutting board and the veggies. "If you don't mind helping ... the burgers are almost ready. I'll make this quick call, and then we'll eat." He wandered into the backyard, talking to Dezy for a few minutes.

It's obvious they connected because Doreen watched Mack on the phone, talking animatedly. When he put away his phone and joined her again, a harder look was on his face.

She looked at him and sighed. "I suppose you talked to Dezy, didn't you?"

"Of course I talked to him," Mack snapped, "and, yes, he did talk to this guy."

"And did the stranger ask about me?"

"Yes. He noted to Dezy that he saw a woman with a parrot on her shoulder, and Dezy told him who you were."

"*Great*," she muttered. "So the animals once again get me in trouble."

"Absolutely. More than that, they make you easily identifiable," Mack stated. "The trouble is now, what will we do about it?"

"Do you really think this guy is dangerous?"

He cast her a look and asked, "What about you? You tell me. This stranger talked to Dezy *before* this guy came to talk to you in the parking lot. So the stranger knew exactly who you were, and he didn't say anything about speaking to Dezy."

She winced at that. "In other words, it was a setup."

"Exactly, and you can't give me a description beyond

baseball cap, glasses, and a beard."

She added, "Six-two maybe, smaller than you, not as heavy"—she paused, rummaging her brain for anything more—"but that's about it, yeah."

"In that case," Mack replied, "I won't be so bold as to say that it was *definitely* Bob Small, but I will say that you need to watch it. Stay out of trouble and stay out of everybody's way because there's a good chance that this guy and his actions were much less than innocent."

She frowned, as she thought about that. "It's weird to think that every time somebody's nice now that I must look at it from a negative point of view."

"Not a negative point of view but a realistic one. We must keep you safe."

"Right." She frowned. "I guess he couldn't have been somebody who was just friendly, right?"

"Doreen, he asked about how to get a burial plot. Why didn't he ask Dezy?" She frowned. "Do you really want to take that chance with your life? With the lives of your animals? How would Nan react to that?"

She winced, shook her head. "That doesn't sound like anything I want to do at all. But, if you're right, and this was a disguise, I won't recognize him next time."

"And that's what he's counting on," Mack stated, his tone serious as he studied her. "So please, for God's sake, stay out of trouble for a while." He hesitated. "What are the chances this guy followed you home?"

She winced and looked outside. "Now that is guaranteed to make me not sleep again."

"I'm not trying to scare you," he said, "but I do want to make you sit up and pay attention to what's going on around you."

She nodded. "Okay. I wasn't trying to attract his attention."

"No, but the trouble is, once you *are* on his radar, he now has to decide whether you are a danger to him or not, and you know what'll happen if you are."

She sighed. "Yeah, I do know. Thanks for the reminder. I'll become another Ella."

He pulled her tight into his arms. "Not if I can help it, but, for that, I also need your cooperation."

She glared at him. "And what does that mean?"

"It means, I need you to stay out of trouble," he snapped. "Stay home, locked up inside."

"But, if he knows where I live," she noted, "this could be the worst place I can be."

Chapter 14

The Next Morning ...

DOREEN DID WORK hard at trying to stay safe today. She stayed at home. She worked in her garden. She phoned Millicent and then headed over there via the river, going in a circular route so that nobody would be following her and have even a clue what she was up to. Heck, even Doreen had a hard time even figuring out where she'd gotten to. By the time she got home from that job, she was tired and sweaty and stressed.

She put on coffee and ran upstairs and had a quick shower. It had been an unusually hot day, and then, adding the hard work that she'd done at Millicent's today, which was more digging and edging along the sidewalk, she'd worked up quite a sweat.

As soon as she was showered, she quickly braided her hair. She grabbed a lightweight T-shirt and shorts, then moved slowly downstairs. The physical exercise today would wear on her tomorrow. But, for now, she'd had a hard-working morning and, although tired, felt good about the exercise and the effort she'd put in. As she poured herself a coffee, she opened up the back kitchen door, propped it open for the animals, and sat out on the deck. She'd had one piece of toast for breakfast, but she needed something else.

She walked back to the fridge to see what was there. Mack had cooked hamburgers last night, and they'd polished everything off, so none of that was left. It would be a sandwich again for her. She shrugged. Good thing she liked those.

She quickly whipped up two big sandwiches and, with her plate, moved out to the deck. Mugs followed her, staring avidly at her food. She winced. "Hey, buddy. I guess you haven't had any treats in a little bit, have you?" She got up, walked back into the kitchen, grabbed a couple treats for each of the animals, and headed back outside again. Mugs danced around, more excited than he should have been, and Thaddeus hopped up onto the table, looking for something himself. Goliath, hearing the treats container shaking, had come running but, even now, was lying there, staring at her with that mesmerizing golden gaze of his.

She gave everybody treats and then sat down to work on her sandwich. When she'd finished one, she began to feel a little more human again. She ate the second one slowly. By the time she was done, she was stuffed. But it was a good stuffed. Now all she needed was time to digest and a bit of a chance to relax. She'd spent all morning determinedly putting this nightmare of meeting Bob Small out of her mind.

And yet it wasn't her fault. Still, as Mack would say, it was never her fault, and yet somehow it always ended up being her fault. She didn't quite understand how that worked, but it seemed to end up that way. As she sat, with her cup of coffee, she pondered the information that she had on Ella's murder and everything that she still needed to find out. When her phone rang, she wasn't at all surprised to see it was the penitentiary. She answered it.

"Did you talk to the sister?" Gary Wildorf asked.

"I did. That's a pretty messed-up family."

"So will you do something to help me now?" he asked in an aggrieved tone.

"Not sure there's anything I can do. So far we don't have very much that's helpful with this Bob Small guy. So what if both sisters dated the same man? That's hardly criminal."

Frustrated, he cried out, "Why not? Do I have to get out of here and do the job for you?"

"Maybe. We aren't getting anything that's adding up to a case against him."

"How is that even possible?" he asked in amazement. "This guy murdered so many people."

"Yeah, did you ever write down a list of everything he told you?"

"I did somewhat, yeah," he mumbled.

That was the biggest shock of the day for her. She stared down at the phone. "Now that's interesting," she said. "I don't suppose you have a picture of him, do you?"

"I probably have that too. Don't you even have that much?" Gary asked her. "He served time here, so he must have a mug shot."

"Yeah, but it's a little hard looking for a ghost, someone with no name and no photo," she shared.

"A ghost," he muttered. "Yeah, that's him all right. Even when he was here, so many of the guys don't even remember who he was or what he was or how he looked."

"Of course not, because the only way to survive is to keep a low profile. Was he ever the kind to get into a fight?"

"No, he wasn't big on confrontations. But believe me.

Lots of guys gave him a wide berth. There was something wrong with him."

"Got it. Lots of guys are like that, aren't they? Particularly where you are."

"They are, and it makes no sense that this one keeps getting away from you."

"It's not that he keeps getting away from us," she clarified. "We haven't even found him because we don't have a picture, an ID, or anything yet."

"He was in the penitentiary with me," Gary reminded her, with a snort. "How hard can that be?"

She thought about Mack's problems finding that too. "I can also tell you that his name isn't Bob."

Shocked silence came from the other end. "What?" Gary asked.

"You call him Bob Small, correct?"

"Yes."

"Nothing is there for a prisoner named Bob Small."

"You should check who was in my cell back then."

"Sure, but you didn't give me any dates."

He swore fluently through the phone. "Can't you guys do anything on your own?"

She picked up a pen and a piece of paper. "I've got a pen in my hand. Give me something I can use."

And he started swearing again. "Fine, but this time you need to give me something."

"If I get anything from you, then maybe."

"He used the name Bob Small. I don't know if that's the one the penitentiary used or not, but he wouldn't respond to any other name."

"So," Doreen suggested, "maybe he had the guards hoodwinked to thinking that was his name. He would only need to be a hard-ass about it at the beginning. Once everybody adapted to the name, they wouldn't even question it."

Gary pondered that. "You're probably right about that," he acknowledged. "So I don't know what his name is, but he's got to have a legal name tied up with his conviction."

"That's true," she replied, kicking herself as to why she hadn't even checked with Mack on that angle. "What year was he there with you though?"

"That's the problem," he told her. "I got moved around a lot."

"Which *is* a problem," she agreed.

"Right," he muttered. "It was about fifteen years ago."

"Are you sure? And were you there in that same penitentiary?"

"I was," he confirmed. "That much I know."

"That's good. Did you have a lot of new roomies at that time?"

"Too many," he snapped. "I would just as soon have a room to myself, but I don't even get that."

"Of course not," she said. "Prison is not exactly a luxury hotel." For some reason he thought that was pretty funny, and he snickered. She shook her head at that.

"So now you can track him down, *huh*?" Gary asked.

"I don't know if I can or not," she hedged. "Depends on how many names we must wade through in the paperwork to find all your cellmates' names, then go through their histories. You said you have a picture."

"Yeah, yeah, yeah," he grumbled. "What's your email?" She gave it to him, and he said, "Okay, I'll find it and send it. I have it. I emailed it to myself. So I should be able to attach it."

"Forward the email," she suggested. "Then you don't need to attach it."

"Does that work?" he asked.

"Yeah, it does."

"I'm taking computer courses," he admitted, his tone almost apologetic.

"That's good," she stated. "You'll need it when you get back out again."

"Yeah, I will, won't I?" he said. "Now find something so I can get out of here," he demanded in frustration.

"We're working on it," she replied. "However, just like you, I need something concrete too."

He groaned. "I'll find it, just give me a little bit." With that, he hung up.

What she really needed was a visual confirmation from Gary's photo and that his cellmate, while using the fictitious name Bob Small, had been in the same penitentiary as Gary Wildorf's roommate back about fifteen years earlier.

With the information she'd written down, she quickly sent Mack an email with the details. Then she sent him a text, wanting to know if he'd seen her earlier email. When he called her a little bit later, he asked, "What is this?"

"Those are the dates that Bob Small was a prisoner, supposedly in the same cell with this Gary Wildorf guy, who keeps calling me from the penitentiary."

"He called you again?" Mack asked, his tone sharp.

"Yes. I managed to bluff him by saying that we didn't have anything."

"We really don't," Mack confirmed.

"So it's not much of a bluff, but it felt as if I were bluffing."

"That's because you're a softie," Mack stated, his voice

gentling.

"Gary's really hoping to get something to ease the situation in his world."

"Maybe, but I hope you didn't promise him anything."

"No, I didn't. He's just really hopeful."

Mack sighed at that. "When this turns bad," he began, "which, given this guy is in prison and the fact that you can't exactly get him out of there, you must be strong because he might get pretty ugly."

"I haven't promised him anything," she repeated. "So I can see how that is possible, but that would be his fault, not mine."

Mack chuckled at that. "Easy to say that, but Gary won't believe it when that happens."

"No, of course not," she muttered. "Still, not my problem. He will send me a picture though."

"He's got a picture of Bob Small?"

"Yeah, apparently. Not sure where it is from though, or how old."

"Right, and that'll be the next thing. Just because he has a picture doesn't mean that we've got anything better than what you had for a description on your stranger in the cemetery. Nelly has a picture too. I need to go grab that."

"Hey, I showed you my picture of her photo, which was *worthless*, as you said. You can't keep bugging me about that. I tried to get the original picture from her, but she held tight. You can get her to give it up though."

He chuckled. "Send me the photo from Gary when you get it."

"Will do," she said. "Can you phone the penitentiary and go back through the records to find out who was Gary's cellmate at that time?"

He laughed. "I'll get right on that," he said in a snide tone. "Not to worry. I will. Eventually."

"Considering we have this tidbit, I would think it's pretty well on top of the priority list."

"It's pretty far-fetched that Bob Small's even involved in Ella's murder. Remember?" Mack added, "However, I could get somebody to phone down there and see if we can get some answers."

"Good, because, if it isn't far-fetched, you have one killer to consider."

"But that doesn't necessarily mean he's Ella's killer."

"And yet it's not all that far out of line either. You certainly must consider it's a possibility."

"Absolutely. But then, if we look at it from that point, so is her sister."

Doreen groaned at that. "You're still thinking Nelly might have done that?"

"I talked to her, and, according to her, she did hit Ella pretty hard."

"What? So Ella got hit, and somebody comes along and shoots into a dead body? That won't wash."

He chuckled. "No, it won't wash," he agreed, "but I'm not sure that Nelly isn't smart enough to have orchestrated this on her own."

"I'm not either," she muttered.

Hearing that from Doreen surprised Mack. There was a momentary pause before he asked, "Seriously?"

"There was way too much family interaction going on between the sisters to make me happy," she muttered, "and not all of it nice."

"*Siblings*," Mack noted. "Sometimes they get along great. Sometimes they can't stand each other."

"And I get that, even as an only child," she murmured. "I really do. I just wish it was a little bit easier to sort through."

"Me too," Mack agreed, "but you're doing fine. If you get anything else, let me know." And, with that, he rang off.

She just sat here, looking down at her phone all over again. When her phone buzzed, she knew an email had come in, and, sure enough, there was the photo attachment. She stared at it, frowning, because—just like Mack had explained earlier—it was pretty hard to see who this guy was. She forwarded it to Mack.

He called her back. "Not a great photo."

"No, it sure isn't. Looks like a newspaper print or something."

"Yeah, it does, doesn't it?"

She added, "Not a lot of cameras in the cells, I presume."

"I'm not sure, but I would highly doubt it," Mack stated. "Some prisoners get all kinds of things, but I don't think that would have been an option where he was."

"So this is likely to be either something that he got from the prisoner himself or …"

"Or what? Like from a newspaper in the prison?"

"That's possible too," she said, "and it's old. So it's too old to really identify him. So there goes that theory too."

"Maybe," Mack said, "but I've got somebody looking up the dates at the penitentiary, so hopefully we'll get a name from that."

"Chances are it'll be more than one though."

"Why do you say that?" Mack asked.

"Wildorf told me that he got moved around a lot for a while."

"*Great,*" Mack muttered, "because then, if you're right, Wildorf could have had quite a few cellmates. But we'll cross that bridge when we get there."

She smiled at that because that was such a Mack saying. When he rang off again, she got up and made herself a second cup of coffee, and her phone rang again. Expecting it would be the inmate all over again, she picked up the phone and answered before she checked the Caller ID. It wasn't Gary. Instead it was heavy breathing and nothing else. She straightened in her chair, glared down at her phone. "Who is this, and what do you want?"

And then realizing that she probably sounded like a fool, she snapped, "Go take a hike and leave me alone." And, with that, she ended the call and slammed down her phone. She knew, if she phoned Mack and told him, she'd be in trouble. The trouble was, if she didn't phone Mack and tell him, she would also be in trouble.

Finally she decided she had better let him know, and that would probably be the lesser of two evils. She quickly sent him a text, and then decided that it was laundry day and bedding day, plus a whole pile of all the other household chores that she needed to get done—particularly if Mack would reply in a tirade.

Taking her coffee with her, she headed up to her room and gathered her laundry, then sorted it. At a sudden urge, she pulled out a few of Nan's clothes that Doreen had hung onto and then decided that she really didn't want. So that would necessitate a trip to Wendy's consignment shop.

Which, as Doreen thought about it, was a good thing to do. She quickly bagged up several of the items to go to Wendy's, so that she could carry them easily. She double-checked another one or two pieces but couldn't decide just yet. She put on some laundry to wash, and, with that done, she stripped off her bed. After remaking it with fresh linens, she piled the previous bedding in front of the washing machine, so she could put it on next. Then snatching up the bags of clothing, she called to the animals and asked them if they wanted to go for a walk.

Although they'd already been out to Millicent's, they were all more than eager to head out again. She smiled down at them, as they wiggled all over the place, but Thaddeus gave her that look.

"Don't." She pointed a finger at him. "Mack told me to be careful, but he didn't say stay at home." But Thaddeus wouldn't let up with that look. Man, he could make her feel so guilty, so fast.

"I need to get these to Wendy's," she argued. "It's a walk we do all the time. It's hardly a problem." She could have driven, but that wouldn't work away some of the uneasiness settling inside her.

With the animals quickly leashed up, she looked at Thaddeus and asked, "You want to stay here?" Almost as if he understood, he gave a squawk and flew up onto her shoulder.

"Good," she replied. "I didn't really want to go without you." He tucked his head up against her neck and whispered, "Thaddeus loves Doreen." She absolutely loved when he did that; it nearly broke her heart. She tucked him up close, and, then locking up the house, she headed out again.

Chapter 15

DOREEN WAS ABOUT ten minutes into her walk when Mack called.

"What kind of message is that?" he asked her, disgruntled.

"It means, I got a prank caller of some kind," she explained.

"What do you mean, a prank caller?"

"Heavy breathing on the other end of the phone."

"Ha. Could have been kids," he replied cautiously.

"Could have been," she admitted. "Could have been all kinds of things. I told him to leave me alone anyway."

"I'm sure that'll be effective," Mack noted, with a hint of humor.

She glared down into the phone. "I honestly didn't know what to say. I should have hung up immediately."

"Next time it happens, if it happens again, do that. Other than that, like I said, stay home and stay quiet."

"Oops," she muttered. She wouldn't mention that she had already been out earlier this morning to Millicent's. Doreen frowned. He'd be mad when he heard about that from his own mother.

"*Oops?* What does *oops* mean?" he asked, his voice rising. "What do you mean, *oops?* There's no room for *oops* here, Doreen."

She sighed. "I'm outside, walking toward Wendy's right now."

"That's not an *oops*," he roared into the phone. "How is that staying at home?"

"I was getting frustrated and upset," she explained, "so I thought I'd make a quick run to visit with Wendy. I have some more clothes to sell."

"You've got more clothes to sell? How is that even possible?"

"Nan had a ton of clothing, and I wanted to keep a few of the pieces. They are really nice pieces and a really awesome vintage, but they didn't feel the same on me anymore. I've changed, I guess."

"Yeah, you definitely have," Mack grumbled. "You used to listen when you were told to do something."

She snorted. "In your dreams. That was when I was married."

First came silence on the other end, and then he groaned. "How will I keep you safe if you keep wandering around town?"

"I figured it was probably better to wander around town and act as if nothing was wrong," she stated, "than to hide away in my house, petrified to get out. I don't want to be a prisoner in my own house."

"No, but you do want to live, right?"

"Sure." She sighed. "You always pull that line, and it makes me feel terrible."

"And yet it still doesn't make a bit of difference," he muttered.

She smiled into the phone. "It does, … maybe not enough."

"*Not enough* is no joke," he said, with a sigh. "Let me know when you get to Wendy's, and let me know when you get home. And, if you feel anybody walking behind you, following you, even a weird noise, you call me. You hear me?"

"Okay," she said happily. "Glad you've got nothing better to do than babysit me."

"It would have been better if you'd stayed home," he muttered. "But instead …"

"I'll pass through the grocery store on the way," she shared. "Do you want me to pick up something for dinner?"

"What? Am I coming over for dinner again?" he asked, a note of humor evident.

"Oh, I should have rephrased that, shouldn't I?" She winced. "Hi, Mack. Do you want to come for dinner tonight?"

"Thank you, Doreen," he said in mock exaggeration, "I would love to."

"I even heard from a birdie that your birthday was coming up," she blurted out.

"Yeah, my birthday is coming up but not for a while." He asked cautiously, "Why?"

"I wondered if you wanted to spend the day together and maybe have dinner. I'm not a great cook, as you well know, but I could give it the good old college try and cook you dinner," she offered hopefully.

He chuckled, but his tone was now warm and silky, which made her smile. "That would be lovely," he replied, "but keep in mind my brother might be there."

"That's fine. He can come too."

"You really think so?" he asked.

"Yeah, I really think so. I can poison him as easily as I can poison you." And, on that note of laughter, she rang off.

It took about a good ten to fifteen minutes to get to Wendy's, and the whole time all Doreen's animals were completely calm and relaxed. When she stepped into Wendy's store, she stopped at the entranceway. Wendy looked over at her and came running.

"Are you okay?" she cried out.

"I'm fine," Doreen replied, staring at her. "Are you okay?"

"I'm fine now," she beamed.

"I didn't want to come into the store because I've got the animals. Here," she said, as she held out a bag. "Some more clothes from Nan. I wasn't sure whether you could sell them or not."

Wendy smiled. "If you hung on to them, I presume they are good pieces."

Doreen nodded. "But these don't fit right, don't feel right, you know?"

Wendy nodded. "Absolutely I do know. I'll go through them, and, if there's anything that I can't sell, I'll let you know. How's that?"

"That sounds good," Doreen stated.

"Are you okay for money right now?"

"I am at the moment," she replied cheerfully. "I did get that reward."

"Oh, right," Wendy nodded. "In that case you don't need a check today, right?"

Doreen shook her head. "No, and it's not time yet, so it's okay."

And, with that, Wendy smiled. "After all you've done for

me, I am quite prepared to break the rules, if you needed a little bit."

"No, that's okay, but thanks anyway."

"Anything new on the horizon?"

"Yeah, a lot's new," Doreen said, "but nothing I can really talk about yet. Hopefully nothing too big goes wrong, and we can get it solved pretty quickly."

"I heard about Ella."

Doreen froze, frowning at her. "Did you know her?"

"She was a politician in town, so I grew up knowing about her. I didn't know her myself, though. She's a generation older than I am."

"Right, did you ever know a Bob Small?"

Wendy considered that name but shook her head. "No, can't say I did."

At that, Doreen nodded. She hadn't really expected her to. "Anyway, it's pretty sad about Ella."

"It is, indeed. We all have things that we don't like about people, and, in her case, it was justified since she was a politician," Wendy added, with an eye roll. "Still, you don't want to see anybody taken down too early in life."

"No, definitely not. It should be our choice right up to the end." At least as far as Doreen was concerned. With a wave of her hand, she headed back out with her animals in tow. She stopped outside the storefront for a few minutes, looked around, and smiled. "You know something, Mugs? It's a lovely day, so let's take a meandering way home and learn something new about the town."

It was one of her favorite pastimes. She picked a new route to go home, so she passed a new block, some new people, something different every day. As much as Kelowna had shown its dark underbelly, it was also a town that had ended up being full of good people, most of them trying to have a simpler life. And, with that, she headed off toward home.

She hadn't gone much more than a few steps around the block and to the crosswalk, heading slowly home, when Mugs started to growl. She looked down at him, frowning, then slowly searched for the source of his agitation, but she couldn't find it. "What's the matter, Mugs?" she asked.

He kept growling, his hackles rising, staring straight ahead, but she couldn't see anything. Not sure what his problem was but knowing that he most definitely had a problem with whatever it was, she was willing to take heed. Therefore, she crossed the road to a more populated area among other storefronts.

With Goliath on his leash and staying fairly close to Mugs, Doreen wondered at their behavior. When a man called out from behind her, Doreen turned, startled, but it was the owner of the Chinese food place that she visited often. She smiled at him. "Hey."

"I haven't seen you around town lately," he noted, with a smile. "You used to come by with the animals over at the restaurant but not lately."

She nodded. "Lately I've been so busy that I haven't eaten out."

"Always busy, always busy." He chuckled. "That's a good thing."

"It certainly is for me," she admitted.

He quickly waved as he passed her, and, while they had been there together, Mugs hadn't been upset, but now that she was alone again, Mugs was not happy.

"You make me nervous," she said. "Knock it off, will you?" But there was no stopping him and his growling. They kept walking, even though nobody was around. She reached down and gently stroked him, taking time to calm him, so that he would stop that low growl in the back of his throat. Some people stared at her oddly, as they passed Doreen.

Finally when he stopped growling, she sat down on one of the side fences made out of stone, petting Mugs again for a few minutes. "It's okay, buddy. It's okay. We're not far from home." He may not be growling anymore, but he kept looking around, and the ruff was still raised on his neck.

He started to bark as a vehicle went past. Maybe it was a scary vehicle, she wondered, as it drove by, but the driver wasn't even looking at her. She looked down at Mugs. "Okay, now I'm really worried about you. What is the matter?" He was getting more and more agitated again.

"Fine, let's go," she said, hating to admit it, but his behavior alone was enough to set her nerves on edge. By the time she raced toward her cul-de-sac and reached the house next door, she and her animals were almost running. By the time they got up to her front door, and she had the security off and then bolted inside, she was almost in a full-blown panic. She leaned against the front door, panting, staring down at Mugs. "What was that all about?" she cried out.

He looked at her, barked once, almost as if to say, *Now stay home.* Then he sauntered a few steps into the living room and collapsed in a heap on the carpet, as if exhausted.

That's when she remembered she hadn't picked up groceries for dinner. She shook her head at him. "If that was because Mack told us to stay home"—she glared at Mugs in accusation—"that's not fair. We needed to get out a little bit." But Mugs was ignoring her completely. Frowning at that, and not at all happy at his behavior and yet not sure what was going on, she walked into the kitchen and put on a cup of tea. And realized that the rear kitchen door was wide open.

She stared at it in shock. "*Uh-oh.*" She raced outside, and everything looked normal, but it didn't feel normal. She quickly phoned Mack.

"Now what?" he asked. She explained about the kitchen door first. Then he asked, "Did you leave it open?"

"I don't think so," she said hesitantly, "but I was outside most of the morning."

"*Of course.* I'll log off a little bit early and come by. I want you to stay outside until I get there."

"Fine," she muttered. "It's probably nothing."

"Maybe," he noted, "but I'd rather be safe than sorry at this point. Now you heard me, right? Stay outside. I'll be there in five." With that, he hung up.

Chapter 16

DOREEN WAITED OUTSIDE, pacing nervously all along the back of her house, even going as far down to the creek and then back up again, waiting for Mack. When there was still no sign of him fifteen minutes later, she started getting worried. She didn't want to call him, but was he on his way or was he caught up in something?

Getting even more nervous, she decided to go down to the creek and wait. As she sat on her butt on the grass there, Mugs came over and leaned up against her, giving her a soulful look.

"I know, buddy," she murmured. "Not quite how we expected our day to go, did we?" She sighed, as she sat here. When she heard a man call out, she turned to see Mack on her deck. She bolted to her feet and raced toward him. As she got closer, he opened his arms. She didn't even think about it; she dashed right in, and Mack closed his arms around her securely.

When she finally had her nerves under control, she heard him chuckling. She leaned back, looked up at him, and frowned. He immediately gave her a mimicking frown back. She shook her head. "Are you laughing at me?"

"Nope, but, … if the only way to get you to run into my arms is to have somebody come and scare the bejesus out of you," he explained, "I may contemplate setting up that ploy myself."

She glared at him and shook her head. "It's a good thing I know you're joking."

"I am joking, and you know that too. Your house is empty. I've gone through it, top to bottom. Whether somebody was here earlier, I can't say. However, all I can tell you is, right now, it is empty."

She let out a long-suffering sigh. "That's something, at least."

"It is, indeed, and I'm not sure what's going on, but you do need to make sure that your doors are locked at all times. And put that alarm on and keep it on."

"I can't imagine not having locked them," she told him. "But I was out here this morning, so I guess it's possible."

"Oh, it's definitely possible," Mack noted. "The question is, is somebody keeping an eye on when you're coming and going, or did they casually walk by and wandered inside to check out the house, or was this a targeted B&E?"

She looked at him in shock and then bolted from his arms into the kitchen. As she ran around the kitchen, she felt the panic setting in. Finally she turned and whispered, "It's gone."

"What's gone?" he asked.

"The journal," she cried out. "The journal's gone."

He stared at her in shock. "Are you serious?"

She nodded. "I had it here." She pointed at the kitchen table, where she had notes too. "My notepad with my notes is gone too." She stopped, looked at him, tears welling up in her eyes. "Does that mean Bob Small was here?"

He stared at her. "Let's get back outside. I want to bring forensics over here."

"Forensics won't believe you," she muttered.

"If the journal is missing, … let's make sure it's not anywhere else."

"Okay," she agreed. With him at her side, they went upstairs, checked out her bedroom, the spare bedroom, every other place that she could think of, but it wasn't here. She knew in her heart of hearts that it was gone. "I was down at the river, thinking about the journal. So I came inside to read it again, while making notes this time, all at the kitchen table," she told him, "trying to pick up any nuances and to see if I could sort out anything else about it."

"Of course." Mack shook his head. "Yet I doubt anybody was watching you at the river. He could have heard from Ella about the journals, or maybe he knew about the journals already. Maybe that's why he actually …" Mack stopped.

"You mean, that's why he killed her?" Doreen whispered.

"It's possible, but we don't know that."

"No, we don't know it for sure," she murmured. "Yet it's pretty hard not to come to that conclusion, isn't it?"

"Take it one day at a time," Mack suggested reassuringly.

She nodded. "I would like that, but this is getting more than a little bit disturbing." He stared at her, and she raised both hands. "No, I'm not giving up."

He closed his eyes, pinched the bridge of his nose. "I wonder what it would take for you to give up."

"More than this," she muttered, and then she sighed. "And I get it. I really do. This is bad enough."

"But apparently it isn't bad enough for you," he said in exasperation.

She nodded, as she walked around her deck. "It is pretty bad though."

He asked, "You did scan in all those pages, didn't you?"

"I did, and I sent them to you as well," she stated, looking over at him. "So all is not lost. It depends if you need that original journal for a conviction."

He shrugged. "We may have the scanned pages, but have you looked to confirm the scanned pages were legible?"

"I did. I had to open the spine out quite a bit in order to make sure the pages lay flat. It's not a perfect copy by any means."

"I don't need a perfect copy," he stated, his tone grim, "but we do need legible."

"I think we've got that," she replied.

He nodded, gave her a smile. "We'll leave, while forensics is here."

"Chances are he came in the back door, saw the journal, and left," she noted. "It wouldn't even have taken him two seconds to find it."

Mack nodded. "Then we'll check the door handle and anything in the kitchen. Do you think he wandered through your house?"

She thought about it, shrugged. "I'm not sure why he would care. He came for the journal. Ella had the other two journals, which he must have found and taken from her house. The question is whether he'll go after Nelly to ensure that she can't talk either."

"But that also means he'll come after you, so you can't talk," he pointed out.

She winced. "As much as I love that logical mind of

yours, there are times when it's much nicer when you don't make things quite so clear."

"If I don't make them clear," he replied calmly, "you tend to ignore me."

She glared at him. "That's not quite true," she muttered. He gave her a flat stare, and she sighed, raising her hands again. "Fine, maybe it's somewhat true."

He snorted at that.

She wrapped her arms around her chest. "Which also means that I guess we can't have dinner, *huh*?"

He nodded. "Not at the moment, not here. What about going back to my place for dinner?"

She slowly nodded. "I can do that."

He hesitated and then asked, "How do you feel about staying the night at my place?"

She stared at him in shock. "Do you think that's necessary?"

"Let's say that I'm not feeling very comfortable now that something potentially so dangerous has been found in your house."

"I guess the next question is, … does anybody else care?"

"What do you mean?" he asked curiously.

"Would anybody else know that I have the journal? Would anybody else care enough to come and break in and get it?"

"Meaning, it wasn't him?"

"What if it wasn't him?" she asked Mack. "What if it was somebody else entirely?"

He scratched the side of his head. "You have any idea who?"

She shook her head. "No, I really don't, but we should still consider that."

"Absolutely we should," Mack confirmed. "I'm just not sure who or what else could be involved in this."

"What about Ella Hickman?" Doreen asked. "Maybe she told other people. She must have an awful lot of people in her world."

"And she does," Mack stated. "It's one of the problems with her murder case. She knew a lot of people and not always made the best of friends."

She stared at him. "Ah, so, in other words, there could be a lot more suspects for her murder than we thought originally."

He nodded. "And that is just another problem. There could be any number of suspects that we weren't even considering before."

"God," she said, "that really muddles everything, doesn't it?"

"It sure does."

"Imagine if I had been killed today. Think how muddy the waters would be now," she suggested. "A lot of people didn't appreciate my nose in their cases."

"Thankfully most of those people are already in jail." Mack frowned at her.

"Yeah, they sure are, except for the people out on bail or the families of the people who may have died through all this or the families who think their child had been railroaded into this mess, et cetera, et cetera."

He stared off in the distance and slowly nodded. "What that means is, this break-in isn't all that clear-cut either."

"I was wondering about that too," she admitted. "I've had nothing to do for this last twenty minutes but to wonder."

"Any conclusions?"

"No," she replied. "I still keep coming back to one person in particular who needed that journal, however. It does not mean that he's the one who came here and took it. Lots of people know where I live now, apparently. Easy even to hire someone."

"That is true," Mack agreed, his tone sober, "and that again complicates everything."

"Not my fault," she murmured.

Chapter 17

WITH THAT DECISION made, at least for dinner, Doreen wasn't so sure about staying overnight. Despite her B&E, she really wanted to be back in her own home. Still, Mack loaded her and her animals into his truck, explained the situation to the two cops who had arrived, and shared that he was taking her away for a bit, while forensics worked on her kitchen area. With that done, he hopped into the truck beside her. "Ready?" he asked.

She nodded. "Still not so sure about this."

"It's dinner. You've been there before."

She looked at him and then chuckled. "I'm not talking about you and your house," she cried out. "I'm worried about who would have come into my house."

"Maybe forensics will get some answers."

"Maybe. ... Still feels weird though."

"All of this feels weird," Mack declared. "And that's what whoever it is is counting on. Hoping that we don't find any answers, that we're not getting anywhere, that this weirdness is just confusing the issue. Throwing us a bone, so they go dogging off in the other direction. Red herrings are common with criminals."

"Right. Wouldn't it be nice if they would turn around and tell us exactly what we need to know?" she muttered, then gave him a fat grin. "Think how busy I would be then."

He shook his head in mock horror, as he drove out of the cul-de-sac and headed toward his house.

"When is your brother coming?" she asked him. Mack glanced at her, surprised. She shrugged. "I wondered, considering your birthday."

"Right, well, that is this weekend, so I don't know if he'll make it or not. He did say he was pretty crazy busy."

"I imagine his world's about as nuts as ours, *huh?*"

"I don't know about just as nuts," Mack clarified, "but it's definitely crazy, and that's one of the reasons why I try not to bother him too much."

She snorted at that. "And then you gave him to me as my divorce attorney."

He laughed. "I did explain the scenario, and he did understand."

"He *used* to understand. I'm sure he's wondering what he got himself into now, though."

"Maybe, but he's also in full agreement that this needs to be settled."

She smiled. "I know that. I really do. I did hope that it would have been done by now."

"Me too," Mack agreed, grinning at her. "Having this guy always in the background sucks."

"Yeah, it really does." She wondered about telling him that Mathew had called but decided against it. They had enough to deal with now. By the time they pulled into his house, she asked him, "Did you happen to consider if you have food for dinner?"

Mack looked a bit sheepish when he replied, "I generally

have food. It might not be fancy, but it would be more than sandwiches."

She frowned at that. "Are you insulting my sandwiches?"

"Nope, your sandwiches are great, when you make them."

"I don't have a ton of money these days," she explained. And then she had to stop and reconsider her own words. "No, wait, wait. That's wrong."

"Yes, it is wrong." He glared at her. "You're doing fine. You must remember that. Bernard gave you that reward money, and, even though you shared it with Esther, you have lots left. Don't you?"

"True. I've seen him several times since. He's quite a sweetie."

Mack frowned at her, as he leaned across the front seat, edging closer to her, and asked, "What?"

"What? Bernard is a nice guy. I've seen him a couple times, and he seems lonely. He's one of those nicer people in the world."

Mack nodded slowly. "Yeah, I'm sure he'd like you to think that."

She snickered. "He would very much like me to think that, but, no, I'm not prepared to be anybody else's arm candy," she stated. "I went that route already. Remember?"

"Yes, I'm still trying to forget that part," he muttered.

She hopped out of the truck, frowning, wondering if it really bothered him. Not that there was anything she could do about it at this stage. As she walked up to his front door, Mugs wandered the gardens and the lawn, taking a moment to urinate on a bush and then sniffed out another one. She noted, "He's checking out your yard. I hope you don't mind."

Mack shrugged. "He's a dog. That's what they do."

She grinned. "Yeah, and what about the cat?" Who was even now rolling in some mint.

He watched Goliath for a moment and replied, "I presume, from the way he's acting, that's catnip."

"My husband used to put catnip on the neighbor's yard to keep the cats on their side and away from his yard."

Mack snickered. "I bet the neighbors loved it."

"One of them really did love it, which really made my husband upset because he was trying to upset her. Instead it had the opposite effect."

"Oh, anything that pisses off your husband, I like the idea of," Mack declared. "If there was ever somebody who needed to have a comeuppance, it's him."

She wouldn't argue with Mack on that point. Doreen wanted Mathew out of her life. And, so far, it seemed as if that was getting harder and harder to accomplish. "I wonder how long it'll take for this to come to an end."

"Hope not much more." Mack unlocked the front door and let her in. With the animals now inside, she undid the buckle on their leashes and let them go. Mugs immediately raced around, barking. She stared at Mack. "I wonder if Mugs is looking for your brother."

"It's possible, but he's not here. Sorry, Mugs."

Mugs raced up the stairs, came running back down again into the kitchen and around.

"I think he's excited to be here." Doreen laughed at his antics.

"Good, as long as he's happy, then you'll be happy." When she frowned at him, Mack laughed. "As if I don't know where your heart lies."

"Obviously the animals are very close to me."

"Of course they are, and I certainly understand that."

She still wasn't sure if something else was in his comment, but Mack appeared to be happy and cheerful, so she was more than happy to let it go. The last thing she needed was a problem between the two of them. She wandered into the kitchen and announced, "Food?"

He sighed. "You are always so hungry."

"Yeah, I am, and I keep trying to fix that, but …"

"We're getting there," he said comfortably. He opened the fridge and nodded. "I did take out food for dinner tonight."

"You did? I thought you were coming to my place?"

"I took it out before that," he noted, "so we have pork chops."

"Oh, that sounds good." She gave it some thought and asked, "What do you do with pork chops?"

"Cook them," he quipped, waggling his eyebrows at her.

She sighed. "What can I do to help?"

"You can prep veggies." He pulled out a bunch for her to work on.

By the time they had a meal on the table, ready to eat, she was starved. They sat down, and she tucked in with an appetite that surprised her. She shook her head. "I don't even know why I'm always so hungry," she muttered.

"There could be all kinds of reasons. Stress is one. Some experts say that, if you don't get enough protein, you keep eating and eating, until you get enough of the nutrients your body requires. If that's your case, then your body ingests other food because that's what you have available, trying to get you to the right level."

"So that's how people get fat," she muttered.

He chuckled. "Hardly your problem."

"Not yet," she stated, "but it does make you wonder."

"No," he disagreed. "Don't even start thinking about your weight. You've got a long way to go before that becomes an issue."

"But I don't want it to become an issue either."

"Good." He now glared at her. "So don't even mention it again." Still she shook her head. Mack raised a hand and continued. "I've seen too many cases of women who became anorexic and sick because they were so worried about their looks. You went through all that with your husband already. Don't go back there."

She patted his cheek gently. "I wasn't planning on it. I'm not anywhere near that mind-set," she replied, "and I enjoy my groceries way too much. So, if I get fat, you'll deal with it."

He burst out laughing. "You'll probably look cute as heck when you get fat." She gave him a look of absolute horror, and he burst out laughing again. "See? Look at you. Even that thought is enough to send you running."

She laughed. "Not really, ... but I don't think *cute* and *fat* are words I want associated with me."

"Too bad. I kind of like them."

After dinner they sat outside on his deck in his quiet backyard, and she smiled. "You have a nice place here too," she commented.

"It is nice," he agreed. "It's very centrally located. It's easy to get in and out of." He shrugged. "It was fine at the time, but not sure I want to stay here long-term."

She stared at him. "Long-term? Meaning that you want to leave Kelowna?"

He shook his head. "No, not at all. I just meant that I don't think I want to stay in this house long-term."

"Okay. So you do want to remain in Kelowna?"

"Right," he confirmed.

She nodded, understanding what he meant now. "But houses can be changed."

"Exactly," he said, with a smile.

She added, "And sometimes you need to change things."

He nodded. "For you, for your house, it's all about freedom. It's all about new beginnings. It's all about security, and so was my house a statement of independence for me back then." Mack chuckled. "Now it's a place to drop my head at the end of the day."

"How long have you been here?" she asked curiously.

"Close to a dozen years."

She nodded. "And I understand that. Not everybody your age even has a house now. So back then I'm sure there weren't all that many people with them."

"We were all trying to get into our own homes at that time," Mack shared. "Most of my friends got married and settled in pretty fast. I was one of the long-term holdouts."

"You and your brother," she pointed out.

"Exactly, and that didn't make my mother very happy at all."

"Not to mention she had children very late in life herself."

"Exactly," he said, "and so that made it even harder because she's still very much hoping for grandkids." He winced. "Not sure that'll ever happen."

"I had the same problem for a long time, but my ex didn't want kids, so ..." She shrugged. "If he didn't want something, then it didn't happen."

"What about you? Did you want any?"

She thought about it and then slowly shook her head.

"Back then, no, because of the life they would have had. It's different now. I'm not even sure who and what I am and what I want yet, but sometimes I think two would be lovely."

"With the divorce though, causing you a headache, it's not as if you've had a chance to get clear of that and figure out what you want for a future."

"That's what I keep telling myself." She smiled, as she gave him a direct look. "Sometimes that gets a little harder to listen to."

"You don't have to tell yourself anything," he declared. "Life is all about living in the moment. Right now, for you, that means keeping you safe, while you go off and create all kinds of chaos."

She snorted. "As if you don't do the same."

"Except that I signed up for this as a career," he pointed out. "You didn't."

"And that's one of the things that's been really bothering me lately—the fact that I effectively have no career. I have no way to make a living. I don't have any way to keep that roof over my head, outside of what I'm doing. Sure, that's been successful to a certain extent, but I was trying to figure out whether I needed to have a career. That way, I could—when people ask, *What do you do?*—I could say, well, hey, *I'm a secretary. I'm a writer,* or *I'm a hygienist* or something."

"A hygienist?" he asked, looking at her. "Are you thinking about going back to school for something like that?"

"No, I'm not," she stated emphatically. "I really hate going to the dentist."

He burst out laughing. "You and many others. That's probably one of the biggest phobias going."

"I can understand why," she agreed, with a mock shudder.

Mugs came over and dropped his head on her foot.

"What's the matter, big guy?" she asked him.

At that, almost immediately, Thaddeus repeated, "Big Guy, Big Guy."

Doreen groaned. "All right, I'm sorry. That was a bad choice of words," she muttered.

However, Thaddeus wasn't having anything to do with it. He started pacing back and forth, screaming, "Big Guy, Big Guy."

"Do you ever wonder if he's picking up something from that other parrot?" Mack asked her.

"No, I think at the moment it's literally my choice of words. Like, when you have a toddler, and you make the mistake of saying, *candy* or *dessert* or *cake*, or you have a dog, and you make the mistake of saying, *going for a walk.*"

At that, Mugs bounded to his feet and woofed at her several times. She groaned, closed her eyes, and sighed. "That's the same kind of mistake, yeah."

He chuckled. "Why don't we take them for a walk? We can go around a few blocks, give them a chance to relax."

"Have you checked in with the guys?"

"Yes, they're done," he stated. "We can get you home after this."

She nodded but went quiet. Did she want to go home? That was the question. Of course she did, but what she didn't want was to go home to an intruder. But considering her intruder already got everything he wanted from her, chances were that he wouldn't return.

"You're thinking he'll come back," Mack noted, easily interpreting her silence.

"I don't know what for. He got the journal, so I can't

imagine anything else matters to him."

"Except for whoever may have read them?"

"There is that," she confirmed, with a nod. "So I guess that would be a possible problem."

"Ya think?" Mack asked in a wry tone.

She grimaced. "I must be a big girl and go home and deal with this."

He stared at her and shook his head. "No, you can stay here for the night. I have a spare room. You're quite welcome to stay there."

She pondered it, frowning. "No. … As much as I appreciate the offer, I don't think it's necessary." He didn't like her answer, that's for sure. She smiled. "It's got nothing to do with you. It has to do entirely with not wanting to become too dependent on anyone."

And that seemed to make him even more upset.

She groaned. "I'm not doing a good job of this," she shared, "so why don't we take the animals for a walk?"

Mack hopped to his feet and didn't say anything and led the way out the front door. Mugs immediately followed, quite excited to walk in a new location.

As they did, she tried to formulate what was in her mind. "I'm not trying to stay distant from you," she began. "I'm still trying to let go of the shackles of my husband."

Mack still didn't say anything.

She frowned. "And maybe that doesn't even explain it very well either," she added. "I don't know. I feel as if I need to go home."

"And this time we'll let it happen," Mack finally said. "However, I don't want you to feel that you can't stay here or that you aren't safe in any way or that being here will compromise whatever independence you feel that you must have right now."

She looked at him, startled.

He shrugged. "It's not hard to understand where your mind's going. However, for me, it's hard to accept that it's still going there."

She sighed. "I'm really not trying to be a problem."

He laughed. "And that's something else you must get rid of."

"Yeah, well, by the time I get rid of all these hangups," she noted, "there won't be anything left of me."

Surprised, he looked down at her. "I think that what would be left is the real you. The one on the inside, dying to come out. The fact that you're even thinking about all this and working your way through it is huge," he noted. "Don't get down on yourself for doing what you need to do."

"Did anybody ever tell you that you're very patient and a very good person?"

He shrugged. "I deserve a medal for being so patient," he announced. "Everybody else from work is bugging me constantly."

"Oh, ouch, I am sorry about that. I'm sure that's not fun."

He sighed. "They can say whatever they want. I don't really care."

"And I appreciate that about you. I feel like such a fool sometimes. It doesn't help to know that other people agree. And I get upset about that."

He burst out laughing. "Nobody thinks you're a fool. They're all trying to figure out how your mind works, how you can come up with some of this stuff."

She considered his words in surprise. "I don't think my mind works any differently than anybody else's."

"I'm here to disagree with that." he muttered. "Your mind has a very unique twist to it, and it's working out well for solving these cases. You just need to cut yourself some slack and to keep doing what you need to do."

"Even if it's not what you want me to do?" she asked gently.

He looked down at her, put an arm around her shoulders, tucked her up close, and declared, "I don't have to like what you're doing. I must accept it and do my best to keep you safe. That's what I'm trying to do. I'm not trying to lock you in, lock you down, keep you as a prisoner, or force you to do anything," he explained. "I worry that you'll cross a line and get yourself seriously hurt—or worse, killed."

"Definitely not in my plan," she muttered.

"Nope, never is, and yet I've seen it happen time and time again. Those people had no plans to die early, but it still happens. Plans change, life happens, the best we can do is hopefully avoid everything that's coming our way when it gets ugly like that."

"I hadn't considered that," she said. "The trouble is, if I stay at your place tonight, that'll feel as if I'm giving in to the fear. If I give in to the fear, when I go back tomorrow night, nothing will have changed. It'll still be the same kind of ugly."

"And maybe not. Maybe in another twenty-four hours we'll have caught this guy."

She smiled up at him. "He's gone decades, literally decades, without being caught. As much as I would like to think the next twenty-four hours would make that kind of a difference, I'm not at all sure I can believe it." He sighed loudly, one that she'd come to understand. She turned to face him with a forceful gaze. "And thank you."

"Thank me for what?"

"For understanding. I have come a long way. However, I still have a long way to go."

"And that's fine," he acknowledged. "Just keep moving in the right direction."

She burst out laughing, and he grinned at her. "I'm getting there, but I would like to go home."

"And before I let you go," he said, "I want to go through your house and make sure that everything is completely fine."

"I won't say no to that," she agreed immediately. "Enough is going on here right now that I would appreciate it if you did do a full house search."

He nodded, and, with the animals loaded up again, he took them back to her house. As she walked into the living room, she looked around and nodded. "Even though I know that strangers have been here, even though the cops have been here," she said, "it still feels like home."

He considered her for a moment. "Most people feel the opposite."

"I get that. I need to be here. This has to be a sanctuary for me."

"Even though somebody has violated that sanctuary?"

She turned to him with a wry look. "Have you counted the other people who have violated my sanctuary as well?"

He chuckled. "Good point. Now I'll do a full search. Why don't you put on the teakettle?"

She walked into the kitchen, winced when she saw some of the fingerprint dusting powder on the cabinet handles, but she filled the teakettle first, then grabbed a cloth and started to wipe off things. She didn't know what it would take to get it cleaned up, but hopefully the stuff would come off fairly easily. When Mack came back downstairs again, he went to the basement and out to the garage, checking every corner, every nook.

She always forgot about the basement. The fact that it had been filled with antiques and would hopefully bring her a ton of money always made her consider it with joy. Still, somebody may know about it or may have found it. The idea of being robbed or taken out while she was sleeping because they had a hiding spot may have also filled her intruder with joy.

As Mack walked into the kitchen, he studied what she was doing. "Did they leave much of a mess?"

"No, I don't think so. They must make some mess, so it's all good."

He smiled at her. "Are you good? Because I'll skip tea and head home if you are."

"I'm fine." She waved him off. She walked to the front door with him.

"Remember to lock the door."

"Will do," she said.

He leaned over, kissed her gently, and, just like that, he was gone. She locked the door and set the alarm behind him, as soon as his truck drove out of the cul-de-sac.

Mugs was watching her every move.

"What did Mack do? Put you on extra guard duty or something?" she joked. He woofed at her a couple times, and she smiled. "You are the best of dogs," she murmured. And she quickly gave him a big hug. When he protested and wiggled free, she laughed. "Fine, but don't think you'll get away from my hugs all the time." And she headed back to the kitchen. The teakettle had popped, but she wanted to finish up the bit of cleaning first.

With that done, she fixed a cup of tea and slowly made her way upstairs.

Chapter 18

The Next Morning...

DOREEN WOKE THE next morning and felt a sense of well-being at a good night's sleep sliding though her. She rolled over, stretched, pulled Mugs closer, and gave him a great big hug. He woofed and wiggled in her arms, cleaned her face briefly, then stretched out, as if to say, *Leave me alone. I must sleep.* She chuckled at the tired pup and then decided that maybe a hot shower would be the perfect thing for her. She checked her cell phone to see it was already seven thirty.

"Look at that," she noted. "We had a great night."

She sent a quick text to Mack. **Had a lovely night.** He sent back a thumbs-up. And she wondered if he'd gotten any sleep. She sent him a quick text back, asking how his night was. And in response she got a thumbs-down.

She wasn't sure whether he was busy and couldn't talk or was busy and didn't want to discuss it. At least he'd answered, so that was all good too. She had a shower, quickly dressed, and went downstairs, where she propped open the kitchen door, stepped out onto the deck, and sighed with joy at the beautiful morning.

Something was so comforting and so beautiful about being outside first thing in the morning, especially when she was close to the river like this. Ducks and birds and animals always wandered about, as if she'd caught them unexpectedly by surprise. Although on this morning, it seemed as if her wildlife was already awake and gone. But then she'd taken her time with her shower, and here she was even now trying to get herself some coffee. She chuckled at that. If only coffee wasn't such a necessary part of her life, but it was, and she wouldn't change it one bit.

With coffee in hand, she slowly meandered down to the stream, feeling a new lease on life. She got through the night, no problems, had a good night's sleep, and today the world looked great. When her phone rang, she thought it was Nan's phone number, and she quickly answered, singing out, "Good morning."

At first came silence on the other end for a moment, and then came a growl. "Why are you so happy?" her ex asked.

She winced, looked down at the Caller ID number, and realized that she hadn't checked close enough. "What's this? A new phone number?" she asked suspiciously. "Trying to avoid people catching you?"

He snorted. "Last thing I need is mockery from you."

"I'm not supposed to talk to you, so if you've got something to say, say it fast because I'm gone," she muttered.

"Don't hang up on me," he barked.

"Yeah, why not?"

"Because things are going on here that you don't understand, and I need you to back off."

"It's not me doing anything," she declared. "You need to come to terms with the fact that a divorce, particularly after you pulled the stunts that you did, means it'll cost you.

That's all there is to it." And, with that, she disconnected. She wasn't at all sure if she should have hung up because she did note the desperation in Mathew's tone. Worried, she immediately phoned Nick.

"Wow," he answered. "We're talking lots these days. Remember the time when I couldn't even get a hold of you?"

"Am I bothering you?" she asked.

"No, not if you have a reason for calling."

"Mathew called again from a number I didn't know," she began, and she quickly reeled off the number. "He also sounded quite desperate but a different kind of desperate."

After a momentary pause, Nick asked, "And you think he's in danger?"

"I don't know what to think," she admitted. "I don't want to be sympathetic. I don't want to get involved in any way emotionally. Still, I don't know what to think, but it was very strange."

"Okay, thank you."

Nick didn't say anything more, so she ended the call.

She wasn't at all sure what she could have done differently, but it sounded as if Mathew was in trouble. As much as she didn't want anything to do with the man, neither did she want him killed because of his poor business decisions. Still, they were his business decisions, not hers. And yet he had always been the one to spell out how well he knew the business world and how she knew nothing. She shrugged, determined to put it out of her mind.

When Nan phoned her a little bit later, Doreen smiled and said, "I thought you called a couple minutes ago."

"I would have, but it got a bit crazy."

"Yeah, that was my ex instead."

Nan gasped. "You're not supposed to talk to him."

"*Thanks*," she noted in a wry tone. "I do know that."

"So why did you talk to him then?" Nan cried out. "It'll really hurt your chances of getting out of this."

"I hope not," she stated, "because I'm rather desperate to get this resolved."

Nan sighed. "Men like your ex, they just keep getting to be more and more of a problem. You must cut him off."

"I'm trying. It would be nice if people would believe me."

"I guess then you must try harder," Nan replied in exasperation.

Doreen shook her head, wondering how this had become everybody else's problem. "Did you have a reason for calling?" she asked carefully.

"Yes," Nan stated. "I wanted to invite you down for tea."

"I'm sitting at the river, having coffee," Doreen replied, with a smile. "Enjoying the beautiful morning."

"Enjoy it for as long as you can, dear," Nan said. "So is that a yes or a no?"

"Of course I'll come down for tea," Doreen noted. "Do you need me down there right now or can it be when my coffee is gone?"

"Oh, heavens, make it when your coffee is gone. You're quite grumpy without it. I'll see you in about half an hour then." And, with that, she hung up.

Doreen stared down at her phone. "Am I really that grumpy without coffee?" As if understanding the question, Mugs barked at her. She glared at him. "That's enough out of you," she muttered. But she had to consider, was she really that dependent on coffee?

She thoroughly enjoyed it, that was her definite drink of choice, but was it a problem for other people? She pondered that, as she walked back up to the house and poured herself a second cup of coffee. Instead of going back down to the river, she sat on her patio near the deck and enjoyed the view. She wondered whether she was supposed to eat before going to Nan's or not. Doreen hadn't had breakfast yet, just her coffee. As it was midmorning now, Nan would have snacks if not a basketful of goodies.

If she ate until she was full and went to visit to find some of the good food Rosemoor offered, then she'd be upset. She couldn't eat much after a meal here. However, if Doreen didn't eat here first and no food was offered at Nan's, then Doreen would be hungry. Then she snorted. *When did Nan not have food that she pushed on me?* So she decided that the best course of action would be to have a little bit here. And, with any luck, she could have a little bit more with Nan.

She smiled at that because the last thing she wanted to do was become dependent on Nan for food, but it seemed the more she went down there, it was almost a given that Nan would have something. Of course that became something that she worried wouldn't be there the next time she went. Life was like that.

She put on one piece of toast, had a little bit of gooseberry jam with it, smiling. The jam already reminded her of her grandmother. For that thought alone, she thought she should hang on to a couple jars and never use them. Sometime later Nan wouldn't be here, and the jam would make Doreen remember her grandmother with a smile.

Nan was in great health, except for the memory issues at times, and, as long as Doreen could keep Nan safe, then she had a lot of good years left.

After feeding her animals and then eating a piece of toast and jam and having one last cup of coffee, Doreen cleaned up the kitchen, locked up, and she and her pets headed outside. Thaddeus walked this time, as he pranced down the path, Mugs in tow. Doreen shook her head at Thaddeus and chuckled.

"Glad to see you so happy today," she muttered. He called at her a couple times, she was not sure what he was trying to say, but he appeared to be quite happy. And they were always happy when heading down to Nan's. As soon as she reached Rosemoor, Doreen found her grandmother, sitting outside, waiting for her. Doreen waved, brought the animals across the lawn, always looking for the gardener who was likely to yell at her.

Nan chuckled. "Are you still afraid of that gardener?"

She shrugged. "The first one was scary. The second one I didn't want to get off on the wrong foot with, but he doesn't like animals either."

"Anybody who doesn't like animals isn't to be trusted," Nan announced.

Doreen frowned at her. "We can hardly make such a clear-cut statement."

"I can make any statement I want," Nan declared. And then she smiled up at her granddaughter. "Be a dear and bring out the teapot, will you?"

"Sure." Doreen walked into the kitchen and found the teapot and cups on a tray. She picked it up, brought it out, and set it on the patio table. "Are you tired today, Nan?"

"A little bit," she admitted. "It was a busy day yesterday, starting with Ella."

Doreen nodded. "What else were you up to?"

"What weren't we up to?" she said, with a sigh. "Lawn bowling, bingo, and then I got into a pool game last night with Patsy. I never should have done that. That woman always beats me."

"And sometimes," Doreen noted, looking over at Nan, "I think you let her beat you."

Nan chuckled. "That's very smart of you, my dear, but don't tell anybody else."

"Nope, I won't," Doreen stated. "I'm pretty sure that's all part and parcel of the fun, isn't it?"

"It is, indeed," she muttered.

"Did you gamble at the same time?"

"Not with her," Nan said. "Patsy's a mean gambler."

"You were supposed to let her back in your good books."

"No, *you* wanted me to let her back in my good books," she corrected. "I am still thinking about it."

Doreen sighed. "That's sad. … I was hoping that, when Patsy helped me so much, that you would have let her back in."

"I'm still thinking about it," she announced.

"Think about it faster," Doreen suggested.

Nan glared at her, then shrugged. "Fine. She did help, but I don't want her thinking she's part of our club."

"Oh? What club is that?" Doreen asked curiously.

"*The* club. *The* club," she repeated, with an eye roll. "My dear, sometimes …"

"I'm still not exactly sure which club you're talking about," Doreen admitted, "but that's all right."

Nan looked at her and chuckled. "It's hardly all right when you're the president."

"I'm what?" she asked, looking at Nan in shock. "How can I be president of a club I don't even belong to?"

"Oh, you belong," Nan confirmed. "You're an honorary member."

"Honorary members don't get to be presidents," she

muttered.

Nan waved her hand. "Details, details. Besides, you're the one who solves the cases, and we're just on the inside, trying to help."

"Oh." With a sinking heart, Doreen realized what Nan was talking about. "You're talking about *that* club."

"Exactly," Nan noted, with quiet satisfaction. "And it's lovely to be on the inside."

Doreen shook her head. "A lot of people might think that," she began, "but there are certainly some costs to being on the inside."

"Yeah, and *you* keep paying it," Nan declared, frowning at her.

"I'm fine. I'm fine." Doreen knew that Nan would immediately go off on a warning, *Be careful.* Yet it was Nan who had got hit on the head recently. Speaking of which, Doreen asked, "How is your health?"

Nan patted Doreen's hand. "It's totally fine," Nan said. "Besides, that hit on the head was well worth it. The food's much better now."

Doreen groaned. "Says you." She sat down and asked, "Is the tea ready, do you think?"

"Oh, absolutely." Nan leaned forward and poured the hot tea into the awaiting cups. Frowning at the tray, Nan added, "I forgot to put the treats on the tray."

Doreen raised an eyebrow. "And here I thought maybe there weren't any," she said humorously.

"As if that'll happen," Nan muttered. She got up, headed into the kitchen. When she returned, she had a basket in her hand. "I put them in the oven to keep them warm," she shared.

"To keep what warm?" Doreen had already lifted the

towel, sniffing the basket's contents. "Pastries again," she noted, with a delighted smile.

"Breakfast time," she murmured. "I can't really go nick some lunch food if it's still breakfast time."

"Of course not," Doreen agreed. "What are these?"

"Assorted mini quiches," she replied. "They taste delicious though, so I don't really care what they call it."

Doreen immediately chuckled. "No, I'm right there with you. As long as it's good food, we don't care what it's called." She lifted one and placed it on Nan's plate.

Nan immediately waved her back. "No, no, no. I've had several for breakfast. Matter of fact, I had way too many. It's probably why I'm tired now. It's an awful lot to digest at once."

Doreen studied Nan first but put the pastry on her plate. Doreen wasn't sure if that was a ploy to ensure Doreen ate more or if it was truly a case of Nan having eaten too much. It wasn't something Doreen had ever seen her grandmother do before, but it could still be possible. "How many of these did you eat?"

She chuckled. "At least four." At Doreen's incredulous stare, Nan nodded. "See? As I told you, I certainly don't need any more." She shooed at her. "Eat, eat, eat."

Doreen shook her head but picked up the one on her plate and took a bite. Immediately the taste of cheese and ham and egg filled her mouth, wrapped up in a luscious pastry. "Oh, wow," she cooed, once she swallowed so she could talk. "This is delicious."

"Right? So it's a good thing that our previous cook was bad news," Nan stated. "Believe me. People do come up and thank me for having taken one for the team." Doreen didn't want to laugh, but it was hard. When one finally escaped,

Nan looked at her with a note of satisfaction. "See, see? That's how it should be," she declared. "You should be smiling and laughing all the time."

Doreen chuckled. "Personally I think I do an awful lot of that."

"No, not enough," Nan corrected, "but we're working on it. And Mack is too."

"Oh, did you enlist Mack's help in trying to make me laugh more?" she asked, with a smile.

"We would if we could, but he's always so busy. It's hard to pin him down."

"That's true enough," Doreen admitted, "but he does work on it anyway."

Nan nodded. "I'm glad to hear that. We gave him quite a talking to."

She winced. "That's not necessary, Nan."

"You never know."

There was absolutely no point talking Nan out of trying to get Mack involved, because Nan would do it regardless. Doreen needed to accept it, to realize Mack was a big boy, and could say no at any time. Nan was doing this because she loved Doreen.

When the first quiche was done, she looked down at the second one and wondered if she should hold off until later.

"Eat," Nan demanded. "You do not need to save that for later."

Doreen frowned at her grandmother. "How did you know what I was thinking?"

Nan rolled her eyes at her. "Anybody could figure that one out," she muttered.

Doreen smiled, picked up the second one, sat back, and slowly savored it. "It's really good. You guys are truly blessed to have this kind of food here."

Nan smiled. "Believe me. We know, and we're very appreciative of it."

"And that makes all the difference, doesn't it?" Doreen pointed out. "Knowing you'll get good food can make such a difference in your day."

"It's always been that way with people," Nan said. "Everybody needs to have a place where they can be well-fed and looked after. Food is a comfort for the body, but it's also food for the soul," she stated, "and that's very important."

Doreen certainly wouldn't argue that point. She also firmly agreed with her grandmother that she was blessed enough to have cooking like this ready-made. "I wonder what it would take to get Esther into a place like this."

Nan stared at her. "Do you think she'd come?"

Doreen thought about it and then admitted, "I don't know. I think she's lonely. I think that she would very much like to be a part of something, but I also think that change is hard for her."

"Change is hard for all of us," Nan declared. "People like Esther even more so."

"Why people like Esther?"

"Because of her age. She's got that many more years living on her own, so it's hard to let go of her lifestyle as she knows it," Nan explained.

"I suppose so. Still, when I saw her, it was so hard for her to walk and to get around. Yet she's out there, chasing the magpies and yelling at them. In a way, she seemed to be having fun."

"She's been having a battle with those magpies for at least thirty generations of magpies," Nan stated, with a quiet complacency. "Personally I think she's very fond of them. I think she goes out there and feeds them."

"Then why would she chase them off, if she feeds them?"

"Because they come back again, and she's lonely."

Hearing that, Doreen's heart broke a little bit more. "I wonder if we could coerce her into Rosemoor."

"I don't think so," Nan replied. "It's always been an option for her."

"I'm not sure she has the money though," she murmured.

"That's often the problem here, isn't it? You want to think that everybody has enough money to live in this place, but they don't. Plus it's not even one of the highest priced places."

Doreen wasn't sure about that. Rosemoor seemed to be plenty pricey, and she certainly had met lots of people around town and when working various cases where the cost had been too much for most of them. But then Nan had money, and, as long as Nan didn't give it all away to Doreen—and that was always a constant burden on her—then Nan would continue to have money.

"I want you to always have enough money to be here," Doreen shared. "And it does worry me when you are always giving money away."

"Oh, hogwash," Nan replied. "Giving money away is a joy, particularly to you."

"And yet I don't want you to get caught short."

"When you get the antiques money, then you can help me out," she murmured, "but I won't be happy if that day ever comes."

"Why not?" she asked in confusion.

"Because it means I didn't plan well for myself," Nan explained. "And my mind's been a steel trap all these years, as I worked out the angles of everything that needed to be done and how much money it would all cost." Nan smiled at her granddaughter. "Don't you worry about me. I've got this down pat."

But still it was hard to accept that, with the rising inflation rate that nobody could have predicted, how could everything still be okay for Nan? Doreen hoped that, if it ever did come to that, she would find out ahead of time and could do something about it. She had already mentally earmarked a chunk of money from the antiques to go toward Rosemoor and her grandmother's care.

"Now stop worrying about me and tell me what's going on with Ella's case," Nan said. "Nelly's been beside herself. She's kept to her room and been given medication to calm her down."

Doreen frowned at this news. "Still?"

"Yes, still, and it seems as if nothing is calming her down. Nothing is really working."

"Do you think something else is going on?" Doreen asked her grandmother.

"I do, but she won't talk to me," Nan said, with a wave of her hand. "She won't talk to anybody. I think she feels guilty about something."

Doreen knew exactly what that was, but she'd hoped Nelly would have calmed down somewhat by now. However, that was hard to do when you thought that you were responsible for somebody's death.

At that, Nan leaned forward and asked, "Do you think you could talk to her?"

"I could talk to her," Doreen pointed out, "but no guarantee that she would talk to *me* though."

"Yet you seemed to have gotten through to her last

time."

"I don't know about that, but I'm certainly willing to try." She hesitated, then said, "Maybe I should go now."

"Absolutely, leave the animals here," Nan told her. "Knock on her door, tell her who it is, and see if she'll talk to you. It would mean a lot to the rest of us to know that you care."

"I certainly don't want her suffering any more than she has to over this. It's hard enough to deal with the loss of her sister, without anything else coming into play."

"If I had an idea what's coming into play, I would do something about it," Nan offered. She stared at her granddaughter shrewdly. "You, however, *do* know something about it."

She looked at Nan and then shrugged. "Maybe. ... That doesn't mean that I can say anything about it though."

"No, I'm sure you can't." Nan nodded. "Yet you can do something to make Nelly feel better."

Chapter 19

DOREEN WASN'T SO sure that it would be all that easy, but she got up obediently and took a sip of her tea before the cup went cold, then walked toward Nelly's room. When Doreen got up to the door, she placed an ear against it. She couldn't hear anything but gave a smart rap on the outside. When she got a soft answer, Doreen said, "Nelly, it's Doreen. May I come in?"

The silence went on for a long moment, and Doreen wasn't sure Nelly would even respond. Then the door opened, and Doreen saw Nelly. The poor woman was distraught, her face flushed and teary and swollen, as if she hadn't slept, and was beside herself.

"I'm so sorry," Doreen said immediately. "You're really struggling, aren't you?"

Nelly's eyes filled with tears, and she nodded.

"Do you want to talk?" Doreen asked.

Nelly looked around hesitantly to see if anybody was watching.

Doreen muttered, "Nobody knows I'm here."

At that, Nelly opened the door wider, and she let Doreen in. Nelly shut the door immediately behind her.

"Did you talk to the police?" Doreen asked.

Nelly nodded and then whispered, "They weren't very nice."

Doreen winced. "No, from their perspective, not telling them years ago means that other people died," she explained to Nelly. "But you also must let some of this go because it was a long time ago."

"And yet it doesn't feel so long ago," she muttered. "It feels as if it's right now."

"Of course it does, especially with your sister's death."

"A death which I don't know if I caused or not," she muttered.

"Have you seen him again?" Doreen asked the one question that had been bothering her the whole way over.

"No, but now I'm looking for him everywhere. I stay in my room. Even the cops told me not to go anywhere and to stay where it's safe. Safety in numbers and all that."

"Exactly," Doreen murmured. "And of course safety in numbers is one thing, but it still feels like a prison, doesn't it?"

Nelly slowly nodded. "And the guilt is crippling me," she muttered in a faint whisper. "As if I don't have any right to live, particularly now that my sister's gone."

Doreen didn't really have anything that she could say to make Nelly feel any better about that. "The only thing you can do now is make the best of it. Try not to get sick yourself. Plus try to understand that the police are doing what they can, but now they're dealing with the problem of time and not being able to identify this person."

"I showed you the picture," she said, looking at Doreen.

"Oh, and I have a couple more pictures, but they're all old," Doreen added. "The problem with that is, people can change their appearance."

"And he was very good at that," Nelly stated. "Ella used to laugh because sometimes he'd come here looking as if he were bald, wearing some weird scalp cap, and sometimes he'd come to her, and he'd have this full beard and glasses and a baseball cap," she shared, with a shrug.

Doreen froze. "Interesting," she murmured. "He liked disguises, did he?"

"Of course. That made more sense when thinking about the *hobby* he had," Nelly said, with sarcasm. "I can't believe I didn't do anything to help all those years ago."

Doreen couldn't believe it either, but what was she supposed to say? Nelly was already traumatized. "Did the police give you any insight into what they were doing?"

She shook her head. "No, basically they were pretty upset and took my statement in cold disdain and then left."

Doreen winced because, well, what could she say? The cops were upset. A lot of cases were attributed to this one man, but they also understand the fear factor and how somebody like Bob Small would wield their fear of him with a very capable hand. "They also know what you went through and how scared you were," Doreen said. "Judgment on their part is easy. They weren't there at the time."

Nelly looked up at Doreen gratefully. "That's the thing. Nobody understands what it's like."

"And I'm sorry because it seems as if everybody is judging and criticizing you, and yet there's nothing you could have done at the time," she tried to say in a soothing manner.

"Or I could have," Nelly argued. "I could have told them about the journal back then. And, when I had the journal, I should have done something then too," she murmured, "but I didn't." She shook her head. "I never thought I was a mean person or a bad person. I always thought that was Ella. However, now? Well, now I must look at my own actions in a completely different light. And, … and it sucks."

To hear the words come out of Nelly's mouth made Doreen pause.

Nelly shrugged. "It does," she repeated. "You want to leave behind a legacy of goodness, but here I am, facing the twilight days of my life, and all I see are mistakes made and mistakes that are way too late to do anything to correct," Nelly admitted, her tone hardening.

"If you have anything else that you can give the police," Doreen suggested, "that would be one way you can correct it. There's also your sister's death to avenge and to get justice for her. So, if you have anything, anything you know or remember, then let the police know."

"I don't want to talk to them anymore." Nelly looked at Doreen. "They were mean."

Doreen winced at that. "I don't think they meant to be mean. I think they were tired of dealing with people who seemed to think that the cops are supposed to solve all these things, and yet nobody helps the police, even when they have information."

"Maybe," Nelly relented, "but the end result is, I don't want to talk to them again. Ever."

"Do you have anything else to give them?" Doreen asked curiously.

She hesitated. "Maybe."

Doreen sat down on the closest chair. "If you do, they need it."

She grimaced and repeated, "But they were mean."

Doreen picked up Nelly's hand. "I know this is hard. But again, if there's anything you have for information on this guy, give it to the police."

Nelly looked at her, with eyes filled with tears, and asked, "Would you take it to them?"

"Take what to whom?"

"Take it to the police."

"Yes," Doreen said immediately. "Absolutely I will."

"And will it stop them from coming back and talking to me again?" she asked in a caustic tone.

"I'm not sure that it would," Doreen replied. "You must look at it from their point of view. They're doing everything they can to solve your sister's murder. They talked to you, and you didn't give them that information. So now they don't know what to think."

"Then it's better off if I don't give it to them," Nelly snapped.

"No, it isn't, because your sister's murder may never get solved, not if we don't get the information that we need."

Nelly sniffed at that. "They weren't very nice."

"I don't think anybody in this situation is very nice. A lot of people have died, and, for all you know, it could have been people the police knew and loved. And, if they had any personal connection to this case, it'll be very hard for them to hear about it."

At that, Nelly closed her eyes and whispered, "That would be terrible."

"Exactly, so why don't we work on the premise that they were doing the best they could, and I suggest you give me whatever it is you didn't give to the police, and I'll make sure that they get it."

She nodded. "I don't know if it's of any value."

"Oh, I'll tell them that you forgot about it, and then, when we were talking, you remembered."

Nelly studied Doreen. "You think they'll believe you?"

"Yes," she lied. "And honestly they know that you're distraught about your sister's death, so there's really no way for anybody to know the truth about it. What's important is that you hand it over."

Nelly got up very slowly, as if she were on her last few minutes of life, and toddled over to her bed. There she picked up a small notepad and brought it over and handed it to Doreen.

She looked down at it. "What's that? A series of numbers? What is that?"

"It's the numbers that my sister would call when she was here, and then she swore and said something about *wrong phone*."

"Wrong phone number or wrong phone?"

Nelly eyed Doreen steadily. "I took it to mean *wrong phone*, as in Ella was to only call from a different phone."

Doreen asked, "And you think it's Bob Small's number?"

She nodded. "I've seen it before. She'd written it down a couple times and never would tell me who it was, but, over the years, it's hard to forget it."

And it would be because the last four digits were literally zero, one, one, zero. "Interesting," Doreen murmured, staring at it. "I'll give it to Mack and see what he can do with this. Maybe they can trace it. And that also means ..." Doreen faced Nelly, realizing something. "Nelly, your sister had a second phone."

"She didn't keep it with her. It was always in the house."

"In which case then, I need to go back to her house and

see if I can find that. Did your sister have any hiding places in her house?"

Nelly laughed. "All women have hiding places," she murmured. "I think hers would have been in the closet."

"Fine, I'll see if I can arrange to go take another look then," Doreen replied. "On the top shelves were a bunch of boxes."

"Yeah, that would have been where she stashed paperwork and stuff," Nelly confirmed. "However, for the second phone, it would be somewhere else, somewhere that she could grab easily and fast."

"Oh, that makes sense too." Doreen smiled at Nelly. "Thank you for giving us this."

Nelly nodded. "They won't be mean when they come back, will they?" she asked anxiously.

"I promise they'll be as nice as they can be."

Nelly sighed. "That's not exactly the same thing."

Doreen chuckled. "No, it's not, but it is the police, so they will try."

Nelly nodded again. "Okay, fine." She walked Doreen to the door. "Don't tell Nan."

"No, I won't." Doreen knew how much judgment Nelly would face if anybody found out what she had done. "But it could get out at some point."

"I hope not," Nelly whispered. "I love being here, and I love the people, but I don't think I could handle it if they hate me after this."

"Let's not put that out there," Doreen suggested gently. "There is lots of time and life left for all kinds of good things to happen."

Nelly gave her a sad smile. "It doesn't feel as if there's a lot of time left," she noted. "If feels as if there's no time left, and it's all running away on me."

Doreen looked at Nelly in alarm. "You won't do anything stupid, right?"

"No, I won't do anything stupid. I need to see this through, even if I don't like it."

Doreen slowly nodded, as she searched the other woman's face.

But Nelly gave Doreen a determined smile. "Don't you worry," Nelly stated. "I won't do anything foolish."

Not at all sure about that and definitely not convinced by anything Nelly said, Doreen added, "Please don't. That would make for yet another victim that nobody needs right now." And, with that, Doreen said her goodbyes and headed back to Nan. She was quiet all the way. When she got there, Richie waited for Doreen with Nan.

"Sorry." Doreen stepped up to them. "I didn't realize you guys had plans."

"I didn't think you would be so long," Nan replied, looking at her. "Is she okay?"

"She's depressed and upset, but I'm hoping she'll be fine."

"Hopefully." Nan handed Doreen a little paper bag, "These are your leftover snacks." She handed over the leashes and the animals now. "But we must leave."

"You two have fun." Doreen quickly grabbed her animals and headed to Nan's patio. Once outside, she turned to look, but Nan was already closing the patio door and heading off with Richie. Doreen wasn't sure what was going on today, but, hey, Nan's life was busier and more exciting than Doreen's, and that revealed a lot about her own life.

Chapter 20

WHEN DOREEN REACHED the creek, she immediately phoned Mack.

"What's up?" he asked.

"I came back from talking with Nelly. She's really despondent. Apparently your guys were pretty mean." He gave an exasperated sigh. "I'm not here to tell you off," Doreen said, "but she didn't tell either of us all the truth."

"What?" he snapped. "What do you mean?"

"She withheld a notepad, which I did coerce out of her. However, she didn't want to give it to you guys because it would mean talking to you again, and she didn't want to deal with that again."

"*Great*," he mumbled. "Now we're so scary that nobody wants to talk to us."

"She's a frail old lady at this point."

"And one who made some really bad decisions. Keeps making them, by the sounds of it."

"Yeah, and this was another one. The notepad had a phone number on it. And her sister ..." Doreen quickly explained.

"Good Lord," he snapped. "She has a second phone?"

"Yes, that was my understanding, and she would have kept it somewhere close to her bed, so she could grab it easily. I think it was her connection to Bob Small. And I have what may be his telephone number here on this pad."

"Give it to me," he said briskly. She quickly gave it to him over the phone. "I'll get back to you," he muttered. And, with that, he hung up.

She looked down at the animals. "We did something useful today at least."

Mugs barked, and she undid the leash, so that he could go free. Almost immediately he dashed into the water.

"No, Mugs," Doreen cried out.

But he was having nothing to do with it. For whatever reason, sitting here waiting for her while she was off talking with Nelly had determined that he needed playtime in the river. And playtime it was. Even Goliath joined in. She laughed, splashed them, got soaked herself, and, by the time she called it quits, said, "Come on, guys. Time to go home."

She walked up to the house, grabbed some towels, and quickly rubbed down the animals and then herself. As she hung up the towels to dry, she heard her phone ringing. A little hesitantly, considering that she'd already talked to Mathew recently, she answered to hear another heavy breathing caller on the other end. She groaned. "Really? You haven't got anything better to do than bug me?" she muttered, and she quickly hung up. When it rang again, she frowned, answered it, same thing. She hung up, it rang once more, and the same thing.

"You must be so bored," she declared. "Surely something else in your life is worth doing other than bugging a woman." And, with that, she hung up again. This time there was only silence.

Relieved, she quickly sent Mack a text, informing him that her caller had called three times, each time the same thing—silence and heavy breathing.

He phoned her back. "And you answered it the third time, why?"

"Because I wanted to know what this guy was up to," she replied in exasperation. "Like how does anybody have time for this nonsense?"

He laughed out loud. "Not too many people do. Usually it's very targeted, and they have a reason, which is also why we keep telling you to stay out of trouble."

"I *was* trying," she stated. "Apparently this guy set off my temper a bit."

"Ya think?" he asked, followed by a hard sigh. "When it rings again, don't answer it."

"What if it's you?" she asked in a cheeky tone. He gave a long-suffering sigh. "Fine, fine, fine," she replied. "I won't. Did you get a hold of the number?"

"No, we're still working on it."

"It'll be unlisted, won't it?"

"I'm not saying anything to you," Mack said. "Chances are, you'll get into even more trouble."

"Hey, that's not fair," she muttered. "I'm not responsible for this one."

"No, and, in fact, you got the information for us, which is good. However, it does not make us any happier with Nelly."

"And I think that's why she was petrified about calling you guys back. You also made her feel so guilty that she couldn't in good conscience keep it."

"That's good," Mack noted, "at least something came out of that visit."

"She felt as if everybody was judging her."

"She kept information on a serial killer for decades," Mack stated, his tone flat.

"I know, but, because of how you guys made her feel, she kept that number from you, and that's also not good. You must understand her too. We're trying to solve something, so we need everybody's cooperation. That means playing nice too."

"Yes, ma'am."

She winced, not liking Mack's tone of voice. "I get it. I need to stay out of it," she muttered. "I thought I'd give you what I found," and, with that, she hung up on him.

Chapter 21

Later that Afternoon ...

DOREEN SPENT THE afternoon at Millicent's, changing up little bits and pieces in her garden. Mostly it was a chance for Doreen to get out of the house and to do something. She almost felt bad charging Mack for the hours, but, when she thought about it, she didn't feel bad at all. The least he could have done was filled her in on the phone number and any other information he'd gleaned. The fact that he couldn't was something that she knew but didn't really want to acknowledge. It was one thing to get the information that she needed, and it was an entirely different thing to know that she wouldn't get it whether she needed it or not.

As she finished the gardening work and sat down with Mack's mother, the older woman looked at her expectedly. Doreen studied her face. "Did I miss something?" she asked cautiously.

Millicent laughed. "No, but I did hear through the grapevine that there's a new case in town."

She winced at that. "Your son has a new case," she clarified. "I do too, but, well, it's connected to his case.

Therefore, as far as he's concerned, I don't have a case." And even her best efforts couldn't stop the grumpiness from coming out.

Millicent laughed in delight. "I do like to see the relationship between the two of you blossoming."

Doreen stiffened at that. The last thing she wanted was a heart-to-heart with Mack's mother at this point. Doreen looked over at her casually and added, "There's an awful lot we don't get along about. It's a matter of compromise."

Millicent gave a wise nod. "Absolutely, all relationships are."

At that, Doreen sagged in place. "Hopefully he'll call me back with the information I'm looking for," she muttered, as she stared down at her cell phone.

If the conversation would center around her and Mack, Doreen was more than ready to head out. And more than ready to not come back for a little bit. At least until Millicent changed gears.

His mother chuckled. "He can't."

"I know," she groaned, flashing her a grin. "It still would be nice if he would."

"I'm sure it would, but, considering he's very honorable," she shared, studying Doreen's face with a closed gaze, "he won't."

"Yeah, he is," Doreen agreed. She checked the time and said, "And I should head home."

Millicent nodded. "Are you doing something for Mack's birthday, dear?" she asked out of the blue.

Doreen froze. She turned and looked at her. "Only in the sense that he's having dinner at my place, and we might spend the day together," she shared calmly. "I believe Nick is coming up, and we would have him over as well."

"Oddly," Millicent added, "I have both boys coming here for dinner on Friday." She hesitated and then said, "And I would like it if you would join us."

Doreen was not at all comfortable with that, particularly seeing the look in Millicent's gaze. "I'm not too sure what's going on this Friday," she hedged. "Is his birthday Saturday or Friday?"

"Technically it's Friday."

"Okay," she muttered. "In that case he'll get double birthday dinners. I'll do the other one on Saturday."

Millicent laughed. "And Mack has always liked his sweets."

"*Great*," Doreen moaned. "You do know I don't know how to cook?"

Millicent nodded. "I also know that you've been taking lessons from Mack."

"I'm trying to. He's a good teacher. I'm a slow learner."

"He's always been handy in the kitchen," Millicent murmured, "and he does like his groceries."

"I like his groceries too." And that, for whatever reason, Millicent thought was hilarious. She beamed and added, "Let me know about Friday, dear."

"I will, thank you." And Doreen quickly made her escape. Once she made her way back toward home, the animals in tow, she walked as briskly as she could, as if she could leave the conversation behind with Millicent. Because that invitation meant a whole lot more than coming for Mack's birthday dinner. It's not as if Doreen was against the idea, not in any way. But it certainly made her a little leery about everybody else's view of her relationship with Mack.

She didn't even know how she viewed it. She'd done a darn good job of putting it out of her mind for the moment, much to Mack's dismay. But, until things clarified, it was all she could do to keep functioning on the level that she was at. She really didn't want to have her husband be a part of the equation. As far as Doreen was concerned, she really needed the men in her life to be one at a time.

Most people would say that Mathew wasn't even part of the present equation and that she was using him as an excuse, which she winced at. Yet it seemed to have some merits and probably did, if she cared to delve a little bit deeper into that issue. Which, of course, she didn't.

Matter of fact, she would just as soon not delve into that issue at all. And, for a while, she got away with it, but she wouldn't get away with it for long. She needed to sort it out. For she did know that she didn't want to say goodbye to Mack. If he walked out of her life at this point in time, she would be devastated. That much she knew for sure. She knew Mack was a good thing. All the rest was still up in the air.

As if he heard the thoughts running around in her head, he called her, just as she walked up her driveway.

"Hey," he said.

"Hey," she replied, her voice slightly off.

"What's the matter?" he asked.

"Nothing," she muttered. "Why do you always think something is the matter?"

"Because there almost always is," he replied in a mocking tone.

"There isn't. I came back from your mom's."

"Oh, good. How's her garden looking?"

"It's looking fine. Today was more about getting out of the house and visiting with her."

"So, in that case, you're not charging me, is that it?" he

asked, with a laugh.

"I probably shouldn't," she admitted. "I did a bit of work, but it wasn't very much."

"I'm not worried about it. You know that, right?"

"Maybe not, but my conscience wouldn't allow me to charge you. Besides, your mom brought up something that made me skid out a little faster than normal. And, no, I'm not telling you."

"Oh, great," he said in exasperation. "You drop a bombshell like that, and then you won't tell me what's up?"

"No, I won't. And it serves you right. You won't tell me anything either." And then she hesitated. "Or is that why you're calling?"

"You think I'll tell you now?" he asked, but again his laughter was back.

She groaned. "I'm glad I'm a constant source of amusement for you," she noted, "but there are times when it's not very easy."

"No, there are absolutely times when it's not very easy. There are also a lot of times when having you dump all the information on me is not very easy either. Then you turn around and expect me to get answers for you," he pointed out. "That's also not easy."

She groaned. "*Great*, so apparently we're not very easy together."

He hesitated before asking, "Did my mother say something to you?"

"Lots," she stated, her tone succinct. "I'm not sure how much of it all she meant."

Mack was silent for a bit, then added, "You do know not to take anything she says seriously, right?"

"That's where you're wrong," she declared. "Your mom

didn't say anything, and, for a fact, she was very nice, very friendly …"

"But something rattled you."

"Isn't that great?" she mocked herself. "I can face down serial killers. I can get into trouble and face down criminals after stolen rings, and yet your mom says one thing to me, and I feel as if I don't know what to do."

"And maybe you should tell me what she said," he suggested. "Communication is the only way we'll deal with this."

"*Hmm*, I have to think about it," she muttered.

"*Doreen*," he said in a deep voice.

"Yes, did you check out that phone number?"

"I did."

"And what about it?"

"And remember I have a case."

"*Great. … You* have a case. I would like to have a case, but apparently we're on opposite ends on that case too."

"No, we're not," he argued. "You've got to remember that some of these things can't happen the way you want them to happen."

"If that were the case," she retorted, "it would have happened already."

He chuckled. "You're really not that hard done by."

"I don't have to be that *hard done by* to feel hard done by," she grumbled.

He burst out laughing. "It sounds as if my mother really set you off. Maybe I'll call her and ask her."

"Don't," Doreen snapped.

There was immediate silence from Mack's end. "I presume it has something to do with our relationship?"

"No, yes, maybe. I don't know," she grumbled.

"That's clear as mud," he noted. "Don't let her push you or make you feel uncomfortable in any way. Our relationship is our relationship. Nobody else belongs in there but you and me."

She smiled, something settling in her soul. "Thank you for that," she said. "And your mom didn't say anything to upset me. In a way it was the opposite."

"Okay, that doesn't sound too ominous."

"No, not too ominous," she admitted, "but it does make me realize how other people are possibly viewing our relationship."

"A lot of people are viewing it many ways," Mack noted. "Again, it's just the two of us. Nobody else gets to belong in that circle."

She smiled. "Pretty sure that's a case of *too late.*"

"And it doesn't have to be. The minute it gets uncomfortable, you can back off."

"And I've done that several times," she admitted.

"I know. You don't need to remind me."

She burst out laughing. "I do thank you for being you. It has made this a little easier on me."

"I'm glad to hear that. I'm sorry if she upset you so much."

"And she shouldn't have. There was no need for me to be upset. It's more foolish of me not realizing that what she did say had a little more importance than what I was thinking."

"You do know that you're talking in circles, right?"

"Yeah, I'm working my way through something."

"Okay, in that case, I'll leave it with you to think about."

"Yeah, that'll be good. And when you figure out anything about this phone number, you could pass that on to me too."

"And why would I do that?" he asked in a dry voice.

"So I can phone this guy and figure out if he had anything to do with this case."

"Are you serious? You would call Bob Small?" Mack asked in astonishment.

"Why not?" she replied. "Half the problem in all this is people don't talk."

"The other half of the problem is, these guys are criminals, and, if you tip them off that we're looking at them, you give them time to prepare and to duck out."

"This guy's already figured out that we're after him," she declared. "There's really nothing we'll shock him into doing."

"So why talk to him then?"

"Because he's been evading the law for so long. He might want somebody to brag to."

"And he might decide that you know too much and that you should be taken off the planet."

"I'm pretty sure he thinks that anyway," she stated, with no apparent worry. "My concern is for Nelly."

"And why is that?"

"Because she's the one who's been keeping track of her sister, and I'm not sure that, even now, she isn't still hiding something from us."

"That would not be good," Mack snapped.

"Maybe not, but people are people," Doreen said, "and now there's been two things that she'd handed over. So I wouldn't be at all surprised if there isn't a third, something that she really knows she shouldn't have. Now I don't have any reason to say that, just that inner knowing that's making me a little edgy."

"I trust your instincts any day," Mack noted. "Maybe I'll stop by and have a talk with her."

"I'm pretty sure that'll be a guaranteed crying jag if you do."

"That's what it is then, isn't it?" he asked. "We can't have everybody making their own decisions on what to do and what not to do when it comes to the law." With that, he hung up.

Afterward Doreen did a little housecleaning to keep her mind occupied and then decided to take a walk with the animals. She held up the leashes but didn't put them on, which almost always told the animals that they were heading for the river. And, sure enough, she was heading down there, looking for a spot to sit, to relax, and to contemplate what was going on.

She didn't want to contemplate what was going on in terms of how everybody else viewed their relationship because, like Mack had said, that was up to them. They would make do or make it the way they wanted it. And, if people didn't agree, well, that was just too bad.

As she walked, she tried to put everything else out of her mind and just let herself think about what was going on in terms of this craziness with Ella. Because Doreen was pretty sure something more was to be learned from Nelly than she was saying. But it was up to Mack to go there and talk to her. As much as Doreen would like to, she didn't think it would be quite so easy.

Chapter 22

WHEN NELLY PHONED her about an hour later, she asked, "Did you tell the cops?"

"Tell them what?" Doreen asked in confusion.

"The number."

"Of course I had to tell them about the phone number, and I told you that I was doing that." There was a moment of silence on the other end.

"Oh."

"They must search that number out," she explained. "It's not something I can do because it's unlisted. I don't know if they found Ella's second phone though." At that came a garbled sound on the other end. "Unless you know something about Ella's second phone."

"Why would I know something about her phone?" Nelly asked.

"I wondered if she left it with you."

Nelly gasped. "Are you psychic?"

"No, I'm not psychic, but I do recognize when people are in trouble."

"I'm not in any trouble," she cried out.

"Are you sure? Because I'm not so sure I can agree with

you."

After another moment of hesitation, then Nelly admitted, "I do have her phone."

"And why is it you didn't tell me that before?" Doreen stared down at her phone in dismay.

"I didn't think I should ... because it seemed to be the final betrayal against my sister. Something I already felt guilty about."

"And yet not doing everything you can to try and solve Ella's murder *isn't* a betrayal?" Doreen asked.

"You don't understand. The relationship between us was very complicated."

"I get that. I really do. I understand complicated, but I also don't understand why you've been holding out information over this whole case. If she's got another phone, then why didn't you give it to the cops?"

"Because she doesn't want me to," Nelly stated.

"And why is that?"

"I don't know, but she's telling me that she doesn't want me to."

At that, Doreen stopped, winced, and repeated, "She's *telling* you?"

"Yes," Nelly snapped, "and that's another reason I didn't want to bring it up."

"So you think she's talking to you from the grave?" she asked cautiously.

There was a moment of hesitation. "Do you think I'm crazy?"

"Given your age, you can get away with all kinds of things," Doreen teased in a dry tone, "but that won't be helpful. Why would Ella *not* want you to give it to the cops?"

"Because she says that Bob will know where it came

from."

"So you think she's trying to protect you?" Doreen couldn't believe the conversation she was having, but, given everything else that she'd heard over some of these cold cases, it wasn't all that far-fetched.

"I think so, yes," Nelly said eagerly, "and honestly I gave you the number on purpose."

"So that's the number that she used all the time?"

"Yes, and I figured, if you had the number, then you wouldn't need the phone."

"But once you mentioned the second phone, that's something the cops definitely must know about. They need to know the number of calls, the length of those calls, all kinds of stuff. Will you give it to the police?"

Nelly hesitated. "You'll tell them now, won't you?" she asked, and this time there was almost an accusatory tone to her voice.

"The police need that phone," Doreen stated. "If it's something that you're asking to keep, then, when this is all over with, they might give it back to you. But you must understand. Your sister was murdered, and somebody is still out there running free because of it."

"It's him," she stated flatly. "My sister firmly believes that he'll come after me."

"And did she also say that he won't come after you if you *don't* give up the phone?" Doreen asked, trying to keep her voice calm. "Because that doesn't make any sense either."

"She hasn't gotten that far."

Doreen stared down at her phone, trying to figure out what that meant. "She hasn't gotten that far?"

"No, she hasn't told me about that yet," Nelly stated. "It's not as if I can sit here and talk to her all the time."

Doreen wanted to say something about how that's good, but, at the same time, she also knew that she had to watch it here. Doreen didn't want to alienate Nelly right now. It wouldn't go well for the investigation. "Why don't you give me the phone then?"

"That's the same as giving it to the police," she replied tartly. "It's obvious that you'll turn around and give it to your boyfriend."

At that, Doreen's eyebrows popped up. "You think I'm giving it to my boyfriend?" she asked in shock. "I'm giving it to the police when I do that. You know that, right?"

"Sure, sure," Nelly replied, "but I don't know what your relationship with the cop is like, considering I've already been through this with my sister and her boyfriend. You know these guys are not good for us."

Doreen winced at that. "I get that you probably think a lot of relationships are the same, but I can tell you that my relationship with Mack is a very different sort of relationship."

"Yeah, right. My sister made all kinds of excuses at the same time too," Nelly replied. "I didn't believe her then, and I'm not sure I believe you now either."

"I get that," Doreen noted in a mild tone. "And I can see that some of this is probably bothersome to you. However, the bottom line now is, we have a problem, and it'll either be me who you need to talk to or it'll be them."

She hesitated. "What if my sister won't talk to me anymore?"

"You mean, after the phone is handed over?"

"Yeah, I think it's my only connection to her."

"She loved you, and you loved her," Doreen shared softly. "I don't think whether you have the phone or not will make a difference. If anything, maybe she'll be a little angrier because you didn't listen to her, and she'll come back and talk to you more, so she can tell you off."

"Oh." Nelly thought about that for a moment. "That makes sense. My sister hated when I didn't do what I was told."

Doreen winced at that. "I can see that, but you can't blame me if she doesn't come back very quickly."

"No, she'll come back all right," Nelly declared, her tone positive. "You don't know what she was like."

"No, I only met her once at your birthday party. We need you to stay safe."

"I will be, but Ella doesn't want me to have anything to do with this."

"Of course not, she knows how dangerous Bob Small is. Did she tell you who killed her?" Doreen asked.

"No, she didn't, but I assumed it was Bob. And I didn't even think to ask her. Maybe I will."

"Why don't you do that now? I'll come down, and I'll pick up the phone."

"Okay. … I still don't think it's a good idea."

"Oh, I'm telling you right now, it's a good idea. If you don't do it, it'll be a bad idea."

Nelly started to cry. "They'll get mean again, won't they?"

Doreen winced because, of course, the police would get very unpleasant about it all. "I'll ask them to be as gentle as they can," she offered, "but, from their perspective, you keep hiding things from them. They could have used all this long ago, all this information right off the bat. And maybe then they would have gotten further along with this case by now."

"I gave them the number," she argued.

"You gave *me* the number, but you didn't give it to them." By the time Doreen finally managed to convince Nelly to do the right thing, Doreen hung up and headed toward Rosemoor.

She muttered, wondering if she should be phoning Mack about it. The answer was, of course, yes, she should. Mack should be there to take possession of the phone at the same time. However, given the circumstances, Doreen was afraid that Nelly would become very difficult and maybe even resort to lying and saying she didn't have the phone.

Chapter 23

P ONDERING THE IDIOSYNCRASIES of Nelly's mind, plus how Nelly viewed Doreen and Mack's relationship, it made Doreen realize that everybody had an interpretation of their relationship that she hadn't even considered. She hadn't been focused on what anybody else thought or said. Even now that's the last thing she wanted to think about. And yet it was hard not to, especially when it was being brought up over and over again.

People had seen her and Mack together many times, and it'd never occurred to Doreen that they would have all come up with opinions as to what or how their relationship worked. She was somebody who tended to stick to her own and to not gossip about other people, but, then again, considering the work she was doing now, most people would say it was a love of gossip that had gotten her into it. Yet it wasn't. It was a love of mysteries and a love of helping people. She didn't want to consider why people even looked at her doing these things, especially when they came up with the wrong reasons.

Pondering all of it and not coming up with any solution was also tough. By the time she made her way inside

Rosemoor, she bypassed Nan's suite and then stopped, realizing she really needed to leave the animals with her grandmother while Doreen was here. She stepped back to Nan's apartment and knocked. Nan opened the door, saw her, and squealed with delight. In a low voice Doreen whispered, "I need to go see Nelly. May I leave the animals with you for a moment?"

Surprised, but completely willing, Nan nodded.

Doreen handed over the leashes and Thaddeus, of course—who was always ready to come snuggle with Nan—who walked over onto Nan's shoulder. Nan took them into her apartment, while Doreen carried on down to Nelly's. As soon as she got there, she knocked on the door. When there was no answer, she knocked harder. Finally it opened, and there was Nelly glaring at her.

"I don't want to," she snapped.

Doreen looked at her for a long moment. "You might not want to," she said, "but it is something you need to do."

She shook her head, crossed her arms over her chest, and stated, "I lied."

"You lied to the police, yes. You did not lie to me."

"And that's where the problem is. I should never have mentioned it to you," Nelly admitted. "My sister will get very angry."

Doreen gave her a steady gaze. "I think she would be angrier if you didn't do what was right."

"And how do you know what's right?" she snapped. "It's not always easy to know what's right."

And the trouble was, Doreen was in full agreement. It wasn't always easy to know what's right, but still it was usually a lack of wanting to follow through on what was right and acknowledging it as the problem. Not that one didn't know what was right, but that one didn't want to do what was right. She stepped in and closed the door behind her. "You know perfectly well it's what you need to do," she stated calmly.

"No, I don't," she snapped, turning away from the door, "and you need to leave."

"I can leave," Doreen noted, her voice calm, steady, as she searched frantically in her mind for a way to turn this back around again. "Don't you want to see the man who did this to your sister caught?"

She hesitated and then shrugged. "He won't get caught. He hasn't been caught in decades."

"Says you," Doreen argued. "You don't know that."

"Yes, I do," Nelly claimed.

"Where did you last see him, by the way?"

She looked at her. "Why?"

"I wondered."

"It was downtown, getting Chinese food."

At that, Doreen stopped and stared at her. "What?"

She looked at her and nodded. "Yeah, he was picking up a to-go order of Chinese."

It's such a mundane thing that it threw Doreen. "You're saying that this Bob Small guy was picking up Chinese?"

"That's what I just told you," Nelly confirmed, looking at Doreen in an odd way. "Are you feeling okay?"

Doreen winced. "Yeah, sure, I'm feeling fine. I thought you were staying inside Rosemoor, how did you see him outside on the grounds." But of course Nelly wasn't staying put. Doreen had seen that one man recently, she'd seen many times at the Chinese food place, but he worked there. And this Bob Small guy certainly didn't need to work, or did he? "So you do leave Rosemoor often, even after your sister's murder?”

“I go out for a lot of walks. I came straight home after seeing him.”

Confused but a little bit upset, Doreen stated, “Give me the phone, let me talk to the cops, and we’ll go from there.”

She glared at her. “I don’t want to.”

“I know you don’t want to,” Doreen noted, “but the time to want something like that is well past.”

“No, it’s not,” she snapped, glaring at her.

Doreen wasn’t even sure what to do or to say at this point.

Finally Nelly sagged onto the couch under Doreen’s hard gaze. “They’ll yell at me.”

“I’ll try very hard to get them not to yell at you,” Doreen repeated. “And I think that they can be good too.”

“Sure they can be, but they don’t want to be,” she snapped.

Feeling as if Nelly were caught on an endless loop that had no happy ending, Doreen added, “The other answer is, I’ll call the cops, and they can come here and talk to you anyway.”

At that, Nelly’s eyes widened. “And I’ll say you lied.”

“Maybe, and then they will get a warrant, and they’ll search your apartment,” Doreen stated.

Nelly cried out in horror.

“What do you expect?” Doreen asked her in exasperation. “Your sister’s been murdered, and you’re holding her private phone hostage. A phone that she kept for secret calls. What else did she leave behind?” Doreen asked, looking behind the tiny woman to view her place.

“Nothing,” Nelly declared. “It was in her coat pocket, and, when she put down her jacket for the birthday party, it fell out of her pocket."

It was plausible enough that it was possible, but, after Nelly had lied about so many things, Doreen found it hard to trust her. "And did anything else fall out?"

"No," she snapped. "You think things fall out of my sister's pocket all the time?"

Doreen didn't know what to think, but anything at this point in time was quite possible. Doreen eyed Nelly. "It's important that you tell the truth. *All* the truth."

"I am telling the truth," she stated, glaring at her. "I don't like you anymore."

"That's okay," Doreen replied, with a note of humor. "I get that a lot."

Nelly frowned at her. "Why don't you care?"

"Because I'm trying to solve your sister's murder. I'm trying to take the killer off the streets, and you don't seem to care."

"I do care," she countered, "but my sister will be very angry."

"Do you really think your sister can do anything about that anger right now?"

She stared at her. "She'll be waiting for me on the other side. You do know that, right?"

Doreen let out her breath in a slow exhale because—of all the things that she might consider were driving Nelly to act like this—Nelly's fear was real. "I'm sorry your sister traumatized you so much in this life," Doreen replied. "It sounds as if you had a very dysfunctional relationship."

Nelly snorted. "We did," she confirmed, teary-eyed. "She was mean."

"And yet I think you probably gave as good as you got," Doreen pointed out. When Nelly glared at her, Doreen nodded. "The thing about relationships like that is, they don't just start in full bloom. They tend to develop over time. And you held on to that journal from your sister in order to get what you wanted, and, once you start playing games like that, well, you and I both know how that goes downhill very quickly."

Nelly reached into the couch and pulled out a phone. She handed it over without a word.

Doreen stared at it and whispered, "Thank you."

Nelly nodded. "I really did love her, you know?"

"I'm sure you did," Doreen noted softly. "And unfortunately that love often doesn't show up until some calamity like this happens, when we no longer have the ability to tell them."

"I wanted her to love me. I didn't want her to love that man. He was a bad man."

"From what you say and from what I know about Bob Small, yes," Doreen agreed. "He was a bad man. But, if you're talking to your sister now," Doreen added, trying for a note of comfort, "tell her how much you love her. Tell her that you miss her and that you're sorry. Maybe that will make you feel better, once you get a chance to explain yourself. And, of course, it has a side benefit that she won't be here to tell you off."

Nelly gave Doreen a ghost of a smile. "You could be right. You need to leave now, so I don't change my mind again."

Doreen understood that and walked quickly to the door. She looked back at Nelly and suggested, "Try to find some peace now. It's even more important."

"Maybe," she murmured. "I'm a little worried yet."

"We all are," Doreen admitted. "There's something very

poisonous in the world with this man. We need to stop him."

Nelly nodded. "Too bad we didn't do anything in time to help Ella," she whispered.

There wasn't anything Doreen could say to that because Nelly was right. By the same token, a lot of people had tried to stop Bob Small, but the people who should have helped were the ones who had withheld the information. Thus, there wasn't any saving grace in any of this.

Doreen quickly walked down the main hallway in Rosemoor and out the front door to the parking lot. Doreen ignored Nan's apartment for now, knowing that Nan would ask nothing but questions. In the parking lot, she phoned Mack.

"Now what?" he asked warily.

She hesitated and then said, "You can't get mad."

"Oh, that's a great start," he muttered. "What am I not to get mad about?"

"You'll get mad, but I need you to not get mad."

"*Doreen*," he muttered, with a snap to his tone, "what is going on?" She sighed and quickly explained. "What?" he roared.

"Yeah, I know. The good news is, I have the phone on me. The bad news is, she really, really, really wants you to not yell at her, when you come to talk to her."

"Oh, my word," he whispered in shock. "She had the phone the whole time?"

"Yes, she did, and she's also now talking about having ongoing conversations with her dead sister."

"Meaning?"

"As in, she believes she's talking to her sister now."

"And you believe her?" he asked incredulously.

"Mack, I'm not saying I believe her. I'm not saying I don't believe her. What I'm trying to explain to you is she believes it."

"Right," he said, "and, of course, that's a very different story."

"As long as she believes it," Doreen pointed out, "you must try to understand where her mind-set's at."

He let out a slow deep breath. "Where are you now?"

"I'm standing in front of Rosemoor," she said. "I was hoping you could swing by and grab this phone. Nan has the animals with her. The minute she finds out what I'm down here for, I'll be hard-pressed for explanations."

"I'm in the vehicle. I was heading back to the station," he explained. "I will swing by. Stay where you are." With that, he hung up.

She took out Ella's secret phone and went through the recent calls. With her own phone, Doreen took several snapshots of conversations and texts, and it certainly did look like it was the same man involved in all of them. And he wasn't a happy man either.

Some of the language was dark and forceful. But obviously he also had a good understanding of Ella because he didn't give any explanations, as if he expected her to know.

She knew Mack would do a full info dump on the phone, and that was definitely necessary. Yet, at the same time, if Doreen could get any bits and pieces before she got into trouble, well, that would help too. Of course, when Mack found out what she had just done, he wouldn't be happy. But some things she had to do. By the time he pulled up, she had taken multiple snapshots of the recent conversations with presumably Bob Small. Ella had only two Contacts on her secret second phone, and Doreen had taken a snap of both of them.

When he pulled up, he took one long look at her, spying the phone in her hand, and swore.

"I know," she admitted. "But, hey, on the plus side, at least I called you."

He nodded slowly. "There is that," he muttered. He stared at the phone and asked her, "Now really the question is, did you look?"

"Of course I did," she stated bluntly. "Only two numbers are in this entire thing."

He grabbed the phone and quickly flicked through it and nodded.

"And quite a few text conversations," she added. "Presumably you can do some analysis on everything here and sort it out."

He nodded again. "We should get something off this, something very useful," he said, his voice gaining in excitement. He groaned, looked back at the retirement home. "She really did that, *huh?*"

Doreen nodded. "She really did, and I did honestly say that I would try hard to get you guys to not yell at her."

He pinched the bridge of his nose and nodded. "I will take that under advisement," he muttered.

She smiled. "I know I'm a challenge," she shared, "but I just want to tell you that I really appreciate your patience." She stood on her tiptoes, kissed him gently on the cheek, and then quickly disappeared into Rosemoor, leaving him staring behind her.

Chapter 24

NAN EYED DOREEN with a knowing look. "You want to explain what happened?"

"Not really," Doreen admitted. "I can tell you some of it, but you *must not* share."

Nan's shoulders sagged, but she nodded.

"It's not easy being part of my inner world, is it?" Doreen muttered. "However, most of this has to be kept private."

Nan sighed. "Okay, fine. I won't tell anybody."

Doreen searched Nan's face—looking for that honest expression that revealed Nan would follow through—and there it was. "Nelly had her sister's spare cell phone. The one that she used for her communications with a particularly notorious affair. Nelly didn't tell the police about it, and, of course, when I finally got it from her, I had to give it to Mack, which meant I also had to explain where it came from."

At that, Nan winced. "That would not have made him happy."

"No, it sure didn't," Doreen confirmed. "However, he now has it, and I'm hoping that he will get whatever information he needs off it."

Nan nodded. "It is still kind of shocking that Nelly didn't hand it over."

At that, Doreen hesitated before answering, "She seems to think her sister would be really angry at her if she told somebody."

Nan stared at her. "Interesting," she noted cautiously. "In Rosemoor, we do have an awful lot of people who believe they talk to their loved ones after they're gone."

Doreen smiled. "Whether it's true or not is a different issue. I'll wait until you cross over to find out for sure." Still, she added, with a smile, "And please don't make that anytime soon because I'm not all that anxious for answers. However, you're the only other person who loves me enough to even try."

At that proclamation, tears came to Nan's eyes. She got up, walked over, and gave Doreen a hug. "And believe me," Nan added ferociously, "I will try. If only to let you know where I'll be when you get there."

Doreen chuckled. "And that would be lovely to find you on the other side too," she said. "I do know that Nelly is really struggling with this whole scenario, and I guess I can't really blame her if she needed or needs or even is communicating with her sister. Yet Nelly seems to think she is in trouble if she does tell the police about that phone."

"And it's possible," Nan noted. "This man, Bob Small or whoever he is, none of us really have any idea what he looks like."

At that, Doreen asked, "Do you think there's any reason why Nelly would have gone to the local Chinese food place?"

"She loves Chinese food," Nan stated. "Some days we can check out for meals, and we always go to restaurants and coffee shops. Nelly often would come with us. She does like a good day adventure."

"But has she left recently, since her sister died?"

"*Hmm*, I'm not sure, but I haven't been hitting the restaurants all that often here lately."

Doreen nodded. "And is it the same one I go to?"

Immediately Nan shook her head. "No, another one is not too far from here," she shared. "That's the one we would normally go to."

"Interesting," Doreen muttered. "I should have asked her which one she goes to."

"It's the one that I mentioned," Nan confirmed. "It's the only one she goes to. She used to know the people who owned it."

"*Hmm*. She told me that she saw this Bob Small character there once."

At that, Nan stared at her. "Oh my." Then she sat back in shock.

"Why, Nan? What's the matter?"

"Hinja told me something about thinking that she might have seen him one time, and I thought she was crazy. And she did mention a Chinese food restaurant."

"What do you mean?" Doreen sat down, staring at her grandmother. "You think Hinja saw him in town? I thought she lived down on the coast."

"Yes, but she came up to visit all the time," Nan said. "And honestly I wouldn't be at all surprised if she wasn't still looking for him each time."

"Considering what she went through, I guess it is quite possible," Doreen muttered. "But would she have seen him and not said anything to him?"

"I don't know," Nan admitted. "She did say that she was

eating an awful lot of Chinese in order to try and confirm her suspicions."

"Are we thinking this Bob Small guy has settled in Kelowna now?" Doreen asked.

Nan looked at her and shrugged. "People all around the world want to come here and settle," she replied. "Why wouldn't he? Just because he's a serial killer doesn't mean he isn't thinking in terms of his own retirement."

Doreen rubbed her cheek. "I wasn't thinking he was a resident here."

"I'm not sure he is," Nan replied. "However, it's not something we can immediately discard as not being viable in terms of a concept."

"So Hinja said she thought she saw him at our local Chinese food place?"

"Yes, and then she kept coming back at odd times, getting Chinese food. The thing was, Hinja didn't really like Chinese food. She told me that, over time, she had learned to like it, but it wasn't her favorite. She only bought it hoping to see that serial killer boyfriend of hers, more as a cover than anything."

Doreen wasn't even sure what to say about that. She let out a slow breath.

Nan reached over and patted her hand. "Let me put on the teakettle. This has obviously been a bit of an enlightening conversation."

"Enlightening, yes," Doreen agreed, "but also in many ways difficult. I go for Chinese food too, but that doesn't mean that one of the men there is a serial killer. It's not as if anybody has a picture of Bob Small that's up-to-date or even a clear shot of his face. And this particular man probably has a lot of disguises."

"He probably does," Nan confirmed. "I'm sure he doesn't expect to be seen or to be recognized here. He's gotten away clean for all these years."

And that was something that blew Doreen away too. "I get it," she murmured. "Now what we need to do is make sure that, whatever happens, this guy doesn't get away again. He'll have bolt-holes all over the place, and, if he can escape once more, he'll be gone and never come back."

Nan looked at her solemnly. "We can't let that happen," she murmured. "Not just for Hinja's sake, and her niece's, but also for Ella and for Nelly." Nan shook her head. "They may have had a crazy relationship, but they were still family, and they still loved each other."

Chapter 25

FINALLY BACK HOME again with her animals, Doreen sat curled up on her living room chair, wondering what was going on right now. She hoped that the police would treat Nelly more gently. Yet, at the same time, Doreen understood their frustration. Nelly had withheld evidence—major evidence needed in a murder investigation. Doreen was still stunned with the whole Chinese food thing. She thought about the number of times that she had enjoyed the simple dish of her favorite Chinese food meal, wondering if the customer beside her could have been this Bob Small.

Or worse, was that why Mugs had been so distraught when just the other day she and her animals had been walking around town?

What an absolute irony to think that everybody was looking all over the place for Bob Small, including her, thinking he was down on the coast or off trucking somewhere in the wild blue yonder, and yet he could have been sitting right there beside her.

She didn't even know what to think anymore. And the more she tried *not* to think about anything, the more her mind glommed on to all these useless thoughts. What she really needed was a way to contact this guy. However, if Bob Small had any idea that Ella's second phone had been found and that the cops had it now, then Nelly was in more danger than ever.

Doreen brought up her phone and quickly went through the photos she had taken of Ella's text messages.

Standing alone, one of the texts was pretty confusing. These were intended to be part of a conversation that other people already knew about. It still surprised Doreen to consider that Ella—who had seemed so savvy and so businesslike and with the political acumen that she must have had for her career—would have maintained a relationship with a serial killer, who could have sunk her entire world once anybody had found out.

Why would anybody do that? And, of course, love was the answer, but this relationship seemed more about dependency and victimization. Doreen wanted to say a Stockholm syndrome case but wasn't even sure that that was the same.

She got up, put on the teakettle, waiting for Mack. Yet she had absolutely no way to know if Mack would come. Since his birthday was Friday, and she needed something to keep her mind off everything, maybe she should try and bake him some cookies or a birthday cake. She frowned at that. How complicated would a birthday cake be?

She couldn't do anything fancy, but maybe she could try something simple, like a coffee cake. With that then being *too* simple, would something much more complex be required? In which case, she was too scared to even try any of it. She did need to know that the end result would work or at least be edible. Pondering that, she went to the internet and looked up simple coffee cake recipes.

And that sent her down the rabbit hole. Coffee cakes

versus birthday cakes, what made one more appropriate for an occasion versus the other? Coffee cakes seemed to be simple. One coffee cake recipe went in the Bundt pan into the oven. Then, if you wanted to put a topping on it, you could, whereas birthday cakes tended to be layers and iced. So it definitely wouldn't be a birthday cake, but maybe she could handle a Bundt cake.

Determined to at least get that much accomplished, she got up, confirmed that she had the pan that would work, and then found the simple recipe because *simple* still was the prime consideration for any of this. With that she put on a small pot of coffee and got to work. She was still staring down at the recipe, wondering if what she had mixed was even right, when her phone rang. Distracted, she frowned at the phone, not recognizing the number, debating whether she should answer it, thinking about her heavy-breathing caller, and then finally did. "Hello."

The voice on the other end said, "You're an interfering witch, right?"

It was such a conversational tone that she wasn't even sure what to say in response. She didn't know this person, at least she didn't think she knew this person, but he seemed to think he knew her. "I don't know who you are or what you want," Doreen replied, "but I'm busy, so go away." And, with that, she hung up and went back to the recipe.

She studied the batter in confusion. She wasn't sure she'd done anything wrong, but, in truth, it had seemed way too easy to be a complete recipe. Should she stick everything into the pan and put the pan into the oven or should she go back over the steps again? She was hoping to make this a good first attempt, so she went back over the process of what she'd done. Sure enough, it seemed that this was all there was to it. So she used the spatula to scoop the batter, which was fairly creamy, into the Bundt pan—this weird thing with a hole in the center. She didn't understand that whole concept. Why would you have a pan with a hole in it? It made no sense.

So she scooped it into the holey pan, giggling as she put that name to it, and put it in the oven for the allotted temperature and time. Pretty sure that she would completely forget about it, or she would sit here in the kitchen on the floor and watch it to confirm she didn't mess it up, she set a timer on her phone for the halfway mark and then poured herself a cup of coffee. She looked down at the animals, who were all staring at her, as if she would burn down the house. She glared at them. "That wasn't so bad."

Mugs barked at her, but he didn't seem to have anything else to say. She looked over at Thaddeus, who was wandering back and forth, not frantic but definitely not too sure about this. She glared at him. "Surely I'm not that bad a cook. I can do some things." He didn't seem to be at all that convinced, but then neither was she.

With the coffee pot on, she opened up the back door, stepped out, and sat down on the nearest chair. It was a nice day, and yet, for her, still so much was going on that it was hard to relax.

Finally she decided to phone Nan.

"What's up?" Nan asked. "By the way, the police are here talking to Nelly."

She winced at that. "Let's hope that Nelly reacts well this time."

"I don't think so. An awful lot of caterwauling is going on back there," Nan shared in a dire tone.

"*Great*, now you'll blame me for that too."

"No, not at all. Nelly should have told the truth right from the beginning."

"I think she's worried about her sister."

"Sure, she can worry all she wants, but that doesn't change the fact that sometimes you must step up and do what's right."

"Yeah, I know. So where is the Chinese food restaurant that Nelly favored?"

"The one on Gordon Street."

"Interesting," she muttered. "I don't think I know that one."

"It's good," she said cheerfully. "It's a little bit farther away than some other favorite restaurants or coffee shops, but a lot of us here really enjoy it."

"Good, maybe I'll wander down there."

"You could," Nan replied hesitantly, "but I wish we had a better photo of this killer, so you don't cross paths with him."

"I know, right? I should have something much clearer, but I don't. I've got a photograph from Nelly, but it's very old, and I got a photograph from an inmate, but it's even older. Apparently this Bob Small guy is really good at disguises."

"I did see Ella in town once with a man, who didn't know I was looking at him. I was going to tease her and to tell Nelly about it, but Ella asked me privately not to say anything to her sister."

"So?"

"So I didn't," Nan replied. "I figured that would make good blackmail material down the road."

"Nan," Doreen cried out.

"I'm teasing," Nan said. "Anyway I didn't tell Nelly anything."

"What did the man look like?"

"He was tall, slim, good-looking actually. He had a certain level of charisma, which I wasn't really expecting. However, with her being a strong public figure for a long time, I'm sure she's had a lot of male attention."

"I'm sure she did," Doreen agreed, "but that doesn't mean that this guy was the same guy I'm looking for."

"I overheard them saying they were heading to pick up Chinese food." She giggled. "I can't really accost everybody who goes and picks up Chinese food though."

"Nope, you can't."

"I wondered at the time who he was, and I asked my companion back then. Now who was I with that day?" Nan pondered. "Oh, my memory is starting to go."

"How long ago was this?" Doreen asked.

"Not all that long ago," Nan stated. "It really wasn't."

"I really could use a description," Doreen noted.

"He was driving a fancy truck. That's not much of a help," Nan admitted. "He was missing a finger. That's what got me."

"What do you mean, he was missing a finger?"

"One hand only had four fingers," Nan clarified. "He tried to hide it, but he was holding his cell phone in his right hand, so I saw it clearly. Then Ella noted me nearby. She looked at me oddly for a moment. Then later she said that she'd really appreciate it if I didn't bring up what I saw with anybody."

At that, Doreen straightened. "I wonder if Nelly could confirm that missing finger."

"I don't think Nelly can confirm anything right about now," Nan said. "She's really not happy."

"*Great*," Doreen muttered. "I'll call you later, Nan." Then she immediately phoned Mack, but he didn't answer. So on an off chance, she phoned Nelly.

When the other woman answered, she sounded exhausted.

"Are you okay?" Doreen asked her.

"I'm okay," she whispered. "I'm really tired now. It wasn't fun."

"But were they nicer?"

"Yes, they were. Not very nice, but they were nicer."

Doreen rolled her eyes at that. "There is a limit to how nice they can be."

"I know," she muttered.

"Can you tell me if this Bob Small guy is missing a finger?"

"Oh my," Nelly exclaimed. "Yes, yes, he is. I forgot about that. How did you know that?"

"Never mind how I knew. Do you know how he lost it?"

"No, I don't remember hearing anything about it," Nelly replied. "I don't remember if I was even told."

"Okay, that's good enough," Doreen said. "And Ella, when I saw her once, her hair was up. Was that normal for her?"

"Yes, she wore it up a lot," Nelly stated. "She also told me that he preferred it that way."

"Oh, now that's interesting. I wonder why."

"I don't know, but she has beautiful curls, *had* beautiful curls." Then Nelly started to sob.

"Oh, so I wonder why then he wanted her to keep it up, considering he had this thing for curly hair."

"Yes, but she told me that he liked her to keep it up just for him."

Doreen winced and nodded. "Thank you." And, with that, she got off the phone, called out to the animals, immediately loaded them up in her car, and headed down for the Chinese food place on Gordon Street. When she got there, she parked in the parking lot, and checked out her wallet. She had a whole fifteen dollars. She wasn't sure that was enough to buy anything. She frowned, contemplated it, went inside, and studied the menu. A few things she could get but not much. She ordered a simple dish to take home. Her stomach grumbled just then.

Her server smiled at her. "Sounds as if it's definitely time for you to eat."

She nodded. "It's been a crazy busy day."

He nodded. "And people tend to forget to eat when they're busy."

"How true." She smiled at him, while looking around. "I was supposed to meet somebody in the area, but I don't really know what he looks like. He was a friend of Ella's."

He remembered the name, and a sad look came across his face. "It's too bad what happened to her."

She looked over at him. "Did you know her?"

"I did. She came in here a lot," he stated. "She will be missed."

Doreen wasn't sure if Ella would be missed because of her business here or because they were friends. She hesitated trying to figure out how to progress the conversation, then said, "I'm trying to meet a friend of hers," Doreen added. "I should have asked her for a picture ahead of time. But ..."

He frowned at her. "You're meeting him here?"

"Yes, they used to come here all the time."

He nodded. "She came here a lot, but I don't know of any friend."

"Yeah, he is missing a finger on his right hand," she pointed out. "The second finger in."

"Oh, him." The employee nodded. "He's a regular customer too. That's Troy."

"Troy?"

"Yeah, Troy, I think his name is, maybe. It's something like that, but I'm not sure." He shrugged. "I only go by last names."

"I don't suppose you know his last name, do you?" she asked, with a laugh.

"Yes, Little—at least I think so."

"Good enough," Doreen said. "Have you seen him around lately?"

"He was here this morning, but I wasn't open yet. I told him to come back in a little while. He knows that we don't open too early, but I was a little bit later this morning, so I apologized to him, but today was an unusual day."

"Right, I'm sure that didn't make him happy."

He shrugged. "He wasn't upset though. I think he was inconvenienced."

She nodded, as if that made sense. She quickly ordered her dish and asked, "Did he say when he was coming back?" she asked, looking at her phone.

He shook his head. "No, but he'll be back soon though. I'll go get your order ready," he muttered, and he quickly left.

She sat here, wondering how else she would find this Troy Little, if it were an alias for Bob Small. Regardless it's not as if he needed an ID to pick up Chinese food. As she sat here pondering it, she suddenly remembered the cake in her oven.

She bolted upright, looked at her watch, and realized the

midway alarm she had set had gone off earlier, but she'd had the volume off on her phone. She winced. She must race home as soon as she was done with this. At last, the employee returned with her dish, quickly rang it up, and smiled at her.

"Thank you," she said, prepared to leave.

"If I see him, do you want to leave a message?"

She frowned. "I guess there's no point leaving a message. I'll arrange to meet him again another time." She shrugged. "I forgot I left a coffee cake in the oven," she said, with an eye roll. "So I've got to go now."

"I'll tell him you were here," he called behind her.

She winced at that but knew there was no way she would tell him to not bother because that would make him suspicious too.

Chapter 26

GROANING, DOREEN RACED back home, made it to the kitchen, and pulled out the coffee cake. She stared at it because it was this beautiful high-risen golden mass, with a little bit of a crack across the top, but it was a small crack. Following instructions, she dug for toothpicks and checked the center. It looked almost perfect, but it was still a little soft. She put it back in, reset the alarm, and sighed with joy. She turned, put down the Chinese food, and walked back to the front door, which she had left open in her panic. As she did so, she heard a voice. She turned to see somebody standing in her living room, a lazy smile on his face.

She stared at him. "Hello?" And then looked around. "Where are my animals?" she asked.

"They raced out the back, when you raced to the oven," he replied, his smile genuine. "So I let them go straight through." She didn't believe him. The animals had been in the car with her, and she'd come home with them.

Surely they wouldn't have gone without her, but then, if he had been at the house waiting for her, and even acted as if he belonged here, maybe? She wasn't sure, but then she heard Mugs at the kitchen door. She walked toward the kitchen door, and the stranger called out, "I wouldn't do that if I were you."

She hesitated, knowing exactly who this was now. "Why not?" she asked, as she reached for the door anyway. A gun magically appeared in his hand, but she'd yanked the door open, and Mugs came racing in and stared up at the man. Mugs growled in the back of his throat, but he didn't approach. He was more confused than anything.

"Yeah, I'm confused too, buddy." Doreen turned and looked at the man and the gun. "What are you doing here, and who are you?"

"It's funny you didn't ask the *Who are you* first, but you're becoming a pain in my backside."

She stiffened and glared at him. "Do you think you're the only person to have said that to me?"

"Oh no," he murmured, "pretty sure a lot people have. I've been asking around, and generally you're well thought of but *nosy*." He dragged out the last syllable. "And nosy is really not somebody I want in my world."

She nodded slowly. "Yet you had to go kill Ella?"

His eyebrows shot up, and he stared at her. "You know just know enough to be dangerous."

"Oh, I know a lot more than enough to be dangerous," she stated calmly, as she studied him, trying to figure out what the heck she was supposed to do with him. Now, at the same time, she was also worried about the cake in the oven. How stupid was that? What she needed was Mack, only she hadn't told him what she'd done. Gee, what a surprise.

Once again she was looking for Mack to bail her out of trouble. She looked down at the animals, and even Thaddeus was coming in, wandering around, staring at the new arrival.

"Thaddeus is here, Thaddeus is here."

The stranger stared down at him. "A talking parrot?" he asked.

She nodded. "Yes, this is Thaddeus."

"Hi, Thaddeus. Aren't you a character?"

Thaddeus looked up at him, tilted his head, and repeated, "Thaddeus is here."

Bob or Troy or whoever probably wondered why his language seemed to get even simpler instead of how complicated she knew Thaddeus's could be. But then, something was going on between all the animals because they were looking at this guy, as if understanding something was different about him. They'd certainly seen an awful lot of bad guys recently, but, even for her, something about this one sent chills up and down her back.

Her phone was in the kitchen, but she couldn't reach it easily. Then the alarm set on her phone went off. She turned toward the oven, grabbing her phone along the way to shut off the alarm, also to set it to Record, ignoring Bob's shout to silence her phone. He followed her around the kitchen, Mugs milling around her feet, still uncertain as to what was going on.

"Silence your phone," he repeated. She huffed, but she did as he asked. Then she returned to the oven.

"What the heck are you doing?" the gunman asked.

She glared at him. "I made my first coffee cake today." She pointed an oven mitt at him. "And not even you will ruin it."

His jaw dropped. "You see my gun, right?"

She shrugged. "Yeah, whatever." And she bent down, opened up the oven, and slowly pulled out the cake. She stared at it and then turned and beamed at him. "Look. It's the first one I ever made."

He stared at her in confusion. "How come you've never made them before?"

"Yeah, well, let's just say I didn't have much of a life before." She turned and glared at him. "And somebody like you won't take away from me what I do have." And then she turned off the oven, closed the oven door, moved the cake pan over to the rack that she had out.

He asked, "What are you doing now?"

Both exasperation and confusion filled his tone. She looked at him and admitted, "I'm trying to figure out if I should take it out of the pan right now or let it cool first."

"Let it cool," he advised.

"You think so?" she asked. "I don't want it to break apart."

"Then you let it sit and rest for a little bit, so that everything can hold together."

"But what if I wait, and then it sticks to the sides?" she asked.

He stared at her. "Did you fix the bottom, like spray oil or something on the inside of the pan?"

She nodded. "I did."

"But still," he advised, "put it upside down, wet a cloth with cool water, put it over the exposed bottom of the pan, and that will help release it."

"Do you really think that will help?" she muttered, as she stared at the pan in surprise, wondering what she should do. Then deciding that he might know more than she did, even if it was not necessarily the right information, she walked over and put a cloth under cold water and came back and gently wiped down the underneath side of the Bundt pan. A weird hissing sound made her grimace. "You better be right," she declared. "I won't be happy if you ruin this."

He snorted at that. "You are unbelievable."

"Not me, *you*. You get away with murder for decades, and then you come back into town, whether you've been living here or not," she added, "you probably have been seen. Then you start killing people again. Like what's up with that?"

He glared at her. "You don't know anything about it."

"Hinja is dead. Whether you killed her or not, I don't know. Ella is dead, and, as far as I'm concerned, probably another half-dozen other killings you're responsible for right now."

He stared at her. Then shook his head. "You don't get it."

"No, I don't get it," she admitted. "I keep hoping that you'll tell me, but chances are you won't."

"And why's that?" he asked, looking at her, even more confused.

"Lots of people like to explain what they've done when they get caught," she shared, "but I suspect you're more of the close-mouthed guy."

He shrugged. "Never really seen the benefit to spout off my mouth."

"That's what I figured. You would stay quiet, not explain anything. Now that's really frustrating."

"And I care about your frustration, why?" he asked, with a bitter laugh.

But it was that bitterness that made her turn to look at him. "Do you admit to killing all those young girls?"

He nodded slowly. "It's not as if you can get out of this alive, so, yeah. I admit to killing all those young girls years ago," he declared. "I haven't killed anybody recently."

She stared at him and laughed. "Really? What about Ella?"

He glared at her. "You don't know anything about it."

"No, I don't, but she was a lovely woman."

He nodded. "And you think I killed her." He snorted. "What about Hinja?"

"I loved her too," he admitted, "although things were never quite the same after she got so suspicious."

"That's because you killed her niece," Doreen snapped.

He glared at her. "The niece shouldn't have had curly hair."

She rubbed her temples. "*Right*, so anybody who has curly hair is to blame, is that it? What about all the women who curled their hair with a curling iron?"

He shrugged. "I've had a problem with curly hair for a long time, but I've stopped killing. I decided that I needed to cut it clean in the world, and maybe I could have a different life."

"And you expect me to believe that you've changed?" she asked in astonishment.

He glared at her. "Doesn't matter whether you believe me or not," he snapped. "I have changed."

That was not what she expected to hear. "Wow." She walked over to the kitchen chair, taking her phone with her, absentmindedly hitting the Redial button, then tossing it on the table upside down. "So, if you're planning on changing your ways, I presume a woman is involved."

He nodded. "There is a woman involved. Or at least there was."

She winced at that. "Are we talking about Ella?"

"I really loved her, you know?"

She stared at him. "If you loved her, … why is she dead?"

"Because somebody didn't like it that I loved her."

She whistled silently. "*Okay*, but you're still not making any sense."

He shrugged. "I don't have to make any sense. I must put you out of business because I won't ruin this new life that I set up for myself."

"And what about the love of your life, Ella?" she asked.

"I was lucky enough to fall in love several times in my life," he noted. "All of them lived here."

She stared at him. "What about Hinja?"

"I knew her way back when," he said. "And you're right. She didn't live here, but she was living here for a while. I did try to get back together again with her, but she wasn't too interested. And, of course, I couldn't put her mind at ease about her niece because, well, I did kill her." Again he shrugged. "But I've changed."

"And nobody will believe you," she stated in astonishment. "Particularly with the recent killing spree you've been on."

"Not now," he said.

She stared at him. "You expect me to believe that?"

"I don't care if you believe me or not," he stated bluntly. "It's fine if you don't. I'm not here to explain myself to you."

"No, but it would be nice if I understood what's going on."

He glared at her. "And that's exactly why I'm here," he declared. "You're too much of a nosy body. You must be stopped."

"It's what you do anyway, isn't it? Stopping people?" she asked. "You naturally cause trouble."

"I do not," he snapped.

She shrugged. "Sure seems like it."

"No, I don't. I've been clean for a lot of years. Why do you think there hasn't been another spate of these killings?"

She nodded. "I did wonder about that. I wondered about you being in jail. I wondered about all kinds of things."

"Now I want to be a peace-loving man."

"I see. Yet now we have the fact that Hinja is dead."

"I didn't kill her. I did visit her grave and spent some time there, tried to talk to her, trying to let her know that I'm sorry. I'm sure she's over there now, talking to her niece," he said, with a dismissive wave of his hand. "They'll probably all be waiting for me when I go," he muttered.

"That theory tends to make me not sleep at night."

She stared at him. "Did you expect them to think differently?"

He snorted. "I didn't think about it, honestly."

Doreen wasn't sure what to do with this revelation. "And now that you know they could be over there, waiting for you, is that what made you turn over a new leaf?"

He shrugged. "I don't know if anybody made me do that. I certainly tried to change it all because of somebody I cared about."

"So I've heard you say," she noted, "and that's a little disconcerting too."

"It shouldn't be. Besides, I didn't kill Ella," he stated with great difficulty. "Although I'm pretty sure everybody will blame me for it."

"Yeah, they sure are," she confirmed. "I do want to know what happened."

He sighed. "I fell in love. After all these years I guess I was caught up in more hatred than love, and then, when I fell in love," he admitted, "everything changed for me. I've been in love with Ella for years, but, instead of it fading away, it deepened over time."

"And so why are you still here now?" she asked.

"I can't have you ruining what I have."

"And what do you have?"

"I told you," he said in exasperation. "I finally have peace, and I don't want you ruining it."

"Right, got it." She shook her head. "What about all the people you've killed?"

"I didn't kill anybody recently," he repeated. She stared at him. He smiled and shrugged. "You really don't get it, do you?"

"No, I sure don't," she replied.

He added, "I'm not the one who's killing now."

She stared at him in horror. "You mean, somebody else is killing people right now?" she cried out and shook her head. "Please, no."

He nodded slowly, and then he started to laugh. "Everybody was so locked on me as the prime suspect that nobody even looked for anybody else," he explained. "And that's funny. I didn't really care until it became a problem. And now it's a problem." All the laughter fell away from his face.

"I am still not sure I get it."

"Of course not," he snapped, practically spitting in her face, "because you're seeing what you're expecting to see."

She sat here, staring at him, and then gasped. "Good God. It's her, isn't it?"

"It's her," he said in delight, his eyebrows waggling. "I see you're slowly catching on. Although you're not exactly the brightest."

"I wasn't looking for it," she admitted numbly.

"You should have been," he scolded. "It's a typical

sleight of hand.

"Oh my God," she murmured, as she stared at him, and it slowly worked through her brain. "And nobody knows, do they?"

"Not unless you figured it out," he noted, "and it's taken you a while to get there. Therefore, I don't think anybody else knows either."

She shook her head, still in shock. She rubbed her head. "Nelly killed Ella, didn't she?"

He nodded slowly. "And why is that?" he asked, as if talking to a favorite student.

She studied him, hating that this other woman had pulled the wool over her eyes. And then she got it. "Because you loved Ella?"

He nodded slowly. "It was always Ella," he admitted. "Ella was the lifeline in my world. Sure I dated Nelly first, but, once I saw Ella, well, that was it. Only Nelly didn't accept the switch well." He shrugged. "What can I say? Ella was like a soul mate, although I must admit, in many ways, Nelly was more like me. It did take me a long time to see it. I stayed with Ella, until I needed to move on, and then I came back. She had other lovers. Some I could accept, a couple I couldn't. Finally, as age crept in, I realized I needed to let this hobby/fixation/need of mine go, especially if I wanted a future with Ella. She'd made it clear she wouldn't stay with me while I was occupied with my hobby. Not that she ever knew the details, but I think she suspected. That time won't come now. Nelly was a constant thorn in my side. For Ella too."

"Nelly knew about you and your *hobby*, didn't she?"

"Yes, and spent all these years alternatingly terrifying Ella that she'd be next, then making her jealous that she would snag me away again from her sister."

"And you think Nelly shot her sister?"

"Yes, she did," he said, "and believe me. As far as I'm concerned, she will be my last victim."

She stared at him in shock. "Why would you kill her?"

"Because she's the one who killed the love of my life," he snapped, glaring at her. "How hard is that to understand?"

"It's not hard at all," she agreed. "Yet, if you think about it, you killed however many women in your lifetime, and they all had somebody who loved them."

"Sure," he acknowledged, "but they weren't in *my* world, so that doesn't matter."

She was still trying to get her mind wrapped around that mentality and around the concept that Nelly had killed her own sister. Then she asked, "Did you have anything to do with Hinja's death?"

"I didn't. I think Nelly did though. They'd been friends for a while. Ella was telling me how Nelly and Hinja had a falling out, but then Nelly sent Hinja a collection of loose teas as an apology to clear the air, since they were both getting older, and Nelly didn't want that on her conscience. I wouldn't be at all surprised if she poisoned one of the teas. It's not as if anyone did an autopsy or suspected foul play. That she died in a different location gave Nelly a clear alibi, even if anyone had been suspicious about her death."

He shrugged. "I loved Hinja too, many years ago, but it was nothing like what I had with Ella," he muttered. "And I know people wouldn't have understood. Ella didn't even understand. She couldn't figure out why she hadn't turned me in many times, and it tormented her, but she never did. She also knew about my relationship with Nelly, and that bothered her too. It's why she kept her in Rosemoor, where she could keep an eye on her. The two of them blackmailed each other constantly. Talk about dysfunctional families." He tried a crude sense of humor.

"So Ella was blackmailing Nelly?" Doreen asked.

"Yes, and then Nelly was blackmailing Ella, and then, when Nelly found Ella had left her phone behind at Nelly's place, things blew up. We were going to Vancouver for the weekend, but she had left the phone behind. Only I didn't know that. And when she landed, we spent the weekend together. When she came back home, I phoned her, but I didn't get anybody, not until Nelly answered the phone, and she realized what was going on."

"And then she met her sister at the airport and shot her dead," Doreen added. "The question is, how did she find a gun?"

He hesitated at first. "It was a gun that I had given Ella for her own protection. And believe me. That makes me feel even more terrible."

"So let me get this straight. You had a relationship with Nelly. You had a relationship with Hinja. You had a relationship with Ella, and yet you killed all these other women."

"I can't count the one date with Nelly as a relationship," he protested. "That was all in her mind."

"Do you really think that makes much difference, considering how many people you did kill?"

He stared at her. "I thought maybe it would."

"I'm not so sure that it does," she disagreed gently. "The police would very much like to close all the missing person cases and get a lot of details from you, but the fact that all these women were involved with you while you were killing other women ..."

"Hinja was getting suspicious, once I took her niece." Bob frowned. "I shouldn't have done that. That one's always bothered me. I've never taken somebody close to any of the women I dated."

She stared at him, as he sounded so contrite, so calm. "I find this so hard to believe," she shared. "You have had a chance at a good life and freedom, so why are you here now in Kelowna?"

"I was here because Ella and I were spending a lot of time together, but we had to be so quiet about it. That's why I went to Vancouver to try and find a place for us to live. Ella was trying to make peace with her sister, so Ella could come join me, and you know what happened after that."

"And was Nelly just jealous?" she asked. "Did she want you for herself?" Although Doreen found that very hard to believe.

"I don't think so. I think it was more about control and sabotaging Ella's happiness. And mine. There's nothing I can do to change the fact that Ella's dead, but I don't intend to spend the rest of my life in jail, and neither do I intend to see that woman who killed Ella go scot-free."

"And you're saying she may have also killed Hinja because she realized she was also your girlfriend?"

"That would be my take on it, yes," he suggested. "So you really should be putting your energies into proving what she did, not what I did."

"Honestly I should be putting my energy into both of you," she declared, staring at him. "How do you think that any of these murders are okay? Or why do you think Nelly should pay and you shouldn't? I don't understand."

He shrugged, gave her a small smile. "It was all okay, until I fell in love. Ella knew who I was, inside and out, but she still fell in love with me, and finally that's what changed me."

"Yet you were with her for years and never changed. Why now?" she asked him. Doreen had had a bad marriage, and a lot of people looked at her in disgust for what she'd tolerated for too long, even though she had eventually walked away from Mathew. Still, to think that these two sisters, who had been so closely connected to each other and to Bob, their relationship wasn't what Doreen's relationship with Mathew had been. "You won't get anything out of Nelly anymore. At least I don't think so."

He looked down at his watch, shrugged, and noted, "It should be over by now anyway."

She stared at him in shock. "Did you kill her?"

"No, I didn't have to. We had a long talk, and it was decided that she would do something about it herself."

"How did you have a long talk?"

"On the phone," he replied. "I had smuggled in the poison earlier. So, if she decided to take it, then there's only one small loose thread. *You.*"

"Your word against hers," Doreen noted instantly.

"Exactly," he said, with a smile. "I have written out everything I've done in my life, and I was planning on taking care of business, after taking care of you." He looked around her small kitchen. "But, as I think about it, maybe it'll be better if I didn't." He got an odd look in his eyes.

She frowned at him and said, "Yeah, you're right. That would be a lot better if you didn't."

He gave her a dry look. "This way you can tell the truth."

"I can, especially if you give me a copy of what you have written down." Still she wondered at the sudden turn of events, not sure if it was safe to trust him or not. "What it is you're planning on doing?"

"My life won't be fun anymore, not without Ella. At first I was thinking I would go off and try and be happy again, without her, but ..." He turned to Doreen and shrugged. "I don't think I can be happy without her."

"Please don't kill yourself," she implored.

He frowned at her and asked, "How did you know I was thinking of that?"

"The way you're talking," she said, "but there's no need for that."

He gave her a look. "After everything I've done, you think the prisons will be nice?"

"But you will be alive."

"I'll be in solitary confinement for the rest of my life. That's not what I want either."

She was trying to think fast, but it was so hard. Everything was shifting around her, like a bubble about to burst. "Do you want a piece of cake?" she asked immediately.

He snorted, looked over at the cake, and started to laugh. "No. But I have a gift for you. I've just decided," and he pulled out of his back pocket a small black notebook, one that she'd always jokingly thought of being as a man's little black book of a lot of women's telephone numbers. He handed it over to her gingerly. "You'll want this."

"Will I?" she asked hesitantly, as she reached for it.

He gave her a dry look. "Even if you don't, the cops will. You won't have any sympathy for me or for the women in my life. I'm not sure how I got to this point, but I don't have very many years left. I was hoping to spend it with Ella. But, with that taken away from me, I'm not sure what else I'll do."

She stared at him and shook her head. "Please don't do anything stupid."

He gave her a look, pushed open the kitchen door, the animals milling around again, Mugs starting to bark. Bob looked down at them and said to her, "Keep them back. Otherwise I will shoot them."

She immediately called for her animals. And when she looked back up again, she saw no sign of him. She raced out onto the deck, but he was gone. Even as she ran down to the river, she heard somebody yelling at her. She turned and there was Mack, racing toward her, an absolute look of terror on his face.

As he came flying toward her, cops fanned out behind him. Mugs ran to greet him and tripped him up, sending Mack flying to the ground. Swearing profusely, he got to his feet, looked down at Mugs, who was even now happily rolling on the ground where Mack had been. She ran to Mack, threw her arms around him, and said, "He was here. Bob Small was here." She waved in the direction of the river. "He went that way."

The men immediately scattered and headed out. She looked back at Mack and muttered, "They won't find him."

"Why not?" he asked. "And why did he leave you alive?"

"You wouldn't believe it. You are *so* not going to believe it."

He sagged in place, his arms tightening around her. "Try me."

"You need to go to Nelly," she added, "because Nelly killed Ella."

He stared at her in shock.

She nodded. "According to Bob Small, he left Nelly some poison to take care of business herself."

"Oh, good God, I don't even want to leave you here alone." He walked back into the kitchen, stopped at the coffee cake, then turned toward her.

She beamed. "First time ever," she declared, "and all by myself too."

He chuckled. "I'll be back." With that, he was gone.

She stepped out onto her deck, listening as the cops raced around the area, searching. Mugs, Thaddeus, and Goliath all sat beside her on the deck, as she watched. She looked down at them and said, "At least this time nobody got hurt."

Almost immediately she heard a gunshot.

She winced when she saw Arnold coming toward her, his face grim. And she knew. "I guess you found him, *huh?*"

He nodded. "He pointed the gun at his neck and pulled the trigger, when he saw us getting close. Damn, this is not how our day was supposed to go," he said, staring at her accusingly.

She winced. "I'm sorry. But don't you look at me with those accusatory eyes. The only consolation is that the dead guy was Bob Small."

Arnold stopped in his tracks and asked, "The serial killer?"

She nodded slowly. "Yeah, *that* serial killer."

"Good God, and you're okay?"

"I'm okay," she murmured.

He glared at her. "What? Why? How?"

She raised both hands. "Is it too much to think that somebody might not have wanted to kill me?"

He looked at her and nodded immediately. "Yes, it is too much," he declared. "Everybody wants to kill you." And, with that, he shook his head. "I've got to meet the coroner and another team. We have a lot of forensics work to do." As if it were her fault, he glared at her again, before he raced around the corner of the house.

Her phone rang ten minutes later, and she knew. "What happened?" she asked Mack. "Is Nelly already gone?"

"She is, indeed," he confirmed, his voice heavy. "I'm sorry."

"Yeah, me too. You should know that she likely killed Hinja with poisoned tea, and she killed Ella with the gun Bob Small gave Ella for protection, and, yeah, I need to give another statement."

"Sometimes I think we need to bug your entire house," he muttered.

"I had my phone recording while trying to dial you, so I'm not sure how that worked."

"Yeah, I think it did work," he noted. "It's still recording, but I don't know what will happen to the rest of the message."

"That's up to you to figure out. By the way, the cake is for your birthday."

"Are you telling me that I can't get a piece now?" he asked in outrage.

"You're not here," she noted, "so it's really not an issue. By the way, I think Bob Small killed himself," and, with that, she ended the call. Still laughing and mostly out of relief, she got up and put on coffee. By the time it was done dripping, she knew Mack would be here.

Although maybe not when he had to deal with Nelly now.

Doreen sat here in silence for a long moment, wondering at the craziness of sister rivalry to that extent.

And when Nan called, she cried out, "My God, Doreen,

what happened? The place is swarming with police."

"Nelly is dead," she said. Nan started to cry on the phone. Doreen gave her a moment, then added, "I hate to say it, but Nelly likely killed Hinja and Ella."

"What?" Nan cried out. "That can't be."

"I wasn't thinking that Hinja's death was even suspicious, but according to Bob Small ..."

"Oh goodness, ... did you talk to Bob Small? Now you must tell me everything."

"I would say, come up for tea, but you can't because the river is blocked off as forensic teams are coming here." Doreen stood at the creek, staring down toward Nan's place. "And the cops will be all over my place soon too. So sit tight."

"I expect a full report later," Nan announced.

"Will do. Have to give a statement to the cops first though, so not until tomorrow." With that, she disconnected.

Doreen slowly moved toward her house. As she stepped inside, Mack was pouring coffee.

He looked at her and said, "Boy, do we have a lot to talk about."

She winced and nodded. Then she saw the huge piece of the coffee cake in his hand. "You can't have that," she cried out. "It's your birthday cake. And it's not your birthday yet."

"Good, early birthday cake then," he said, giving her a fat grin. He leaned over, kissed her gently, and added, "So happy birthday to me." And, with that, he took a big bite out of the piece in his hand.

Epilogue

Early October ...

DOREEN HAD SPENT days giving statements, while the police tried to get things straightened away, lining up flights where Ella had met Bob Small in Vancouver, tracking down hotels where he'd stayed, confirming Bob's story, sorting out where he was staying in town, and finding the apartment that he'd rented under his alias of Troy Little. Days of going through his little black book with names and dates of all his victims. And then Doreen needed some days of recuperation.

When Mack stopped in the following Friday, he sat down on the patio beside her. "The captain wants to know if you're done creating havoc yet."

She winced. "He knows I don't do it on purpose, right?"

"He does know that." Mack smiled. "We're getting quite a bit of notoriety for having closed all these cases. However, the backlog and the number of jurisdictions and all the provinces involved now is insane," he noted. "We have a lot of cases being examined along both sides of the border. Washington and Oregon mostly."

"Oh, ouch," Doreen replied. "Then we get into all that

lovely cross-border niceties too, *huh*?"

"The provincial government's forming a task force to go through every one of the Bob Small murders to ensure that everybody he took down gets justice and that every family gets answers to what happened," he murmured. "So, although it won't be an easy job, it will be a thorough one." Mack shook his head, adding, "The fact that Bob Small had a notebook and left you that piece of evidence? That's what blows everybody away. I still don't understand why he didn't kill you."

"I don't either," she admitted calmly. "He intended to. He had a gun with him, pointing it at me. I think that's what he was here for, what he was planning on doing, but then ... I don't know. Something about making your birthday cake maybe ..."

Mack stared at her in surprise.

She shrugged. "I know. It makes no sense."

"No, it doesn't, but then it can be something as simple as ice cream melting in the vehicle that stops a depressed woman from jumping off a bridge and committing suicide. The little things in life can throw a switch and make you do something, right or wrong."

Doreen nodded. "Something about that coffee cake. I cannot remember it all. I told him it was the first one I had ever made and that I was really proud of it, and he's the one who told me how to get it out of the cake pan."

He stared at her, slowly rubbing his face. "Good God," he murmured.

She patted his hand. "Now that you already ate your birthday cake ..."

He burst out laughing. "I also didn't get my birthday this year at all, thanks to you," he noted. "Then you tell me that the cake you made for me, first time ever, a serial killer helped you make it …"

"Helped me get it out of the pan," she corrected. "So it wouldn't break or stick to the pan."

"Okay, so with all that craziness, we pushed off my belated celebration until tonight—in case you didn't realize it."

She frowned. "But I made you a cake already."

"You mean, you didn't make me another one?" he asked in mock horror. Then he grinned. "I really enjoyed it. You did a great job on it."

"That was my first coffee cake," she muttered, "and it might very well be the last. So don't hold out hope for more."

"I don't know about that." He laughed. "Maybe it was a fluke, and you should try again."

"*Hmm.* You would say that, just to goad me into baking you another cake." Then she smiled. "Besides I have learned that there's absolutely nothing quite like the joy of seeing other people eat the food you make."

"Exactly," Mack agreed. "That's how I feel when I cook for you."

"Too bad you stopped doing that too," she replied mournfully.

He burst out laughing. "It goes along with that whole, you know, *too much work* thing."

"I'm sorry about that," she said, "but hopefully nothing else will go wrong, with your belated birthday dinner, so it can go off without a hitch."

"Yeah, Nick flew in last night. We had dinner together as a family, and now he's coming over today."

"Oh, *great*," she said, with an eye roll. "He won't be terribly happy with me."

"Why? Have you been avoiding him again?" he asked.

"No, I haven't, but my ex keeps trying to get a hold of me."

"And you haven't been answering, right?"

"No, other than that one time, when I thought it was Nan's number, I haven't been answering," she confirmed, with a big fat smile. "And it's making Mathew angrier and angrier."

"And that," Mack noted, a dark cloud over his face, "isn't a good thing."

"No, I understand," she said, a note of worry in her tone. "It is something that I want to talk to Nick about."

Mack nodded. "Nick told me something about he had news, so with any luck ..."

"With any luck, my ex signed the papers, and I'm free and clear."

"That's the dream," Mack stated, with a smile.

"So any other cases?" she asked, looking over at him.

He glared at her. "No—no cases," he snapped, "no cold cases, nothing. That Bob Small case tangentially involved in Ella's death was the big one. And we'll be dealing with the headaches surrounding it for months, if not years."

"It was a big one," she agreed, "and I'm sorry that it turned out to be as rotten as it was."

"Believe me. Everybody is pretty shocked about Ella's and Nelly's personal involvement with Bob Small, not to mention that Nelly killed Ella," he shared. "And it'll take quite a while to still get to the bottom of it all."

WANTING TO GET out before his belated birthday dinner

later today, Doreen and Mack drove down to City Park. As she wandered toward the beautiful pergola encased in flowers, she smiled in delight as she pointed them out. "The wisteria blooms are so gorgeous."

He looked up at them and smiled. "I don't think I've ever noticed them before."

She laughed, walking under the massive flower-covered square-shaped structure. "That's because you're always worried about cases." She shook a finger at him. "You've got to have a life outside of crime, you know?"

He rolled his eyes at her. "You're the one telling me that?"

She gave him a fat grin. "Of course I am. Let's sit down over here on the hill." And tucked up on the corner of the wisteria, they sat down on the side and sipped the coffee they had picked up a few minutes earlier while driving through downtown.

"It's a really nice area," she noted, with a sigh of contentment.

He nodded, looked over at her. "Are you worried about my brother tonight?"

"No." She gave an airy wave of her hand. "As long as this divorce is progressing, we're all good."

He nodded. She heard something behind her. As she turned to look, Mack asked, "Is something wrong?"

She shrugged. "No, not necessarily, just hearing people talking."

"It would make sense, if people *are* talking," he said in a dry tone. "Look where we are. It's a city park. We're up on a hill where the wisteria are, and you're overlooking one of the most beautiful sections of town," he noted. "People are everywhere."

She chuckled. "I know."

"Besides, … you're supposed to be relaxing and not getting into trouble anymore."

She batted her eyelashes at him. "I thought I did really well last time," she pointed out. "We didn't get into trouble. I didn't get attacked, and nobody got hurt."

He gave her a look.

"Okay, so Nelly died by her own hand, and this guy killed himself, but honestly it's …" She hesitated and then backtracked. "It sounds terrible, but it's not a bad outcome."

"No, it's not a bad outcome," he agreed. "Obviously we had a lot of questions, and it would have been really nice if we had gotten all those answers."

She nodded. "Somehow I don't think you would have got him to talk though."

"No, I'm not sure we would have either. He's not the kind to have handed out answers without reason." But then he looked at her and frowned. "Except in your case, where apparently he was quite happy to talk to you."

She shrugged. "I don't know what it was, but he did give me enough for us to sort out a bunch of his cases," she acknowledged.

He nodded. "And we're still puzzled over that too."

She shrugged. "I don't know either. I guess I just said the right things."

"Yeah, that's the problem. It's as if you have a silver tongue, and people spill their guts to you."

In the background behind her, she thought she heard something about *death* or *dead*. She tilted her head to the side, listening intently, even as she sipped her coffee. When she didn't hear anymore, she relaxed. He looked over at her, squeezed her hand, and she smiled. "Sorry, I keep hearing things."

"Hearing things or imagining things?"

"Either. Both. At least I get it right most of the time."

"*Yeah*," he said, "unfortunately too often. Our workload is showing it. It's almost as if you have your own private police force now."

She burst out laughing. "Now, if that were the case, we could solve a whole pile more."

"I don't want to solve a whole pile more," he argued, groaning. "We need to catch up on what we're doing now."

"Okay," she said. "I'll give you a little bit more time." When he glared at her, she burst out laughing again. "I'm teasing. Don't take it personally."

"Anything to do with you is something that we must take personally," he admitted. "I've never met anybody who can get into the trouble you get into."

In the background she heard more whispers. She turned her head slightly so she could hear more, and then she heard it.

"I don't care. She's dead. We must do something."

She turned to Mack, placed her fingers against her lips, got up, and crept toward where she heard the voices.

"She's dead I said. I don't know what to do."

She caught sight of a tall, slim man talking on his phone.

"Don't you understand? When I said dead, I mean dead. As in, we have a body we need to dispose of." And then he froze, turned ever-so-slightly, caught a glimpse of Doreen, and ran in the opposite direction.

Mack was at her side in a heartbeat. "What was that?" he asked, frowning at her. "I thought I heard something about *dead* and *a body to dispose of.*"

"Exactly." She repeated what she'd heard. "But, of

course, we didn't get a good look at him, didn't get a chance to talk to him, and we have no idea who's dead."

He stared at her, looked all around at the park. "He's long gone now. You also don't know that they were talking about a human body," he pointed out.

"That's true," she admitted. "He did look a little bit familiar though."

He groaned, closed his eyes, and added, "That won't be good."

With the heavy scent of the wisteria coming down on her, she looked up and chuckled.

He glared at her. "Now what's so funny?"

"*Whispers*," she began. "*Whispers in the Wisteria*." She threw her arms around his neck and gave him a great big hug. "The next mystery for me to solve."

"There is no mystery," he snapped, even as his arms wrapped around her securely. "We don't have a body. We don't have anything."

She gave him a big fat smile and added, "Not yet. But we will soon."

This concludes Book 22 of Lovely Lethal Gardens: Victim in the Violets.
Read about Whispers in the Wisteria: Lovely Lethal Gardens, Book 23

Lovely Lethal Gardens: Whispers in the Wisteria (Book #23)

Riches to rags. ... Some things stay buried. ... Some things don't, ... and it's chaos once again!

Spending time with Mack is always fun, but, when Doreen overhears a conversation that sounds like a murder confession, he disagrees, ... until a body shows up. Then he's suddenly a whole lot more interested. The deceased young man had planned to attend the local college and had hoped to rekindle a relationship with an ex-girlfriend.

Corporal Mack Moreau knows he can keep Doreen out of this current case, but, when the young man's grandmother calls and says it could be related to the unexplained disappearance of the young man's parents, ... then all bets are off. Doreen and her entourage are smack in the middle again.

When the case suddenly ties to her neighbor, Richard, it comes home in a big way.

Find Book 23 here!

To find out more visit Dale Mayer's website.

https://geni.us/DMSWhispers

Get Your Free Book Now!

Have you met Charmin Marvin?

If you're ready for a new world to explore, and love ill-mannered cats, I have a series that might be your next binge read. It's called Broken Protocols, and it's a series that takes you through time-travel, mysteries, romance... and a talking cat named Charmin Marvin.

Go here and tell me where to send it!
https://dl.bookfunnel.com/s3ds5a0w8n

Author's Note

Thank you for reading Victim in the Violets: Lovely Lethal Gardens, Book 22! If you enjoyed the book, please take a moment and leave a short review.

Dear reader,

I love to hear from readers, and you can contact me at my website: www.dalemayer.com or at my Facebook author page. To be informed of new releases and special offers, sign up for my newsletter or follow me on BookBub. And if you are interested in joining Dale Mayer's Reader Group, here is the Facebook sign up page.
http://geni.us/DaleMayerFBGroup

Cheers,
Dale Mayer

About the Author

Dale Mayer is a *USA Today* best-selling author, best known for her SEALs military romances, her Psychic Visions series, and her Lovely Lethal Garden cozy series. Her contemporary romances are raw and full of passion and emotion (Broken But ... Mending, Hathaway House series). Her thrillers will keep you guessing (Kate Morgan, By Death series), and her romantic comedies will keep you giggling (*It's a Dog's Life*, a stand-alone novella; and the Broken Protocols series, starring Charming Marvin, the cat).

Dale honors the stories that come to her—and some of them are crazy, break all the rules and cross multiple genres!

To go with her fiction, she also writes nonfiction in many different fields, with books available on résumé writing, companion gardening, and the US mortgage system. All her books are available in print and ebook format.

Connect with Dale Mayer Online

Dale's Website – www.dalemayer.com
Twitter – @DaleMayer
Facebook Page – geni.us/DaleMayerFBFanPage
Facebook Group – geni.us/DaleMayerFBGroup
BookBub – geni.us/DaleMayerBookbub
Instagram – geni.us/DaleMayerInstagram
Goodreads – geni.us/DaleMayerGoodreads
Newsletter – geni.us/DaleNews

Also by Dale Mayer

Published Adult Books:

Shadow Recon
Magnus, Book 1
Rogan, Book 2
Egan, Book 3
Barret, Book 4
Whalen, Book 5
Nikolai, Book 6

Bullard's Battle
Ryland's Reach, Book 1
Cain's Cross, Book 2
Eton's Escape, Book 3
Garret's Gambit, Book 4
Kano's Keep, Book 5
Fallon's Flaw, Book 6
Quinn's Quest, Book 7
Bullard's Beauty, Book 8
Bullard's Best, Book 9
Bullard's Battle, Books 1–2
Bullard's Battle, Books 3–4
Bullard's Battle, Books 5–6
Bullard's Battle, Books 7–8

Terkel's Team

Damon's Deal, Book 1
Wade's War, Book 2
Gage's Goal, Book 3
Calum's Contact, Book 4
Rick's Road, Book 5
Scott's Summit, Book 6
Brody's Beast, Book 7
Terkel's Twist, Book 8
Terkel's Triumph, Book 9

Terk's Guardians

Radar, Book 1
Legend, Book 2

Kate Morgan

Simon Says... Hide, Book 1
Simon Says... Jump, Book 2
Simon Says... Ride, Book 3
Simon Says... Scream, Book 4
Simon Says... Run, Book 5
Simon Says... Walk, Book 6
Simon Says... Forgive, Book 7

Hathaway House

Aaron, Book 1
Brock, Book 2
Cole, Book 3
Denton, Book 4
Elliot, Book 5
Finn, Book 6
Gregory, Book 7

Heath, Book 8
Iain, Book 9
Jaden, Book 10
Keith, Book 11
Lance, Book 12
Melissa, Book 13
Nash, Book 14
Owen, Book 15
Percy, Book 16
Quinton, Book 17
Ryatt, Book 18
Spencer, Book 19
Timothy, Book 20
Urban, Book 21
Hathaway House, Books 1–3
Hathaway House, Books 4–6
Hathaway House, Books 7–9

The K9 Files
Ethan, Book 1
Pierce, Book 2
Zane, Book 3
Blaze, Book 4
Lucas, Book 5
Parker, Book 6
Carter, Book 7
Weston, Book 8
Greyson, Book 9
Rowan, Book 10
Caleb, Book 11
Kurt, Book 12
Tucker, Book 13

Lovely Lethal Gardens

Poison in the Pansies, Book 16
Quarry in the Quince, Book 17
Revenge in the Roses, Book 18
Silenced in the Sunflowers, Book 19
Toes up in the Tulips, Book 20
Uzi in the Urn, Book 21
Victim in the Violets, Book 22
Whispers in the Wisteria, Book 23
Lovely Lethal Gardens, Books 1–2
Lovely Lethal Gardens, Books 3–4
Lovely Lethal Gardens, Books 5–6
Lovely Lethal Gardens, Books 7–8
Lovely Lethal Gardens, Books 9–10

Psychic Visions Series
Tuesday's Child
Hide 'n Go Seek
Maddy's Floor
Garden of Sorrow
Knock Knock...
Rare Find
Eyes to the Soul
Now You See Her
Shattered
Into the Abyss
Seeds of Malice
Eye of the Falcon
Itsy-Bitsy Spider
Unmasked
Deep Beneath
From the Ashes
Stroke of Death

Ice Maiden
Snap, Crackle…
What If…
Talking Bones
String of Tears
Inked Forever
Insanity
Psychic Visions Books 1–3
Psychic Visions Books 4–6
Psychic Visions Books 7–9

By Death Series
Touched by Death
Haunted by Death
Chilled by Death
By Death Books 1–3

Broken Protocols – Romantic Comedy Series
Cat's Meow
Cat's Pajamas
Cat's Cradle
Cat's Claus
Broken Protocols 1-4

Broken and… Mending
Skin
Scars
Scales (of Justice)
Broken but… Mending 1-3

Glory
Genesis
Tori

Celeste
Glory Trilogy

Biker Blues

SEALs of Honor

Axel: SEALs of Honor, Book 25
Baylor: SEALs of Honor, Book 26
Hudson: SEALs of Honor, Book 27
Lachlan: SEALs of Honor, Book 28
Paxton: SEALs of Honor, Book 29
Bronson: SEALs of Honor, Book 30
Hale: SEALs of Honor, Book 31
SEALs of Honor, Books 1–3
SEALs of Honor, Books 4–6
SEALs of Honor, Books 7–10
SEALs of Honor, Books 11–13
SEALs of Honor, Books 14–16
SEALs of Honor, Books 17–19
SEALs of Honor, Books 20–22
SEALs of Honor, Books 23–25

Heroes for Hire

Levi's Legend: Heroes for Hire, Book 1
Stone's Surrender: Heroes for Hire, Book 2
Merk's Mistake: Heroes for Hire, Book 3
Rhodes's Reward: Heroes for Hire, Book 4
Flynn's Firecracker: Heroes for Hire, Book 5
Logan's Light: Heroes for Hire, Book 6
Harrison's Heart: Heroes for Hire, Book 7
Saul's Sweetheart: Heroes for Hire, Book 8
Dakota's Delight: Heroes for Hire, Book 9
Tyson's Treasure: Heroes for Hire, Book 10
Jace's Jewel: Heroes for Hire, Book 11
Rory's Rose: Heroes for Hire, Book 12
Brandon's Bliss: Heroes for Hire, Book 13
Liam's Lily: Heroes for Hire, Book 14
North's Nikki: Heroes for Hire, Book 15

SEALs of Steel

SEALs of Steel, Books 1–4
SEALs of Steel, Books 5–8
SEALs of Steel, Books 1–8

The Mavericks

Kerrick, Book 1
Griffin, Book 2
Jax, Book 3
Beau, Book 4
Asher, Book 5
Ryker, Book 6
Miles, Book 7
Nico, Book 8
Keane, Book 9
Lennox, Book 10
Gavin, Book 11
Shane, Book 12
Diesel, Book 13
Jerricho, Book 14
Killian, Book 15
Hatch, Book 16
Corbin, Book 17
Aiden, Book 18
The Mavericks, Books 1–2
The Mavericks, Books 3–4
The Mavericks, Books 5–6
The Mavericks, Books 7–8
The Mavericks, Books 9–10
The Mavericks, Books 11–12

Standalone Novellas

It's a Dog's Life

Riana's Revenge
Second Chances

Published Young Adult Books:

Family Blood Ties Series
Vampire in Denial
Vampire in Distress
Vampire in Design
Vampire in Deceit
Vampire in Defiance
Vampire in Conflict
Vampire in Chaos
Vampire in Crisis
Vampire in Control
Vampire in Charge
Family Blood Ties Set 1–3
Family Blood Ties Set 1–5
Family Blood Ties Set 4–6
Family Blood Ties Set 7–9
Sian's Solution, A Family Blood Ties Series Prequel
    Novelette

Design series
Dangerous Designs
Deadly Designs
Darkest Designs
Design Series Trilogy

Standalone
In Cassie's Corner
Gem Stone (a Gemma Stone Mystery)

Published Non-Fiction Books:

Career Essentials

Career Essentials: The Résumé
Career Essentials: The Cover Letter
Career Essentials: The Interview
Career Essentials: 3 in 1

Printed in Great Britain
by Amazon

27501465R00165